HORROR AT HIDEAWAY COVE

CRITTER CATCHERS
BOOK 6

HANK EDWARDS

MITTEN GINGER MEDIA

CONTENTS

Chapter 1   1
Chapter 2   13
Chapter 3   22
Chapter 4   37
Chapter 5   54
Chapter 6   67
Chapter 7   81
Chapter 8   102
Chapter 9   121
Chapter 10   134
Chapter 11   144
Chapter 12   152
Chapter 13   163
Chapter 14   173
Chapter 15   185
Chapter 16   203
Chapter 17   210
Chapter 18   225
Chapter 19   236

Dread of Night   245
About the Author   247
Also by Hank Edwards   249

SUMMARY

A wedding on a budget. A honeymoon booked last minute. An urban legend that rises to the surface.

After dealing with a sneaky otter and an expanding guest list, Cody and Demetrius manage to get married without a single monster crashing the event. Afterwards, Cody whisks Demmy away on the honeymoon trip he planned all on his own… after putting it off until the last minute and booking it all online, sight unseen.

To their happy surprise, the cabin Cody reserved is quite comfortable and very secluded, situated on an island in the middle of the deep Heaversford Lake, and accessible only by boat. But as usually happens to the guys, trouble has a way of finding them. For not only is the lake home to Esther, a monster similar to the one in Loch Ness, but shortly after they arrive a storm knocks out the power and a local resident drowns under mysterious circumstances. The clues all point to Esther being somehow involved, and Demetrius and Cody quickly realize they're going to have to get involved and do their own style of investigation.

Before they realize it, their peaceful honeymoon is shattered and they find themselves fighting for their lives in the cold, dark waters of Heaversford Lake.

This is a work of fiction. Names, characters, businesses, places, events and incidents are either the products of the author's imagination or used in a fictitious manner. Any resemblance to actual persons, living or dead, or actual events is purely coincidental.

Horror at Hideaway Cove ©2018 Hank Edwards
Cover design by Ron Perry Graphic Design
Book design and production by Hank Edwards
Editing by Jerry Wheeler

First Publication, 2018

CHAPTER ONE

Demetrius surveyed the elaborate network of wires before him. Thicker than piano wire, but still flexible, it criss-crossed the yard dangerously close to neck level. He had no idea where Cody had gotten the stuff, but he'd strung it from the branch of a small crabapple tree in the middle of the yard to a swing set where it went around a support pole, and then returned to the tree, but a different branch this time, before dropping down to end at the door of a live animal trap.

It looked like an insane Transformer had taken a basket-weaving class.

Demetrius wanted to ask a question, he just wasn't certain what to ask first. Before he could open his mouth, Jugs spoke up from where he stood to Demetrius's left.

"This is some crazy shit, Cody."

Darnell Perramon—known by the name Jugs because of the size of his pectoral muscles—was the same age as Cody and Demetrius, but had attended Harriettville High School, the nearest school to Parson's Hollow and its biggest sports team rivals. Though on opposing football teams, Jugs and

Cody had formed an easy-going, causal friendship based on mutual respect for the other's athletic abilities. When Jugs had been laid off from his managerial job at a Harriettville furniture store, Cody offered him part time work with their business. That part time work had recently turned into a full-time position which allowed Cody and Demetrius both a chance for some time away over the last year.

Cody popped his head out from behind the tree. His huge, boyish smile warmed Demetrius even as a burst of cool wind made him shiver. Pennsylvania couldn't seem to make up its mind this spring. The temperature had been in the seventies the last week of April, and once the month changed to May, dropped into the forties.

"It's not crazy," Cody said. "It's an intricate design that your simple brain can't follow."

Jugs turned to Demetrius with a skeptical expression. "Do you understand his intricate design?"

Demetrius opened his mouth, closed it, opened it again as Cody disappeared behind the tree, then closed it and shrugged. "Let's see if he can explain how it works."

"You know he's crazy, right?"

"Oh, I've known that for years now."

"And yet you own a business with him. And you're going to marry him in a few weeks." Jugs arched an eyebrow. "That might make you about as crazy as him."

"I thought the definition of crazy was doing the same thing over and over and expecting a different result." Demetrius tipped his head toward the spiderweb of wire. "I can safely say I've never seen him do anything like this before."

Jugs looked back at Cody's handiwork and said under his breath just loud enough for Demetrius to hear, "Crazy is as crazy does."

Demetrius grinned as Jugs shook his head, and they both

looked back at the cat's cradle of wires. A slightly out-of-body feeling came over Demetrius, and he spread his feet a little wider and made sure his knees weren't locked so he wouldn't pass out and fall over.

He and Cody were going to get married in just over two weeks.

He was going to be Cody's husband.

Husband.

It had been a lot to comprehend when Cody had proposed to him in Denver while they had been looking out over the Red Rocks Amphitheater buried under snow. Now as the day approached, it seemed like some long, really involved dream he was going to wake up from and discover he was still just fifteen-years-old and trying not to crush too hard on his straight best friend.

His straight best friend who hadn't been adverse to wrestling with him even after Demetrius had come out to him.

And who had disapproved of every guy he'd ever dated.

And who still thanked him every year for being such a good friend on the anniversary of the day they had met.

Life was sometimes one fuck of a wild ride.

Cody stepped out from behind the tree and approached where they stood. His cheeks were flushed and his eyes shone with excitement as his smile widened.

"Hey. How was the job you guys went on?" Cody asked. "Everything go okay?"

"Yeah, it was fine," Demetrius said.

"We didn't have to string a bunch of wire around a yard like some kind of steampunk knitter," Jugs said. "We just opened up the attic door, caught the raccoons, sealed up the entry point, and got the hell out." He waved a hand at the wires as he scowled at Cody. "Did you hit your damn head?"

"Not yet." Cody laughed. "But I understand why you'd

ask me that. I do. Let me just explain. Okay, so the trap is here." He pointed to the trap secured on the ground with plastic tent stakes. "The wire holds the door open and goes around the tree and back to the swing set and then over to the fence where we think it's getting into the yard."

"Question," Demetrius said, raising his hand.

"Yes, the young man in the front row who's obviously paying attention," Cody said.

"Hey, I'm paying attention!" Jugs said.

"Apparently not closely enough to ask a question," Cody said.

Jugs put his hands on his hips. "Well what if he asks an obvious question, like why did you decide to string wire all around the yard instead of just depend on the spring of the trap?"

"Demmy would never ask an obviously unnecessary question like that."

"Um, sorry, but that was the exact question I was about to ask," Demetrius said.

Cody hung his head. "So disappointed. But, I'll overlook it for now." He waved a hand toward the display of wire. "We're dealing with a crafty and intelligent critter."

"It's an otter," Jugs said in a flat, unimpressed tone.

"Precisely! This is something we have yet to come up against."

"It's not an arch villain," Jugs said. "It's an otter."

"If you would allow me to explain?" Cody looked at Jugs, his eyebrows raised so high they were almost halfway to his hairline.

Jugs gave him a long, droll look and Demetrius had to bite the inside of his cheek to keep from laughing.

"Please. Explain," Jugs said.

"So we have a crafty and intelligent critter who is gaining entry through a number of loose boards in the privacy fence.

It could be any loose board depending on his approach vector."

"Approach vector?" Demetrius said.

Cody ignored him and continued with his explanation. "Once inside the yard, the otter makes its way to the koi and goldfish pond where it feasts on the fish."

"Yeah, we know all this," Jugs said. "I took the initial call, remember?"

Cody put his hands on his hips and looked between them. "The two of you are really harshing my buzz, you know that?"

"We're very sorry," Jugs said, not sounding at all apologetic. "Please continue."

"Thank you." Cody cleared his throat and turned back to his project. "The wire is connected to each loose board in the fence I could find. When the board is moved, the wire is pulled taut and it opens the door of the trap."

"Why not just leave the trap open?" Demetrius asked.

"To avoid catching something other than the otter," Cody said.

"Nothing else gets in through the loose fence boards?" Jugs asked.

"Not that I'm aware of."

Demetrius exchanged a look with Jugs before returning his attention to Cody. "Okay. So now the trap is set. What are you using for bait?"

"Tuna fish."

"Oh?" Demetrius crouched down and peered into the trap, noting several chunks of tuna on the spring plate. "That's a good idea."

"Well, one out of a dozen isn't bad," Jugs said.

"I heard that," Cody called as he followed the wire from the trap to the fence and checked that it was secure.

The sound of claws scrambling along a tree made

Demetrius and Jugs look up. A squirrel clung head down to the bark of the tree, twitching its whiskers as it peered at them.

"You've got a visitor," Jugs said.

"What?" Cody looked back and forth along the fence. "Is it the otter? Do you see it? Where is it?"

"Squirrel," Demetrius said. "On the tree behind you."

Cody turned and the three of them watched as the squirrel climbed another foot down the tree. It stopped at one of the wires and put both front paws on it. This length of wire extended to the swing set, looped around one of those poles, and then went to a fence picket near the back corner.

"Uh oh," Jugs whispered.

"No!" Cody shouted and waved his arms in an attempt to send the squirrel back up the tree.

But his actions only startled the squirrel into a mad dash along the wire toward the swing set. Its fluffy tail twitched back and forth to help it stay balanced as it raced away from Cody, the wire bouncing and thrumming beneath it.

The pressure of the squirrel's sprint caused the wire to lift and lower the door of the trap several times, until it finally slammed shut and locked.

"Oops," Demetrius said.

As Cody chased the squirrel toward the back corner of the yard, one of the pickets along the fence across from where Demetrius and Jugs stood bumped open. An otter squeezed through the small opening and waddled across the lawn toward them.

"Cody?" Demetrius said.

But Cody was too intent on pursuing the squirrel and didn't hear him. The squirrel leaped from the wire onto the swing set support pole, and then onto the ground. Cody chased after it as the squirrel darted back and forth along the ground at the bottom of the rear fence.

The otter made its way up to Demetrius and Jugs. It paused to sniff the toes of their boots and sat up on its hind legs to peer up at them, whiskers twitching. Apparently satisfied they weren't a threat, it dropped to all fours once again and hurried to the edge of the pond where it slipped into the water and dove beneath the surface. Demetrius looked at Jugs, and they both looked at Cody who had scared the squirrel to the top of the fence and now stood clapping his hands at it as it sat on top of a picket glaring at him and twitching its tail.

"Think the net will hold the otter?" Jugs asked.

"It should. Want me to get it?" Demetrius said.

"Nah, you enjoy his show. And just remember, he's all yours."

Demetrius grinned as he watched Cody continue to clap at the squirrel. "I'm so proud."

Jugs snorted. "You're crazy is what you are. I'll be right back."

In minutes, Jugs had returned with a long-handled net. Demetrius watched as Jugs swooped the net through the small pond until he had ensnared the otter. He pulled it squeaking and thrashing out of the water, half a goldfish gripped in one paw. The otter's crying finally caught Cody's attention and he turned to stare.

"What is that?" Cody stomped up and looked from the otter squirming and dripping inside the net to Jugs and then to Demetrius. "Where did this thing come from?"

"The pond," Demetrius said.

"It came in under the fence while you were chasing the squirrel," Jugs said, then looked at Demetrius. "I'll put it in a cage in the back of the truck."

Cody watched Jugs walked toward the gate, then turned to survey the wires he had strung around the backyard. His shoulders sagged as he sighed. "It seemed like a good idea at the time."

Demetrius walked up behind him and gave his shoulders a couple of strong squeezes. "I'm sure it did. Come on steampunk Spider-Man, I'll help you unravel your wire web."

After taking down the wires and collecting the cage, Cody and Demetrius met up with Jugs at the truck. The otter paced inside a carrier cage, squeaking and pawing at the latch.

"Tricky little guy," Jugs said. "I had to put a bolt through the latch and then screw a nut on to keep it from getting free."

"That's what Demmy does to me every night," Cody whispered, loud enough for Demetrius to hear.

Jugs got a pained expression. "I do not want to know the details of whatever sex games you two enact."

Cody grinned. "Cause it would put your sex life to shame?"

"Oh, I don't think so, Bonker."

Demetrius cocked his head and looked between them. "I'm sorry. Bonker?"

Jugs's laugh made the otter squeak louder. "He never told you about the nickname we gave him over at Harriettville?"

Demetrius chuckled. "I can safely say I have never heard anyone call Cody "Bonker" before."

"All right, you've had your fun," Cody said, his face turning red. "You should just take an Uber back to the office now. Bye Jugs. Bye!"

"Look at that blush," Jugs said with a chuckle. "Still gets to him even now."

"What does?" Demetrius said, trying not to swoon at how fucking adorable Cody looked with his steadily deepening blush. "Jugs, you have to tell me. You can't just drop a bomb like that and leave me hanging."

"Yes he can," Cody said, and tried to push Jugs off down the street. "Bye, Jugs. If you don't like Uber, you could always hitchhike and meet new people. See you at another time when you're not full of horrifically embarrassing things to say."

But Jugs was a solid guy, and no amount of pushing on Cody's part could get him to budge.

Jugs started to speak even as Cody kept trying to push him away. "During a game in our senior year, Cody was doing his thing and chasing after one of our receivers. Some fast as fuck kid we called Zip. Anyway, Zip was basically leaving flames in his tracks and Cody was huffing along after him as fast as he could. The quarterback threw the pass and it looked perfect, spinning through the air just as pretty as you please. And then it landed point-down right on top of Cody's helmet. Caused a hell of a racket we could all hear over the crowd as it hit, too. Just a big "bonk!" that seemed to echo around the field."

Jugs started laughing so hard he couldn't continue, and Demetrius joined him.

"All right," Cody said, finally giving up on trying to move Jugs and instead busying himself by adjusting the wire in the back of Demetrius's truck. "You've had your fun. Good seeing you, Jugs. How are you getting back to the office?"

"Aw, don't be like that, Bonker," Jugs said as he wiped away tears. "It's been years since I've called you that."

"I know. Let's make it a decade this time, okay?"

"All right, I can see you're still hurt by the wily and clever super villain The Otter foiling your elaborate plan to trap him," Jugs said. "How about you drive me back to the office and we stop by the Hollow Leg and I'll buy you a beer to apologize?"

Cody looked at Demetrius. "Do we have any other jobs this afternoon?"

"Nope. Go ahead with Jugs. I'll release the otter out at

Parson's Pond and then meet up with Amelia to discuss flowers and other stuff."

"You don't need me to go with you?"

"No, it's okay."

"Which, when translated, means, 'I don't want you there because then I can make some actual decisions,'" Jugs said with a chuckle.

"Hey, I've made decisions about our wedding," Cody said as he shot a glare at Jugs. He looked back at Demetrius and said, "Isn't that right?"

Demetrius nodded. "You have. Your brother Dave is your best man, Jugs is your groomsman, and your bachelor party is going to be this weekend at the Hollow Leg."

"And I chose the flavor of the cake, and found us a cheap venue for both the ceremony and reception." Cody put his hands on his hips and shook his head. "I get no respect, I tell you."

Jugs gave Demetrius a skeptical look. "He did all that?"

"He did. And he found us a deejay."

"Well, look at you, Cody Bower, all grown up and eager to get married." Jugs smiled. "You really do need a beer, don't you?"

They all laughed, and Demetrius waved for them to go. "Go have a beer and enjoy yourself."

"But not too much," Jugs said, holding up his index finger. "Right?"

Demetrius shrugged. "He can enjoy himself as much as he wants. He's an adult and can make his own decisions."

Cody gave Jugs a satisfied smile. "I'm an adult."

"You know you can't keep fooling him like this," Jugs said. "I'll wait in the truck so you two can make out in private."

"Out here in the street is private?" Demetrius said as Jugs walked off toward Cody's truck. He looked at Cody and smiled. "I liked your wire weaving skills."

Cody blushed, looking more adorable than ever. "Yeah, all right. It would have been a good idea."

"It was. Maybe a little overboard."

"Like me."

"Just the way I like you." Demetrius gave him a quick kiss on the lips. "Go have a beer with Jugs."

"One beer?"

"Less than three."

Cody grinned. "I love you."

"I love you, too. Can you believe we get married in a few weeks?"

"Nope. Can you believe I'm really looking forward to it?"

Demetrius smiled. "Yeah? Me too."

"Tell Amelia I said hi. I'll see you at home."

Cody kissed him again, a little longer this time, and Jugs honked the truck's horn.

"Is it too late to change my selection for groomsman?" Cody asked.

"Nope. Make sure he knows that, too."

"You got it."

With a final quick kiss, Cody crossed the street and got into the driver's seat of his truck. Demetrius waved as they drove off, then went to the door of their client's house to collect the payment. The client had a few questions about the wires Cody had strung around his yard, which Demetrius felt he managed to explain pretty well. After accepting a check, Demetrius got back in his truck and pulled away from the curb.

He had a lot of errands to run and a seemingly never-ending todo list before the wedding.

Wedding.

The word itself sometimes surprised him. Just floated to the front of his mind and bumped into his train of thought.

He was going to get married. Putting the whole subject of

marrying Cody aside, Demetrius was sometimes still amazed to be planning his own wedding. As he'd been growing up, he'd never thought he would one day be able to marry who he loved. Optimism ran strong in him, so he'd always been able to imagine finding a lover, but he'd never even entertained the idea of being able to celebrate their love with a wedding. Not a legal one, anyway.

And yet, here he was. Planning his wedding. To Cody. And, surprisingly, Cody seemed to handling all of this wedding hoopla really well. There hadn't yet been one instance of him freaking out.

CHAPTER TWO

"I am literally freaking out right now." Cody tried to take a deep breath, but his chest was too tight to comply. He tightened his grip on the beer mug and looked across the table at Jugs. "Like, literally."

Jugs gave him a bored look. "I can see that."

"You're not being very supportive."

"I'm waiting for your nervous energy to wind down," Jugs said, and then finished his beer. "After that, I'll astound you with my wisdom."

Cody chugged the remainder of his beer and signaled for another round.

"Easy with that beer, cowboy. This isn't your bachelor party."

"Hardly. Should be interesting to see what Dave comes up with for that."

"And he's your younger brother?"

"Born two years after me."

"There's five of you?"

"Yep. All boys and all over six feet tall. Two older and two younger than me."

"Look at you, stuck right in the middle. Just like with your sexuality."

The statement shocked Cody so much his mouth dropped open but no words came out. Jugs observed him with a satisfied smirk.

"Finally got you to shut up at least."

"That was pretty insulting," Cody said and sat back to give the waitress room to set down their fresh beers.

"But funny," Jugs said. "You gotta admit that."

"Yeah, all right. I'll give you that."

"Like you gave us those points during your homecoming game?"

"Dude, seriously?"

Jugs laughed, and Cody couldn't help but join him.

"You're an asshole," Cody said.

"You're welcome."

Cody held up his mug. "To old friends."

Jugs clinked his mug against Cody's. "To old friends."

They each took a long draught, and when they'd set down their mugs, Jugs leaned in over the table. "What's freaking you out? You having second thoughts?"

"About getting married?" Cody shook his head. "Nope."

"Not even a little bit?"

"Not even a little bit. Surprising, isn't it?"

"I gotta say this is not how I was expecting you to be acting a few weeks before your wedding. To a man."

"I know, right? But the whole marriage thing isn't scaring me. Maybe Demmy and I have known each other so long that it already feels like we're married. Or maybe I'm just old enough to know I'm not going to find anyone else I can tolerate and who will put up with me as well."

"You are over thirty."

Cody glared. "As are you."

"We're not talking about me."

"Fine. I'm over thirty. Whatever."

"Anyway…" Jugs waved for Cody to continue.

"Right. So I'm good with the wedding and spending our lives together and all of that. But what really has me freaked out is the honeymoon."

Jugs sat back and frowned. "You two haven't had sex yet?"

"What? Why would you ask me that?"

"You just said you were freaked out about the honeymoon!"

"Yeah, because I'm the one who's planning it!"

"Well why the hell didn't you say that in the first place?" Jugs put a hand on his chest and let out a breath. "Nearly gave me a heart attack over here, thinking you were going to get married to a man without having tried it out yet to see if you liked it."

"All right, settle down. Demmy and I have plenty of sex."

Jugs made a face. "That is an image I do not want in my head."

"Are you becoming homophobic?"

"No. If anything, I'm Cody-phobic. I don't want to think about you having sex at all, with a man or a woman. No. Just… no."

"Fine. Sex talk is off the table."

Jugs put his face in his hands. "Ugh. Now I'm imagining you two having sex on a table! Curse my vivid imagination!"

Cody laughed and drank some of his beer as he waited for Jugs to recover. When it looked like he had moved past their conversation about sex, he asked, "Are you ready for me to continue?"

Jugs held up an index finger for Cody to wait as he drank half of his beer in several large swallows. He put the mug down and nodded. "I'm ready."

"I don't know where to go for our honeymoon. I have no

idea about Demmy's expectations. Would he want to go to Paris? Or Mexico? Or some tropical island?"

Jugs shrugged. "Why don't you ask him?"

"I can't."

"Why not?"

"He's taken on all the other plans, like, all of them, so I told him to not even think about the honeymoon, that I would manage it all."

"Kind of painted yourself into a corner with that, didn't you?"

"Yet again." Cody took another drink. "Dammit."

"So think about Demetrius. You're the one who knows him best. What kind of trip do you think he'd like?"

"Okay, that's a good point. Let's see, he's never been one for sunbathing, he burns too easily, so tropical island and Mexico are out. He doesn't really like rich food or fancy things, so Paris probably wouldn't be his thing either."

"Good. You've managed to cross off the most expensive trips from your list. What's left?"

"Somewhere in the States, I guess. But where?"

"You were just out in Colorado over Christmas. Did he like the mountains?"

Cody thought about the sasquatch chasing them through deep snow and shook his head. "Not enough to go back for. Plus my family is there and all that drama over Christmas could still be lying in wait."

"What about something closer to home? Lots of cabins for rent in the mountains around here. You could get one with a hot tub on a deck looking out over the valley."

"That's not a bad idea. He does like the woods. When we're not working in them."

Jugs pointed at him as he took another drink of his beer. "There you go. You have someplace to start."

"Cool. Demmy said he had some stuff to get done, so he

shouldn't be at the office. I'll jump on the computer there and see what I can find."

"Look at you, being all sneaky."

"Hey, I'm getting married, I need to get all the sneaky stuff out of my system."

"Or learn how to be even sneakier," Jugs said.

Cody shook his head. "Nope. Not going to happen. This is one and done for me."

"One and done for sure," Jugs said. "You ever been with any other guys?"

"Jugs, I told you, if you maybe ate less deli meat and burritos, you might have been the one."

Jugs gave him an unamused smile. "Cute, but I don't like my dates to have hairy knuckles."

Cody frowned and looked at his hands. He'd never really noticed all those dark hairs. Good thing Demmy liked hairy men.

"I'm actually being serious here," Jugs continued. "Have you been with other guys?"

"I went on some dates, yeah."

"Did any of these dates lead to sex?"

"You're getting really personal here—"

"And for a reason." Jugs leaned closer over the table. "I want to make sure you've investigated all of your options."

Cody moved forward as well. "I'm getting married in a few weeks to my best friend, and I'm really fucking happy about it. I could not imagine feeling this way about anyone other than Demmy. Man or woman."

Jugs sat back. He crossed his arms and pressed his lips together as he looked at Cody who stared right back. Finally, Jugs shrugged and nodded. "Okay. I just had to check, that's all."

"Well, I appreciate it, but I don't want you worrying."

"I'm not worried about you, I'm worried about keeping

my job. I like working for you guys, and if you get divorced that's going to fuck things up for me." Jugs finished his beer and used the back of his hand to wipe his mouth before smiling at Cody.

"Thanks for your concern."

"Anytime, Bonker."

"Asshole," Cody grumbled and finished his own beer.

Jugs checked the time on his phone. "I've got someplace to be. You ready to go?"

"Yeah, let's hit the road. I have some work to do. You left your car at the office, right?"

"Yep." Jugs waved for the check and the waitress nodded at him.

While Jugs paid, Cody paid a visit to the restroom. When he'd finished, he returned to the table just as Jugs was laying cash on the table.

"Thanks for the beers," Cody said.

"Least I could do after you strung wires all around our last client's yard."

"Hey, my plan would have worked."

Jugs just shook his head as he stood and headed for the door.

A short time later, Cody pulled into the parking lot of the strip mall where the Critter Catchers office was located. They got out of the truck and Jugs gave him a wave before getting into his 2003 Ford Escort, which Cody called an old beater and Jugs referred to as a classic. Cody watched Jugs drive off, then let himself into the office. He booted up his computer and opened a search engine to start looking for available cabin rentals. He could do this. He was going to honeymoon the hell out of Demmy.

Forty minutes later, Cody sat back and shook his fists at the ceiling. "Dammit!"

Every cabin that looked even halfway decent was already

booked solid through the summer and autumn. He cursed all the planners and go-getters of the world then got up to pay a visit to the bathroom. After that, he grabbed a juice from the break room refrigerator and chugged it while standing at the sink.

He had to get this trip just right. Demmy deserved a really nice, relaxing, and sexy getaway. Their last two trips had both gone spectacularly off the rails. First their trip to Florida to stay with Demmy's parents where they'd almost been murdered by a swamp monster. After that, they'd driven to Pinesville, New Jersey, where they had stayed in Ollie's grandmother's barn and tromped through woods looking for the Devil of Pinesville. And just a few months ago they'd flown out to Colorado to stay with Cody's family for Christmas and ended up sleeping on the floor of his brother's living room and rescuing his father from a sasquatch.

"We gotta start balancing out these trips," Cody muttered.

Returning to his desk, he scrolled slowly through the search results again, hoping there was something he might have overlooked. Near the bottom of the third page of results, he discovered a link he hadn't tried yet, so he clicked it and leaned in, hoping for a miracle but not expecting much.

The picture at the top of the page was of the outside of a small, tastefully decorated cabin surrounded by trees. A hammock hung between two trees just off of a covered front porch. Some pictures of the interior showed off a stone fireplace, a king-sized sleigh bed, and a large claw foot tub in front of a wide window looking out on woods. More photos showed a dock built in a small cove, a dirt trail disappearing into a stand of trees, and the view from atop a bluff looking out over a wide expanse of blue water.

"Damn, this is nice," Cody whispered. "Where is this place?"

He scrolled down the page and his interest went up even

higher when he read that the cabin was on an island in the middle of a wide, deep lake in upstate Pennsylvania. It was just a few hours away from Parson's Hollow, how had he never heard of it before? The place was called Hideaway Cove, and it was the only building on an island a mile square. The island had a long history, according to the website, but the cabin was relatively new and intended to be a honeymoon retreat. The photos made it appear perfect for them. Neither he or Demmy were big on tent camping, so the well-appointed cabin was a nice find. And with it sitting on an island of all things, surrounded by woods and beaches and trails for hiking, it all seemed too good to be true. And that worried him.

With his hopes cautiously rising, he clicked on a link that read Check Our Availability! A calendar icon invited him to choose the dates he wanted, and when he did he had to sit back and let out a gasp when he saw the message pop up "It's available!"

"You've gotta be fucking kidding me! This place is available?" He leaned forward and frowned as he inspected the picture more closely. "What's wrong with it?"

He clicked on the Make a reservation link and hurriedly entered his credit card number, not even really caring about the nightly rate. He could pay the balance off over time, most likely a couple of years, but he'd never get a second chance to prove to Demmy how committed he was to their relationship. Just the two of them in a small cabin on an island in the middle of a lake sounded like a good way to start their life together.

Or kill each other.

But Cody thought they'd been friends long enough they could handle being in such close quarters for a week. If there wasn't much to do but have sex, Cody was just fine with that.

He went through the confirmation process and moments

later found an email in his inbox that started with the line, "We're looking forward to seeing you soon at Hideaway Cove!"

Satisfied, he sat back in his chair and grinned at the computer monitor. Everything was set. In a few weeks, he and Demmy would be starting their lives as a married couple. And after that, they would be setting off on a relaxing and romantic week away from Parson's Hollow.

CHAPTER THREE

The bank was on the way out of town toward Parson's Pond, so Demetrius decided to go through the drive through lane and deposit the client's check before releasing the otter. The little critter was busy in the back, fiddling with the bolted cage door and squeaking every now and then. He hoped it wouldn't figure out how to unscrew the nut Jugs had put on to keep the bolt in place on the cage door.

As he sat at the bank window, he felt his phone buzz in his pocket and pulled it out to find a text from Aunt Amelia.

You still want to finalize flowers?

He smiled and wrote back: *Yes! Just need to drop off an otter.*

Otter? I want to see!

Demetrius laughed and wrote. *I will pick you up before I release it. On my way soon!*

Amelia was the youngest of his mother's siblings, and Demetrius's favorite relative. His parents had given up on having children and been surprised by Demetrius very late in life, when his mother was forty-seven years old. Now, his mother was seventy-seven and his father eighty-two and they lived in a senior community down in Florida. As he'd been growing up, Amelia had in some aspects felt more like a mother to Demetrius than his own, probably because she was of a more appropriate parent age. She had never married or had children of her own, and she doted on him as he'd been growing up, and even to this day. Because they were so close, Amelia wanted to do something special to celebrate his and Cody's wedding, so she was paying for their flowers.

The teller finished up the deposit and Demetrius pulled out of the bank parking lot. He drove through downtown Parson's Hollow with the window down, enjoying the spring breeze. He waved to people he knew, including Margie, the owner of Margie's Diner, who was setting out the Daily Specials chalk sandwich board she had finally purchased after debating about it for months with anyone who would listen.

A car pulled out of an intersection right in front of him, forcing him to hit the brakes. It was a Cadillac Sedan de Ville from the mid-70s, tan with a white vinyl roof. A real tank of a car, it seemed to take up the entire road, but maybe that was because the driver meandered back and forth across the dotted white line in the middle. Thankfully there was no oncoming traffic as the Cadillac rolled slowly down the street, a yellow bubble light revolving on the roof.

"Fuck," Demetrius muttered and rested his head in his hand, propping himself up with his elbow on the door frame as he slowed to an agonizing fifteen miles an hour. "Every time."

It was, of course, JoAnn Monroe, known around town as Widow Monroe, the wife of the late fire chief who passed away forty years ago, heroically battling a fire at the hospital. Now in her nineties, ninety-eight at least, and refusing to quit driving, the sheriff had installed a revolving yellow light on top of her car as a warning to other drivers and a beacon to help them locate her when she drove off the road.

Demetrius was always amazed as he remembered her running over the steroid-induced monster farmer Reed Wilkes had turned into and saving their lives. She hadn't even realized she'd hit anything, just backed up and drove off, yellow light flashing and not a scratch on her car.

All hail the Widow Monroe.

For eight agonizing blocks he was trapped behind the Widow, and when she finally made a sharp left turn at the last second onto Rosemont, he gratefully accelerated. With the downtown business district of Parson's Hollow behind him, he cruised through the residential section of town, passing bungalows and colonials as well as the apartment building where he used to live. He did not miss that place, and he would forever be grateful to Amelia who had presented him and Cody with the generous offer of her home, long paid off, while she moved into a senior independent living condo owned by her boyfriend, Otis.

The residential area gradually changed from houses with smaller yards, similar to where Demetrius and Cody lived now, to ranch style homes built on larger plots of land. Some of these homes had fenced pastures for horses or cows or other livestock. A few had enough acreage to grow small crops or corn or soybeans.

Tucked between two of the larger farms was the Parson's Pines Collection. This was a senior living center that catered to all levels of mobility for the older generation, which included condos for independent living, apartments with aide service and a dining room, and the Parson's Pines Nursing and Convalescent Home of Serenity, where those requiring more assistance were housed. Cody's grandmother, Felicia, was a resident in the convalescent home, while Amelia lived with her boyfriend Otis in one of the independent living condominiums.

Demetrius drove slowly through the winding streets of

Parson's Pines Condominiums until he reached Amelia and Otis's unit, discernible from all the other look-alike condos because of Amelia's collection of garden gnomes situated in the flowerbeds. When he pulled into the driveway, Amelia stepped out the front door and hurried to the passenger side of the truck. She opened the door and climbed into the cab then leaned over to kiss Demetrius on the cheek.

"It's good to see you," she said as she buckled in, then turned to peer through the back window. "You didn't set him free yet, did you?"

Demetrius chuckled. "Not yet. There's still an otter in the back of the truck."

As if to prove he was right, the otter let out a series of squeaks and scrabbled around the carrier.

"Oh my God, he sounds so cute!" Amelia clapped her hands and giggled like a little girl, making Demetrius laugh.

"So where's Otis today?"

"Out playing golf." Amelia rolled her eyes. "That man chases more balls than a gay man."

Demetrius gave her a wide-eyed look of shock. "Amelia!"

She waved dismissively. "Oh, oak trees. You know I'm right."

"Well, I'm a gay man and I don't think I've chased that many balls."

"See? You just proved my point."

"Anyway…"

"Yes, all right, I'll stop. But he does play a lot of golf. I swear. Anyway, are you excited to look at flowers after this?"

Demetrius shrugged. "I guess?"

"Guess? That's it?"

"It's a lot of money for a short ceremony."

"But it's your wedding," Amelia said in a dreamy voice. "This is one of the most important days of your life."

"Yeah, I get that. But, you know, none of us have a lot of money, so we're trying to keep it within a certain budget."

"Do you think your parents and I would allow you to skimp on your wedding?"

"No. But…" Demetrius trailed off, unsure how to put what he was feeling into words.

Amelia touched his arm. "What is it, honey? Talk to me."

"Let me think a minute. We're almost to Morley."

A few minutes later, he slowed and pulled off the road onto a dirt trail. This was Morley Trail which was an old logging road more than a century old. Morley Trail rode the low hills around Parson's Hollow and wound through the woods that surrounded Parson's Pond, clear and cold, fed by an underground spring. Demetrius hadn't seen many otters around the pond, but he figured this would be a great spot to release their latest captive.

When he reached a pull off, he angled the truck under a couple of tall oak trees and parked. As he and Amelia approached the back of the truck, the otter started squeaking even louder, making them both smile.

"Let me look in at him first," Amelia said as Demetrius lowered the pickup tailgate. She leaned down and peered into the cage as the otter stuck a tiny paw through the wire door. "Oh my God. He's more adorable than Justin Timberlake."

Demetrius laughed and the otter squeaked in response.

"That's a pretty high level of adorable," he said.

"So you know I'm serious." She straightened up and followed as Demetrius picked up the carrier and headed for the shore of the pond.

"Okay little fellow, this is your new home." Demetrius set the carrier on the ground a few feet back from the water. "Lots of fish in there to eat, and maybe some other otters to play with."

"Stay out of the road," Amelia instructed.

Demetrius loosened the nut from the bolt, then opened the door. The otter hurried out of the carrier, squeaking as he ran through the tall grass around the pond before sliding into the water. Moments later, his head popped up a yard or so off shore, and he turned to look back at them.

"Bye little guy!" Amelia said, and waved.

The otter lifted a paw and waved back.

Her eyes went wide. "Oh, sequoia tree, did you see that?"

"I did!"

They watched the otter swim around the pond for a few minutes, then Amelia checked her watch.

"We need to get going if we're to make the appointment."

"Yeah, let's go. He's doing well."

Demetrius gathered the carrier and secured it in the bed of the truck. He got behind the wheel and waited for Amelia to buckle up before he started the truck.

"Have you thought more about how you're feeling toward the wedding?"

Amelia's tone was gentle, and Demetrius smiled over at her. She had become something of a confidant for him over the years, and a very close friend. She knew him as well as, if not better than, Cody knew him, which had its good points and bad points.

"It's nothing tragic, I assure you. I'm not going to pull a runaway groom scenario or anything."

"Oh, I wasn't thinking that, but it's good to be able to cross that worry off the list."

"You have a list?"

"I helped raise you, of course I have a list. And I also know what kind of cases you and Cody get involved in."

Amelia had been abducted by a swamp monster from outside Demetrius's parents' condominium the previous year. The three of them had fought off the monster made of moss and logs and mud as a tropical storm had pelted the Everglades. Alligators had finished the thing off, but ever since then Amelia had taken to checking in with Demetrius a little more often.

"We haven't been chased by a monster since the sasquatch out in Denver."

"I'm still upset I missed out on that one," Amelia said, thumping her fist on her thigh. "Sasquatch is my favorite urban legend."

"He smells bad, so you didn't miss out on much, I can assure you."

"Have you watched the movie they were filming while you were out there? It's all over that sci-fi and horror channel."

"I haven't," Demetrius said. "Not sure I'll be able to get Cody to sit down and watch it."

"But your buddy's in it. Don't you want to see how he does?"

Demetrius laughed as he thought about Augustyn, a tall, lanky stunt man dressed as a sasquatch who kept wandering off from the set of the movie filming nearby and running into them. He'd helped Demetrius and Cody rescue Cody's father from a real sasquatch, and, rumor had it, used that experience to deliver a realistic performance in the movie *Killer 'Squatch!*

"Maybe we'll watch it on the honeymoon."

"Do you know where you're going?"

Demetrius shrugged and blushed a little. "No. Cody said he wanted to surprise me."

"That is so romantic." Amelia sighed. "Maybe he'll take you to Paris. Or Rome."

"Either of those would be nice, but I don't think that's going to happen. I know our budget, so I'm going to assume it's something within driving distance."

"Well, no matter where he takes you, I'm sure it will be lovely."

"Me, too."

They were quiet a moment, then Amelia said, "Have you collected your thoughts enough to talk about the wedding?"

Demetrius shrugged. "I guess so. Sure."

"You don't seem to be as engaged as I would have expected. Are you sure you want to go through with it?"

"Oh, I'm sure. I've never been more sure of a decision before in my life."

"That's good to hear." Amelia gave a nod. "So is it nerves?"

Demetrius thought about the question. He was nervous, of course. Getting up in front of a bunch of people and taking a vow of marriage was, at its core, nerve-wracking. But his nerves weren't the problem. He'd thought about this issue for weeks now, as first Amelia, then his parents, then Cody's parents, then their invited guests had all started asking detailed questions about the event. It had become somewhat overwhelming, but after some heavy consideration, he had come to the conclusion that he had no idea what he should be doing. As he'd come to realize he was gay, he had never expected to be able to get married. Because of this alienation, he'd never thought about the ceremony or reception or honeymoon, and had no preconceived notions of what he wanted for it all. He'd had months to plan the event, but even after talking with Cody about what he wanted for their big day, Demetrius still could not seem to generate any excitement for the planning of what should be one of the most important days of his life.

He realized he had yet to respond to Amelia, so he gave her a quick smile before pulling into the parking lot of the flower shop. After putting the truck in park and shutting off the engine, he sat back and stared at the variety of flowers on display in the shop window.

"I never thought I would be able to do this," he said, and was surprised to suddenly find himself on the verge of tears.

Amelia put a hand on his shoulder. "Oh, honey. I know you didn't. But isn't it wonderful that you can now?"

He didn't trust his voice, so he settled for a few quick nods as he wiped at his eyes.

"Come here."

Amelia leaned over and pulled him into a hug. He surrendered to her warmth and strength as tears ran down his face.

"I'm sorry," he said, voice thick with emotion. "I didn't realize this was sitting so close to the surface."

"It's okay. You're okay. I'm glad I'm here with you. Come on, let it all out."

Memories of his relationship with Cody over the years spun through his mind as Demetrius considered standing before him and saying "I do." Or "I will," or whatever the hell he was supposed to say. He didn't even know what kind of vows he wanted. A flutter of panic followed that thought, and he found it hard to breathe. Pushing back from Amelia, he stared at her with wide eyes.

"The wedding is in three weeks," he said.

She smiled and nodded. "I know, sweetie. That's why I've been pushing you to make some of these decisions."

"We've made a lot of decisions, but, holy shit, Amelia. I'm getting married in three weeks."

"Yes. But, you have your tuxedos, you have your venue, the music, the food, the cake, and your officiant, tah dah!" She leaned back and did jazz hands. "The last detail is the flowers."

"Right. Flowers. Okay." He took several deep breaths and felt a little calmer. "All right. I can do this."

"I know you can. You ready?"

He nodded. "I'm ready. Let's go."

They got out of the truck and Demetrius found he had to

really focus on taking steps. It felt as if he walked on a layer of marshmallows. How was he going to get through the next three weeks, not to mention the wedding itself?

"I heard about this new flower shop from some of the women in the condo association. It's only been open a couple of months, but the owner is offering some good prices on flowers to bring in the customers." She stopped and leaned in closer, lowering her voice to say, "And they say he's quite the silver fox, if you know what I mean."

Demetrius chuckled, and that helped clear some of the stress from his mind. "I do know what you mean."

"Well, just be prepared. He's got a European accent and thick, wavy gray hair and piercing blue eyes."

"Are we here for flowers for my wedding, or are you scoping out the new silver fox in town?"

Amelia pretended offense. "I have no idea what you could mean by that. I am quite satisfied in my relationship with Otis."

"Who you said is playing way too much golf. Besides, just because you're on a diet doesn't mean you can't look at the menu," Demetrius said.

"Oh, sugar maples." She linked her arm through his. "Come on, let's get this last detail done. Then I'm taking you to dinner at Margie's."

A bell above the door tinkled when they stepped inside the shop, and the intense combination of floral scents made Demetrius's head spin. Vases and pots of cut flowers were scattered around the shop on what looked to be antique furniture. Several coolers along a back wall contained more flowers, and shelves of knick knacks and decorative items separated the open space into aisles.

"Welcome to Moonbeam Florist."

The man was a silver fox just as Amelia had claimed. He was tall with an athletic build: broad shoulders and chest that tapered to a narrow waist above a firm bubble butt. A thick mane of steel gray hair fell in waves to his shoulders, and a neatly trimmed beard perfectly matched the color. His light accent sounded European, but not distinct enough for Demetrius to be able to pinpoint which country inspired it.

"I am Nicolae Vianu, the owner of Moonbeam Florist. How may I assist you today?"

"My nephew here is getting married very soon."

Nicolae's face brightened and he clapped his big hands together. "Wonderful! My congratulations to the groom."

"Thank you," Demetrius said, and felt himself blush.

"He's gotten a little behind on his arrangements, I'm afraid," Amelia said. "And we're looking to order some arrangements that we will need by Saturday three weeks from this one."

Nicolae's eyes widened. "So soon." He recovered his composure and held his arms open wide. "No problem! For my new friends, I will make it happen. Come, let's pick out some flowers." He turned away, then back again. "Or should we wait for the bride-to-be?"

"Oh, um, no, that won't be necessary," Demetrius said, feeling his cheeks flush again. "I'll make the decisions on the flowers."

"So progressive," Nicolae said, then winked at Amelia. "I like that."

Amelia giggled. "Oh, yes, me too."

They followed him to a small sitting area tucked into a corner of the shop where upholstered chairs were gathered around a pedestal table on which rested a few thick books. Nicolae set the books aside and waved them to two of the chairs. Demetrius sighed as he sat in the comfortably padded seat.

"Oh, Nicolae," Amelia said. "This is the most comfortable chair I've sat on in years."

"I discovered this entire conversation group at a roadside antique stand run by an elderly woman who would not be talked down from her set price." He produced a leather-bound notebook from a drawer in the table and clicked a pen open. "Now, let us begin with your names."

"I'm Demetrius Singleton, and this is my aunt, Amelia Waugh."

"Demetrius," Nicolae said slowly, enunciating each syllable as he wrote it in his notebook. "A strong and proud name. Where do you work?"

"My partner and I own an animal control company called Critter Catchers."

Nicolae arched one bushy gray eyebrow. "Critter Catchers? I will have to remember that name in case I need a critter to be caught. And who are you betrothing yourself to, Demetrius Singleton?"

Demetrius always felt a little surge of nervousness when coming out to people for the first time. He tried to be confident and at peace with his orientation, but figured he would always experience that feeling. There was no guarantee how people would react.

"My, um, partner, Cody Bower."

Nicolae's other eyebrow went up as well. "This small town is more progressive than I had first imagined when I bought this shop at the beginning of the year."

Amelia patted Demetrius's hands where he had clasped them tight on the tabletop. She smiled at him, then at Nicolae. "Parson's Hollow is more diverse than a lot of people expect from a small town. And that's just the way we like it."

"The more time I spend here, the more I am seeing that. It's a wonderful thing." He smiled at Amelia. "And you surely cannot be his aunt. You must be his younger sister."

Amelia smiled and a blush turned her cheeks pink. "Oh, you sweet man. Aren't you just full of sugar? I am

Demetrius's aunt, his mother's younger sister." She smiled at Demetrius, tears glistening in her eyes. "I've known Demetrius his entire life, and am so proud of the man he's grown into. As his wedding gift, I am paying for the flowers."

"And she's also performing the ceremony," Demetrius said.

Nicolae smiled. "A licensed officiant? How lovely. And a good resource to keep in mind for any couples looking to wed with no church affiliation."

"Oh, I never thought of that. I could have a little side business."

"Precisely!" Nicolae said. "Who doesn't love a good wedding? Now, let's discuss the flowers."

After nearly forty-five minutes, Nicolae had a handwritten list which included two centerpieces for the wedding party's table, four boutonnieres, two for the grooms and two for their best men, and a wrist corsage for each of their mothers plus Amelia.

"I will assemble these pieces myself," Nicolae said as he closed the notebook. "And I will call you, Mrs. Waugh, when they are ready."

"Please, call me Amelia. And it's Ms. Waugh."

Demetrius cocked his head. "Does Otis call you Ms. Waugh?"

"And who is this Otis?" Nicolae looked between them. "Your suitor?"

"Yes, I am involved," Amelia said as she nudged Demetrius's foot beneath the table. "His name is Otis Bogdanovitch."

"Now that's a name with some character!" Nicolae laughed and clapped his hands together before they all stood. He led the way to the door and held it open for them.

"Have no worries about your arrangements, Demetrius,"

Nicolae said. "They will be the perfect compliment on your special day."

"Thank you for getting them completed on short notice," Demetrius said. "I've been dragging my feet a bit on the final details."

"It is customary for a groom to be nervous before the wedding," Nicolae said. "I'm certain you and Cody will make a handsome couple." He looked to Amelia. "I will call the day before the event to establish a time for you to pick up the arrangements."

"Thank you, Nicolae," Amelia said. "It's been a pleasure meeting you."

"And both of you, as well." Nicolae shook hands with each of them before they left the shop.

"What a wonderful man," Amelia said. "I think he'll fit into Parson's Hollow quite well."

"Just don't forget about Otis the next time you see Nicolae."

"Yeah, about that..." Amelia said, and started off about Demetrius butting in on her conversations as she followed him to the truck. She was still talking as they got in and buckled up, and Demetrius couldn't help grinning. He grinned all through her tirade as he drove her back to the condominium.

Amelia wrapped up her rant with a forceful, "So there!" Then she kissed his cheek before getting out and pushing the door shut. Demetrius watched until she had gotten safely inside the condo before he backed out of the drive and headed for home.

He felt better after spending time with Amelia, and getting the last item crossed off his wedding to-do list. Cody was handling the honeymoon arrangements, and Demetrius had refrained from asking him for any updates. He had to trust that Cody would be able to handle getting it done. All

Demetrius needed to know was what to pack and how long he should expect to be gone.

They had three weeks until the wedding. Three weeks until they stood in front of their families and friends and vowed to spend their lives together.

Demetrius took a deep breath and slowly let it out. He could do this; *they* could do this. It was just a short ceremony followed by a big party. After that, it was back to their every day lives. Not much would change, except for everything.

CHAPTER FOUR

The butterflies in Cody's belly had mutated into a flock of pterodactyls. He shifted his weight and cracked his knuckles, then tugged at the collar of his heavily starched white shirt. Sweat slicked the skin of his back. How fucking hot was it inside this building? Did someone crank up the heater?

"You okay?"

Cody looked at the man standing to his right. It was his brother, he knew that, but for a few terrifying seconds he couldn't think of his name.

Dave. It was Dave, his younger brother and best man. And he was keeping Cody company while he waited to walk down the center aisle of the chairs populated with their friends and family inside the Parson's Pines Optimum Life Community Center. The ceremony was being held in the Wickersham Room, while the reception would be across the hall in the Langley Room. Apparently the rooms had all been named after those people who had made the largest donations to the center.

"Huh? Me? Yeah. Fine. I'm fine."

"You're a little pale."

"It's the tuxedo. It's washing out my complexion."

Dave chuckled. "Yeah, I don't think a white tuxedo is going to make you look quite this pale. You look like you're going to throw up."

Cody shook his head. "Nope. Just a little nervous."

"About getting married?"

Cody held his hand up and waggled it back and forth. "Sort of. Mostly just talking in front of everyone."

"Dude, you talk with all of us all the time."

"Yeah, *with* all of you, not *in front* of all of you."

"You'll do great. Just focus on Demetrius."

Cody glanced toward the screen made of black material that Amelia had asked her boyfriend Otis to put together. It blocked his view of Demetrius who stood at the opposite side of the room. Because they didn't want to assign any kind of gender role to either of them, they had discussed with Amelia how to handle the wedding processional. After some long conversation, she had finally suggested that Cody and Demmy each enter from opposite sides of the space, one to the left of the guests, and the other to the right. The wedding party would walk down the center aisle, but a screen would be set up to keep Cody and Demmy from seeing each other until it was time. They would walk in at the same time and come down the far aisles, turn at the front and approach each other until they stood together before Amelia who was offi-ciating.

It had all sounded great and easy and swell when they had been talking about it, but now that it was almost time, Cody was afraid he was going to trip or stumble or fart or belch or throw up or pass out, or any number of other embar-rassing things.

The low and calming music faded out, and Cody's heart pounded. His mouth felt dry and his tongue seemed to have grown to the size of his forearm, complete with hair.

Dave pulled him into a tight hug. "I love you, big brother. And I'm really, really happy for you. You're my best friend, and I wish you and Demetrius every happiness."

"Gark," Cody managed to say in reply.

Dave stepped back, winked, then turned away and lined up behind Jugs and Demetrius's roommate from college, Trent Warburton, who had agreed to be his groomsman. All four men wore black tuxedos, including Demmy's best man, Oliver, who also happened to be his ex-boyfriend. Cody had only griped a little bit when Demmy had told him who he'd wanted to ask to be his best man. The truth was, Cody had gotten to like Ollie over the years, even though he pretended he wasn't very fond of him.

Still, he didn't think he'd want Demmy and Ollie running off on a road trip any time soon.

Now that the music had faded out, Cody could hear the quiet whispering and position shifting of their guests. There weren't that many people, he tried to comfort himself. Just everyone they knew.

Different music started, faster and harder than what had previously been playing. The familiar notes helped to calm him a bit. It was "Rock You Like a Hurricane" by the Scorpions, and it had been Cody's pick for their wedding party to walk down the aisle. The guests all laughed, and some of them went so far as to applaud and whistle as well. Jugs gave Cody a big smile and a thumbs up before he set off on his walk down the center aisle, followed a short time later by Demmy's roommate, Trent. Dave winked at Cody once more before he started walking, and a minute later, Ollie flashed Cody a smile before he set off.

He and Demmy were next.

This was it. He was getting married.

A high-pitched buzzing sound started, and Cody panicked, thinking something was wrong with the sound system. A few seconds later he realized it was happening inside his own head, and he closed his eyes and focused on his breathing. He could do this. Just a few minutes from now the hard part would all be over. He and Demmy would be married, and they'd have a big party in the room across the hall.

Otis, Amelia's boyfriend, approached. "Ready?"

"No," Cody said.

Otis smiled. "Good. Get going. One foot in front of the other. It's as simple as that."

Cody hesitated for a second, but then Otis nudged him and he set off down the side aisle. He kept this gaze locked on the wall in front of him and focused on his steps. Whispers and murmurs throughout the attendees threatened to distract him, but he refused to look at anyone. Just after the front row, he turned to the right and his first step faltered a bit as he saw Demmy for the first time.

He'd known what Demmy would be wearing because it was the same as Cody wore himself: white tuxedo jacket, white tuxedo shirt, black bow tie, black cummerbund, black pants and shoes. But he hadn't seen Demmy dressed up in a really long time, and the sight struck him like a blow to the gut. Demmy's face glowed and his smile was bigger than Cody had ever seen. Cody's cheeks ached and he realized he was smiling just as wide.

They came together in front of Amelia and clasped hands as the Scorpions faded out. Cody couldn't take his gaze off Demmy, and his cock took notice of the blush in Demmy's cheeks.

"You look nice," Cody whispered, but apparently loud enough for most of the attendees to hear, because a good portion of them laughed.

"Thanks," Demmy said. "You clean up nice yourself."

"Are you boys done?" Amelia said. "We've got a time limit on this room."

More laughter, and Cody felt himself relax a little. Amelia read some spiritual and touching words that Cody would never be able to recall. He stared at Demmy as she spoke, focusing only on him.

"Cody?"

He blinked and looked at her. "Yeah?"

More laughter from their friends.

"Repeat after me, please," Amelia said.

"Oh. Right. Yeah, sure."

He recited the standard vows of having and holding, for richer and poorer, in sickness and in health, till death do they part. Dave handed him the ring and Cody slid it onto Demmy's finger. He let out a long, quiet breath as Demmy repeated the same vows and accepted Cody's ring from Ollie. When Demmy slid the ring onto his finger, it felt heavy and strange, but not in a bad way. It was reassuring and comforting, not at all the terrible burden he'd always heard it described.

"You may now kiss your spouse," Amelia said.

"It's about time," Demmy said, and everyone laughed, including Cody just before he pulled Demmy hard against him and planted a long, hot kiss on him.

When they parted, Amelia announced the newly weds to the attendees and everyone applauded, and some people whistled. Cody thought he'd never stop smiling as he clutched Demmy's hand and followed their best men up the center aisle as the Scorpions blared again.

Pictures were taken, people shook their hands and hugged them. They all filed across the hall to the Langley Room where someone pressed a mug of beer into Cody's hand and he drank it gratefully, only to have it replaced with a glass of champagne. Demmy took his hand and led him to the wedding party table set up at the far end of the room and they sat together. A long, low flower arrangement sat before them, filled with red and white roses and a number of flowers Cody couldn't identify.

"Flowers look great," Cody said.

"Yeah, Nicolae did a great job." Demmy took his hand. "You holding up okay?"

Cody nodded, aware he was only managing to retain a few seconds of input. "I think so."

"You look a little spaced out."

"I feel that way. But I'm okay."

"I hope so, Mr. Bower-Singleton."

Cody grinned and leaned in for a kiss. "Have no fear, Mr. Bower-Singleton, I have no regrets or fears."

"Good."

They had hired Margie, owner of Margie's Diner, to cater the reception and bake the cake, and everything tasted amazing. Cody had wanted meatloaf and macaroni and cheese, and Demmy had added the option of rosemary chicken breasts and an eggplant lasagna for any vegetarians. Cody ate but barely tasted the food. He was having a great time talking and laughing with people, but everything seemed to be happening inside a very realistic movie he was watching. The only times he truly felt anything was when Demmy touched him.

"Ready for our first dance?" Demmy asked.

Cody's eyes went wide. "We picked a song?"

"You got to pick the wedding march, and I picked our first dance. Come on, I think you'll like it."

Cody followed him out to the dance floor, very conscious of everyone watching them. Was he supposed to have learned a dance routine?

"Hey, look at me," Demmy said, and Cody met his gaze. "Relax, I did this as a surprise. You had nothing to do with it. Okay?"

"Oh. Okay."

Demmy nodded to Jugs who stood behind a table and wore a pair of headphones. Jugs smiled and pressed a button, unleashing an all-too-familiar fast-paced electronic beat. Cody tipped his head back and roared laughter as the attendees all laughed as well. Demmy grabbed his hand to get his attention back and they started dancing to what he should have known all along would be their song: "Holding Out for a Hero," by Bonnie Tyler.

The night went on with many drinks and delicious cake, dozens and dozens of pictures with him and Demmy, and a variety of guests. Cody danced with his mother, and then Demmy's mother, and then Amelia, and then Lucia Durant, a sheriff's deputy and one of his ex-girlfriends from high school. After Lucia, he danced with Zenona Baldwin, another ex-girlfriend who was a doctor at the hospital. Eileen Berridge, Ollie's grandmother, pulled him out to the dance floor for a couple of songs as well, and Cody couldn't remember the last time he felt so good even though his feet hurt so much.

By the end of the night he was exhausted and very glad they didn't need to stay and clean up. The kitchen manager approached with the bar bill, and Cody started to reach for his wallet, but his father stepped in front of him and handed over his own credit card.

"Have a happy life, son," his father said, and pulled him into a hug. "This is your mother's and my gift to you, remember?"

"Thanks, Dad," Cody said, and hugged his father again.

A short time later, with a final beer in hand, Cody went off in search of Demmy and found him sitting at a table with his parents and Amelia. Demmy smiled as he approached and reached out a hand for Cody to take.

"Mom and Dad are paying Margie's catering bill for us," Demmy said.

"What?" Cody got up and hugged first Olivia then Marshall hard. After he'd sat down next to Demmy again, he said, "My dad just paid our bar bill."

"What?" Demmy jumped up to go find Cody's parents as Amelia, Olivia, Marshall, and Cody all laughed.

"Are you happy, Cody?" Olivia asked.

"More than I ever imagined," Cody said.

"It's true," Amelia added. "I see them all the time, and they're both very happy."

"We're glad to hear that," Marshall said. "And not at all surprised. Olivia and I are both glad Demetrius found someone who loves him as much as we do."

"Rest assured that is definitely the case," Cody said, and looked over to where Demmy was talking with Cody's parents. "Don't know how I got so lucky. But I'm very glad I finally figured it out."

Cody's four brothers approached and Dave pulled him up from his chair.

"We're all heading back to the AirBNB house we rented," Dave said, and hugged him tight. "Congrats, Cody. It was an awesome celebration."

"Thanks for being my best man."

"I wouldn't have wanted to be anywhere else."

"All right," said Grant, the oldest of Cody's brothers, and pulled Dave away from Cody. "Leave some brotherly love for the rest of us."

Grant had his long hair pulled back into a man bun, and when Cody hugged him, he could smell marijuana on him. He really hoped Grant hadn't brought pot with him on the plane, but decided that the less he knew about it, the better.

"Be happy, Codes," Grant said.

"Don't call me that," Cody said.

"I'm going to find Dems and give him a big hug as well," Grant said.

"Don't call him that," Cody said.

But Grant was gone, and Brady, the youngest of all five, was there to pull him into a hug.

"Thanks for inviting us," Brady said. "Hilari sends her best wishes, but she didn't want to leave Erin. I guess three months is just too soon."

"I totally understand," Cody said. "How's fatherhood?"

Brady's smile was dazzling, even with the bags under his eyes from what Cody imagined was lack of sleep. "It's amazing. That little girl has stolen my heart."

"They do that to you," Cody said.

Brady was gently moved aside by Roman, second oldest and the most conservative. He stood stiff and formal in his blue pin-striped suit with red power tie, looking steadily at Cody.

"Thanks for inviting us," Roman said, and gave Cody a stiff hug. "We hope you're happy."

"Shame Madison and the kids couldn't come."

"The kids are so busy with all of their functions, and Madison stayed home to make sure they kept their schedules."

Cody nodded and gave Roman a tight smile. He knew that Madison and Roman hadn't wanted to expose Summer and Brock to a gay wedding. It was actually more than a little surprising that Roman himself had come from Salt Lake City instead of just sending a card or gift. Cody supposed he had his parents and other brothers to thank for that.

"Well, give them our love."

"Absolutely." Roman shook Cody's hand and then turned away.

"Aw, I missed talking to Roman?" Demmy asked as he came up beside him. "That's too bad."

"Yeah, yeah," Cody said with a grin. "You ready to get out of here?"

"I am. But we're not going home. We have a room at the Harriettville Hilton. Our parents are staying at our house tonight."

Cody's eyebrows went up. "They're what?"

Demmy squeezed his hand. "It's okay. I parent-proofed the house and I packed you an overnight bag. Come on, Jugs is going to give us a ride to the hotel."

They made their way through the much smaller, happily drunk group of family and few friends, saying goodbye and receiving hugs. Cody's father pressed a wad of cash into his hand and pulled him into a tight hug that brought tears to Cody's eyes.

"I love you, son," his father whispered. "I'm so happy for you."

"I love you, too, Dad. Thanks."

Cody's mother was next, tears shining in her eyes as she reached up for a hug.

"We love you and Demetrius so much. Have a wonderful honeymoon." She stepped back and handed him a greeting card envelope that felt a little thick. "Just so you know, we rented a car and drove here. We fly back home tomorrow."

Cody felt the tiny bulges in the envelope. "Is this what I think it is?"

His mother acted coy. "I guess you'll have to open it and see for yourself." She kissed his cheek. "Now get out of here."

They managed to escape from the community center and followed Jugs to where Cody's truck was parked at the curb. Just behind Cody's truck, a few guests and Parson's Pines employees were loading gifts into the bed of Demmy's truck.

"Who's driving what?" Cody asked.

"Your parents are driving my truck to our house where both our parents will take our gifts into the house. Jugs is driving us in your truck to the hotel where he left his car in the parking lot."

Cody grabbed Demmy's hand and pulled him to a stop. "You've been pretty sneaky with all of this."

Demmy tried to look innocent. "Who, me?"

"Come here." Cody kissed him, slow and deep.

"Ahem," Jugs said. "Enough with the PDA. Get in the truck and I'll get you to the hotel where you can slobber all over each other in the privacy of your room."

"Jugs is a true romantic," Demmy said.

"I think I just swooned," Cody said.

They laughed together, and then Demmy pulled him toward the truck. "Come on, let's go."

During the drive to the Harriettville Hilton, they talked about the wedding and reception and the upcoming week when Jugs was going to handle any Critter Catchers calls that came in.

"We appreciate the help, buddy," Cody said.

"I'm not taking any skunk cases." Jugs gave him a side-eye. "Once was enough. Enid Helen is still traumatized."

Cody looked away to hide his smirk. Enid Helen was the Yorkshire Terrier Jugs had caught living in a client's crawlspace and ended up adopting. "Are you sure it's Enid Helen who's still traumatized?'

"Oh, look. Here's the hotel," Jugs said, and turned into the lot.

After several hugs and handshakes, Cody and Demmy

stood side by side and watched Jugs get into his old Ford Escort and drive off with a wave. Demmy took Cody's hand and led him into the hotel lobby. It was late, and the only people around were the employees behind the desk who looked up and smiled.

"Congratulations!" called a young man with a trim blond beard.

"Thank you," Demmy called back, and pulled Cody to the elevator.

"We're checked in?" Cody asked.

"I did that earlier. Our bags are in the room."

"More sneakiness."

"I'm a married man now," Demmy said with a grin. "I get to be sneaky."

"Not sure that was part of our vows."

"I guess you weren't listening close enough."

The elevator arrived and they kissed as it lifted them to the top floor. Cody followed Demmy down the hall and waited while he opened the door to the room. It was the bridal suite, and was the largest hotel room Cody had ever been inside.

"Holy fuck, how much is this a night?" Cody asked as he looked around the living room. It was larger than their living room, and fifteen times as fancy. He stuck his head through a door to find a dining room, and beyond that a full kitchen.

"A lot," Demmy said. "And it was a gift from my parents."

"Yeah?" Cody turned and fixed Demmy with a predatory look. "They willingly paid for this room, knowing what I would do to their only child within these walls?"

Demmy's blush sent heat rushing to Cody's cock. "I don't think they really put much thought into that." He made a face. "At least I hope not. Gross."

"Well, I've been putting a lot of thought into it. A lot."

"Oh? Don't you want to shower—"

Cody stopped his words with a hard, hot kiss. When he pulled back, he cradled Demmy's face in his hands and smiled. "Not yet. First, I want to make sure we use the dining room table."

Demmy frowned. "You're hungry?"

"You could say that."

Cody lifted Demmy into his arms and carried him into the dining room where he laid him on his back on the table. Demmy laughed as he kicked off his shoes.

"I'm a sweaty mess," Demmy said.

"So am I. It won't be the first or last time we get off in this condition."

Cody let his tuxedo jacket drop to the floor. His bow tie, cummerbund, and shirt soon followed. He stepped out of his shoes and quickly shucked his pants and underwear, wearing only his socks as his cock jutted out toward Demmy, bobbing with each beat of his heart. Demmy had managed to get his jacket and bowtie off, and had just started on the buttons of his shirt when Cody moved aside the chair between them and stepped close, his cock hovering in Demmy's face.

"God you're fucking gorgeous," Demmy whispered, then grabbed his cock tight and opened wide to suck him in.

"Oh, yeah."

Cody stood for a moment with his hands in fists at his side and his head tipped back, savoring Demmy's mouth on him. He looked down and discovered Demmy looking up at him as he sucked. Demmy's left hand gripped Cody's dick at the base and the light overhead gleamed along the surface of his silver wedding band. Cody put a hand against the side of Demmy's head, thumb stroking his scalp as he watched Demmy take him deep into his throat.

"That feels so fucking good. Makes me hungry for a taste."

Cody pulled back and bent over to kiss Demmy hard, tongues twisting together as Cody fumbled with the remainder of the buttons on Demmy's shirt. He flipped the shirt open and ran his hand up and down through the hair covering his belly and chest. Demmy had unbuckled his belt and opened his pants and managed to shove them and his underwear halfway down his thighs, all without breaking their kiss.

When Cody finally pulled back, he looked into Demmy's eyes and said, "I am so in love with you, I can't even explain it."

"I feel the same way. It's hard to believe you and I have been having sex for almost a year now, let alone just got married."

Cody held up his left hand with his gold band on the ring finger. "Believe it, baby. You're stuck with me now."

"Just the way I like it," Demmy said, and then moved Cody's hand down to where his erection stretched up along his belly. "And you said something about being hungry for a taste?"

"More like starving."

Cody moved to the end of the table, shoving aside chairs as he went. He yanked Demmy's pants and underwear the rest of the way off then removed his socks and threw them aside. He took off his own socks and, finally naked, climbed up on the table to stretch out on top of Demmy. Their cocks lined up perfectly, pre-cum mixing and helping them slide together. Cody kissed Demmy's soft, swollen lips before moving down to his ear and then to the side of his neck. He slid lower, sucking on a nipple and gently tugging it with his teeth. Lower still, pausing to lick the salty sweat glistening along Demmy's belly, and then finally running his tongue down the hot length of his cock, right to his shaved balls. He worked his way back to the tip of Demmy's dick, and extended his tongue to swirl it around the head. With a tight hold on the base, Cody slowly took him into his mouth.

Demmy groaned and rested a hand on the back of Cody's head, holding him in place and thrusting up into his mouth. Cody closed his eyes and let Demmy work, giving him what he needed.

"I want you up here," Demmy said, his voice deep with need. "I want to suck you, too."

Cody got off the table as Demmy rolled onto his side, and he delivered a tongue-heavy, lingering kiss before stretching out alongside him in a sixty-nine position. Their sucking started out slow at first, but quickly intensified. Cody was getting close, but he didn't want to come just yet. He had more things planned for Demmy.

"You okay to take this a step farther?" Cody asked, and tapped a finger against the tight ring of Demmy's anus.

"Oh, yeah. I've been thinking about that all day."

Cody rolled off the table and pulled Demmy to one end. His back left a long smear of sweat along the polished wood surface, and they both laughed.

"Housekeeping is going to love us tomorrow," Demmy said.

Cody leaned in for a kiss. "You have no idea." He pulled back a bit and asked. "Where's my bag?"

"Bedroom. Your side of the bed. But the lube's on the nightstand."

"Oh?" Cody raised his eyebrows. "Did you already make use of our honeymoon suite?"

Demmy smirked. "Nope. I was getting it ready for us for tonight." He pulled him down for a kiss. "Stop talking and go get the lube."

Cody jogged through the suite, cock slapping against his belly and thighs. He grabbed the lube from the nightstand and returned to the space between Demmy's upraised legs, the tube already uncapped and drizzling onto his dick. With slow, easy movements, Cody inserted a slick finger into

Demmy, followed soon after by a second, and then a third. Demmy moaned and whispered encouragement as Cody fingered him.

"Ready for something more?" Cody asked.

"God yes." Demmy lifted his head from the table to look at him. "Get that big cock inside me."

Cody's dick jumped at the growl in Demmy's voice as well as the words. He loved it when Demmy talked dirty.

He applied more lube to his aching cock and then stepped close. The tip of his dick touched Demmy's hole and he pressed forward, sinking slowly inside until he was fully seated.

"Oh, fuck yeah." Demmy's voice was low and deep. He stroked himself and looked up at Cody, pupils so wide they practically covered his irises. "Fuck me, baby."

"Not going to take long," Cody said as he started thrusting, hands tight around Demmy's ankles.

"Me either," Demmy said. "Oh yeah. Right there. Just like that. Go deep."

Sweat ran down Cody's face and he closed his eyes and tipped his head back. Demmy's ass was hot and soft and tight and Cody's dick fit perfectly inside it. It was like they were made to go together.

"Really close," Cody said. "Right there."

"Do it. Come inside me."

A few more thrusts was all it took before Cody let out a deep grunt as his orgasm rushed through him. His cock pulsed inside Demmy, and Cody felt Demmy's muscles tighten around him as he came himself.

"Fuck yeah. Oh fuck."

Demmy's toes tightened as cum splashed across his belly. When he'd finished, he lay gasping and sweaty on the table, and Cody thought he'd never looked sexier. With slow movements, Cody eased out of him and lowered his legs. He leaned over him and delivered a gentle kiss on his mouth.

"What time is checkout?" Cody asked.

Demmy frowned, then said, "I think it's eleven. Why?"

Cody kissed him again. "Because I'm not done with you yet, Mr. Bower-Singleton."

CHAPTER FIVE

"You seriously had no idea about this?" Demetrius took a T-shirt off the rack and held it in front of himself.

Cody glared from where he stood in line at the convenience store register. "I assure you, I had no idea."

Demetrius turned the shirt around to look at the graphic: a line drawing that depicted a boater on a lake with a startled expression as he looked up at a long-necked monster smiling down at him. The caption underneath read, "A big 'Hello!' from Heaversford Lake and Esther!"

"Do you want me to buy you a souvenir T-shirt?" Demetrius asked. "They have several varieties in your size."

Cody turned away from the cashier and approached Demetrius. "I have never wanted something less in my life than one of these souvenir T-shirts."

"I think it would be a nice memento of our honeymoon."

"Your thinking would be incorrect. Come on."

Demetrius replaced the T-shirt and followed Cody out of the convenience store, laughing to himself. During the first few hours of their drive, the conversation had been easy and flirty, with Cody behind the wheel. Cody's mood had changed, however, when they passed a billboard with a cartoon depiction of Esther, and the blurb, "Esther sightings on the rise at lovely Heaversford Lake!" Each new billboard had further soured Cody's mood, and Demetrius had ventured a guess about the reservations Cody had made for them.

Now, he could hear Cody grumbling as they walked to the truck parked at a gas pump.

"This is supposed to be our time away from monsters and craziness. We're supposed to be spending it together, just us."

Demetrius waited until they were inside the truck before speaking.

"All of those billboards and T-shirts and coffee mugs and baseball caps with cartoon Esthers is just a bunch of tourist trap crap. I'm sure there's nothing to the legend. I mean, look at Nessie over in Loch Ness. All of those sightings just keep bringing in tourists hoping for a glimpse, but they've never found any hard evidence that she exists."

Cody shook his head. "That's what they said about the Devil of Pinesville, and bigfoot. And look where all of that got us."

"Yeah, I know. But, I gotta say, this is pretty much par for our course, you know? It wouldn't be a typical trip for us if there wasn't some monster legend lurking in the background."

"I get that. I just wanted to make this trip really special for you. For us. Something different that we'd both enjoy. A way to kick off this new part of our lives."

"So let's make that happen. Come on, where do we go for our reservation?"

Cody looked at his phone. "The Crescent Hill Hotel."

"Sounds perfect. Let's go."

Cody started the truck and pulled out of the lot. As he cruised along the main road that followed the curve of

Heaversford Lake, Demetrius looked out his window at the fishing and speed boats cutting across the water. It was a big body of water, one of the largest lakes he'd seen, and the wind was up which made the lake's surface choppy with small waves. Near the middle of the lake he could see a small island, and he wondered if someone lived out there.

When Cody turned into a driveway, Demetrius looked away from the lake and found a white clapboard house with green shutters and a covered front porch running across the front and around the far corner.

"Wow, this is nice," Demetrius said. "Looks cozy and comfortable."

"Yeah? Don't get used to it, because we're not staying here."

"What? But the sign says Crescent Hill Hotel."

Cody pulled into a spot and put the truck in park, then winked at him before getting out.

"What is going on?" Demetrius asked himself.

He got out of the truck and followed Cody up the steps to the porch and into the hotel. The small lobby was tasteful and warm, with paneled walls and a large wooden registration desk. A woman with long silver hair done up in a bun stood behind the desk and smiled at them.

"Welcome to the Crescent Hill Hotel. Are you checking in?"

"Hi. Yes, I have a reservation for Cody Bower."

Demetrius browsed through the local attraction pamphlets laid out on a side table across the room. There were a lot of Esther boat excursions, an Esther museum, and a haunted hayride featuring, of course, Esther. As he browsed through the information, Demetrius listened as Cody spoke to the woman.

"Oh, you're in the bungalow. It's such a lovely spot. Is it just the two of you?"

The familiar tension coiled into life in Demetrius's gut. Nearly every time he had checked into a hotel with a boyfriend, there was that moment where the person behind the counter had to come to an understanding of what they were going to be doing in that room. And here Cody was about to experience it for himself for the first time.

"Um, yeah. Just us. That's it." Cody stammered a bit, but seemed to get through it okay.

Demetrius joined him at the desk as the woman tapped on a keyboard attached to an old computer complete with a large, fat monitor.

"Well, Rufus will be escorting you to the island." She handed Cody his credit card back and smiled. "You boys enjoy your stay. Keep an eye out for Esther."

Cody gave her a tight grin. "Oh, we won't. But thanks. Where do we find Rufus?"

"He'll be down at the dock. Just take your bags across the road and look for the Crescent Hill Hotel sign. You can sign up for Esther spotting tours right there as well."

"I think we'll pass, but thanks," Cody said and turned away. "Let's go."

"Best get some outdoor activities in quick, they're predicting rain this afternoon and into the evening," she called after them.

"Of course they are," Cody grumbled as he led the way out of the hotel.

"We're staying out on the island?" Demetrius asked.

"Yep. Just us out there. No one else around." Cody handed Demetrius his bag from the back of the truck's cab and waggled his eyebrows. "We can get as freaky as we want to."

"You're not scared of Esther spying on us?"

"Let her look. With all the stuff I've got planned for you, that monster wouldn't know what hit her."

The timbre of Cody's voice made Demetrius's cock take notice. "Oh, my."

"Oh, yeah. I'm going to wear us out this week."

"What the hell are we waiting for? Let's get to that dock!"

Demetrius set off down the driveway at a run and heard Cody laughing behind him. The sound of it made him feel good, and he laughed as well. They crossed the road and made their way down a short flight of wooden steps to the concrete dock that stuck out over the water. It was wide with slips on either side where a variety of boats were tied up. They walked past an enclosed booth where a few people were in line to sign up for an Esther sight-seeing tour of the lake, and Demetrius heard Cody give a derisive snort.

"Think we should tell them about what happened to the documentary crew that went out into the woods near Pinesville?" Cody asked.

Demetrius shivered at the memory of watching the footage of the crew being killed by the Devil of Pinesville, a creature that was part bat, part goat, and completely terrifying.

"I'd rather fly under the whole monster-hunting radar here, if we can," he said.

"Really? I must admit I'm a little surprised. I would have thought you'd be first in line to look for Esther."

"I've already caught my monster," Demetrius said, and gently bumped Cody.

Cody chuckled as they reached a boat slip with a sign above it that read Crescent Hill Hotel. A small fishing boat with an enclosed bridge rode the choppy water, and from somewhere inside they could hear a man whistling. The name painted across the stern read *The Lazy Aye*.

"Ahoy!" Cody called.

The whistling stopped and a man stepped out of the bridge to smile at them. He was a tall, broad-shouldered

Black man, with a round belly and an ass to match. Work gloves made his big hands look even larger, and he pulled off one glove to reach out and shake with each of them. His close-cut hair the color of steel wool and weathered face made him look to be somewhere in his seventies.

"I'm Rufus, but I guess you already figured that out, didn't you? Come on aboard and I'll get you two out to the island."

"Thank you," Demetrius said as Rufus took the bag from him and helped him step across to the boat. "I'm Demetrius, and this is Cody."

"Pleased to meet you both. Put on a life vest and have a seat. The lake's a little mischievous today, but we'll get out there quick as a wink."

In a few minutes, Rufus had the two engines running and the boat bounced across the waves, heading for the island in the center of the lake.

"Do you boys know anything about Heaversford Lake?" Rufus called over his shoulder.

"Not a single thing," Cody said.

"She's a deep, mysterious lady, full of secrets and surprises. Formed by glaciers tens of thousands of years ago, she's almost five hundred feet at her deepest point and supports a wide variety of plant and fish life. Best walleye fishing in northern Pennsylvania, too. Got a nice beach on the far side of the lake from the Crescent Hill Hotel, but the majority of the shoreline is small stones and bluffs. Not a lot of sunbathers or swimmers because of it."

"So more sport fishing?" Demetrius asked as he squinted into the wind and spray.

"Yup. Sport fishing." Rufus grinned. "And monster hunting. You here to look for Esther?"

"Not even a little bit," Cody said.

Demetrius grinned and nudged him, then realized Rufus was still watching. A small flutter of panic went through him as he wondered how Rufus would take their familiarity. But Rufus's grin widened into a smile and he winked.

"Your first trip together?" Rufus asked.

"No. We've traveled together before," Demetrius replied, then decided to take it a step further and added, "We're on our honeymoon."

Cody looked at him with raised eyebrows and Demetrius patted his thigh reassuringly.

"Well I do like to see that," Rufus said with a laugh and shook his head. "Young love. Ain't nothing like it. I was young and in love about a million and a half years ago, when dinosaurs still walked the Earth."

"Like Esther?" Cody asked.

Rufus's booming laugh made Demetrius and Cody join in.

"Exactly! I've lived here all my life and have never caught a glimpse of our girl, but I keep hoping to one day." He looked over his shoulder again. "Not much nightlife in town for men like us."

Demetrius nudged Cody again and grinned.

"But seeing as it's your honeymoon, I doubt you'll be wanting to leave the island much any way, if at all."

"You're right on the money, Rufus," Cody said.

"Do you have someone special in your life?" Demetrius asked.

"Other than Esther?" Rufus laughed again. "As a matter of fact, I do. It's not common knowledge, but it's satisfying in its own way." He waggled his eyebrows. "Nothing better than a man in uniform, is there?"

"Nope, not a thing," Demetrius said, then caught Cody's surly expression. "You wear a uniform, dear, don't worry."

"Really?" Rufus looked between them. "You don't look like policemen. Are you in the service?"

"I believe Demmy is referring to the coveralls we wear when we go on a job," Cody said.

"Hey, coveralls can be sexy. You ever see those pornos set in an automotive shop?" Rufus laughed.

"I gotta say, this is by far the best boat ride I've ever been on," Demetrius said with a laugh.

"Congratulations on your wedding. Was it a big service?"

"We kept it on the smaller side," Cody said. "Around fifty people."

"We rented the activities rooms at the senior citizen complex where my aunt and his grandmother reside."

"I like that," Rufus said. "Keeping it all in the community. That's the way it should be. Uh oh. I need to make a detour, hold on."

As Rufus steered the boat to the right, Demetrius held on tight and looked over the gunwale. An older man with strands of long gray hair floating in the wind around his baseball cap captained a very elaborate boat. The man sat in a seat and peddled in a manner similar to that of recumbent bicycles Demetrius had seen around Parson's Hollow. At the front of the seating area, an opening twice as tall and three times as wide created a kind of suction into the body of the boat. A collection area was being towed behind the contraption, and it looked to Demetrius to be full of trash. Rufus lifted a hand to wave to the boater and he waved back.

"That's Dave Lamond, lifelong resident here on Heaversford. He built that boat himself to try and do something about all the plastic littering the lake." Rufus shook his head as he got the boat back on course for the island. "Damn shame what's happening to our bodies of water these days. If it's not the plastic grocery bags, it's the plastic straws or drinking cups or single use coffee pods. It's really taken a toll on the fish and turtles around here."

Demetrius watched Dave peddling away and gathering trash, then looked over the side of the boat. A plastic grocery bag floated by, followed seconds later by a couple of water bottles.

"Awful," Demetrius said.

"It's gotten a lot worse lately," Rufus said. "Breaks my heart to see the lake come to this. But Dave's got help from an environmental group who come out and scuba dive to clean up the plastic that's sunk too low to get scooped up by his boat." He slowed the engines and smiled. "And here we are. Welcome to Broken Jaw Island. The dock is built in Hideaway Cove, and your honeymoon bungalow is just about dead center on the island."

Through a thick stand of trees, Demetrius caught flashes of a house. The sides and roof were cedar shingle, and a covered porch ran across the entire front. A dock extended from between two large rocks, leading to a series of wooden steps that went up a short hill toward the cabin.

"You've got a two-man boat there at the dock for fishing or a trip into town. Just watch out for the pleasure cruisers, and there's a nasty patch of cross-current out in the middle that might give you a jostle. Make sure you wear your life vests whenever you go out on the water. The engine's a mid-size, so the trip to town will probably take you forty minutes one way. Here we go. Watch your fingers now."

Rufus edged the boat up alongside the dock and cut the engines. He got out and tied the boat up, then helped them step off.

"You okay carrying your bags?" Rufus asked.

"Oh, yeah," Cody said. "Just lead the way."

As Rufus walked up the steps ahead of them, he pointed out different varieties of trees and bushes and flowers.

"There've been rumors of a couple of deer out here, probably wandered over when the lake froze in the winter, so don't be surprised if they come nosing around."

"How big is the island?" Demetrius asked.

"Broken Jaw Island is one mile long and just over a mile wide. The dock extends from the center of the only cove which is mostly hidden from view of the town, which is why it was named Hideaway Cove. Story goes this island was used by the Delaware Indians as a spiritual retreat. After they were relocated, smugglers and mobsters hid out among the trees. The island was owned by a farming family who sold it to the original owners of the Crescent Hill Hotel when they found the soil too rocky to grow crops."

"You know a lot about this place," Cody said.

"I've always liked history and geography," Rufus said, and paused at the top of the stairs to catch his breath.

Demetrius and Cody stood and looked back out over the lake. The overcast sky made the water looked gray and cold. Demetrius could feel the ozone from an approaching storm in the air, and he wondered how it was going to look out here on the island.

"Whew, can't do as many stairs as I used to," Rufus said. "Cabin is this way." He started off along a boardwalk from the steps that led through the trees to the steps of the cabin's front porch. "We just had the boardwalk replaced at the end of the summer last year. When it rains, which it looks like it's fixing to do, the island can get very muddy. Mind where you step if you go off the boardwalk."

"Is there electricity?" Cody asked.

"Yup. An underwater cable was run out here years ago. Comes up out of the ground a ways back in the woods and is strung along poles to the cabin. Might flicker a bit in the storm, but shouldn't go out."

"Shouldn't being the key word," Cody said.

"You've got that right," Rufus said with a wink.

They reached the cabin and climbed the five steps to the porch. The breeze had picked up and tree limbs swayed as Rufus turned the knob and opened the unlocked door. The living room was spacious and populated with a large, comfortable-looking couch and two big armchairs arranged in front of a stone fireplace. A small dining table with four straight-backed chairs sat in front of a big picture window on the side of the cabin, and a narrow kitchen was visible around the side of the fireplace.

"Fridge and cabinets are stocked with groceries, per the emailed list we received," Rufus said. "Plenty of firewood in the woodbox here and outside. Stove is gas and the pilot lights are lit. There's a half-bath off the kitchen, and the master bedroom and bathroom are upstairs. No air conditioning, but there's usually a good breeze off the lake, and ceiling fans in each of the rooms. A shed out back has inflatable rafts, life vests and fishing equipment."

A rumble of thunder made them all look toward the large front window.

"Going to be raining soon," Cody said.

"That's my cue to leave." Rufus headed for the door. "Spotty cellular service out here at best, but there's a satellite dish on the roof and a wireless router on top of the kitchen cabinets, so you'll be able to connect to wifi. If you need anything, there's a shortwave radio setup in the kitchen. Keep it on at all times, just in case some really bad weather rolls in. That way we can get in touch with you."

"Thank you, Rufus," Cody said, and Demetrius saw him slip the man some cash as he shook his hand.

"Thank you." He smiled and nodded to them in turn. "Cody and Demetrius, enjoy your honeymoon. I wish you all the best."

They followed him out the door and stood side-by-side on the deck watching him walk back along the boardwalk. Cody put his arm around Demetrius's shoulders and pulled him close against his side.

"Just the two of us." Cody ran his hand up and down

Demetrius's spine. "No one around. What kind of kinky stuff do you want to get into?"

A brilliant flash of lightning left Demetrius seeing spots. It was followed almost immediately by a wall-shaking blast of thunder that made them both jump. They fled inside to find that the lights had gone out.

"Shit," Cody said.

Rain started falling in a heavy sheet, pummeling the ground hard enough to fling mud and small stones into the air.

"Do you think Rufus was able to leave?"

Before Cody could respond, they saw a figure rushing toward them through the rain, a slicker held up over its head. Rufus climbed the steps and stood dripping onto the boards under the porch overhang. He peered in through the screen door with a sheepish expression.

"Sorry guys, but I need to wait for the weather to lighten up before I can cast off."

Demetrius pushed the screen door open and gestured for Rufus to come inside. "I wondered if you'd had time to start back. Come on in."

"I know it's your honeymoon, but this isn't a good time to be on the lake," Rufus said as he tossed the slicker over a rocking chair on the porch and entered the cabin. "These spring storms don't usually last long. My apologies again."

"Don't worry about it," Cody said. "You're just in time to help us light the fire and some lanterns because the power went out."

"Oh hell, already?" Rufus tried a light switch. "Yep. That's deader than a door nail. I wonder if that lightning struck the utility pole out back? Well, come on. I'll show you where the oil lamps and matches are kept."

Rufus made his way through the living room, wet shoes squelching.

Cody looked at Demetrius and shrugged. "Happy wedding night, husband."

Demetrius squeezed his hand. "I wouldn't want to be anyplace else."

"That's good, because it looks like we're stuck here for a while," Cody said, then flinched as another burst of lightning lit up the cabin, and a powerful boom of thunder followed immediately after.

"If the power's out, that means the pump for the well is out, too," Rufus called from the kitchen.

Demetrius managed a tight grin. "Just the three of us."

CHAPTER SIX

So far, Cody thought the honeymoon was going about as well as one of their Critter Catchers jobs. Rufus had helped them light an assortment of oil lamps as the storm battered the small island and the air inside the cabin grew more and more humid.

"Since the well water pump won't work without power, you'll have to use the hand pump out back," Rufus said. "Once the storm lets up, I'll have a look at the utility pole and see if there's anything I can do to get your power back."

"We'd appreciate that," Demmy said. "In the meantime, would you like something to eat or drink? You said we have a stocked refrigerator and cupboards."

Cody couldn't think of a way to signal for Demmy to take the hospitality down a notch or twelve; he didn't want Rufus too comfortable and possibly over-staying his welcome. Which, if anyone were to ask Cody about it, he already had. Although it wasn't his fault the storm to rival armageddon had rolled in when it had.

Rufus followed Demmy into the kitchen and they took a

quick look into the dark depths of the refrigerator as Cody leaned back into the couch and closed his eyes.

"Cody, do you want a beer?" Demmy called.

"Bring two," Cody replied, then muttered to himself, "I'm going to need them."

With a beer in hand, Rufus sat in one of the armchairs across from Cody, and Demmy sat on the couch next to him, handing over the two bottles he'd requested.

"What do you do for entertainment in town?" Demmy asked.

"Oh, you know. Not much going on in town usually. There's a half hour drive to the nearest movie theater, and an hour to something resembling a mall. Mostly we watch movies at home or go out to eat at the diner. Lot of support for school functions in town, mostly sports events, but the kids put on a heck of a play each spring as well."

"On the boat, you said you have someone special in your life," Demmy said. "Something about a man in uniform. Would that mean you're seeing a police officer?"

"You pay attention to the little details, don't you?" Rufus said with an embarrassed smile.

"You have no idea," Cody said, and received a sharp elbow from Demmy.

"We've been pretty careful about keeping things quiet, but I do take comfort from a member of the Hempstead police force." Rufus took a long pull from his beer. "We've been together for a long time now, so I guess we're somewhat official."

"But just not out to the town?" Demmy asked.

"Not to really acknowledge it, though I'm pretty sure everyone knows what's going on between us. He's just not comfortable with people knowing his business." He scooted to the edge of the chair cushion and lowered his voice. "Plus, he's white, and a bi-racial relationship would probably raise a lot more eyebrows than a gay one."

"When you buck the system, you really go for it," Cody said.

Rufus's laugh was almost drowned out by another rumble of thunder.

"You've got that right, Cody. Anyway, I'm also a few years younger than him, so there's challenges all through our relationship."

"But you've been together a long time, so there's something special there," Demmy said.

Rufus smiled and the flame from the oil lamp shone in his eyes. "Oh, yes. There's something there all right. Now, enough about me. Tell me about the two of you. How'd you meet?"

They traded off talking about their history, and Cody was actually starting to enjoy himself when Rufus looked toward the window and stood up.

"Looks like the storm's about blown itself out. Guess it's about time for me to head back." Rufus carried his empty bottle to the kitchen and placed it by the sink. "I appreciate you boys letting me cramp your style for the start of your honeymoon. I'll check on the utility pole out back before I leave."

"I'll come with you," Cody said. "I want to see where this thing is."

"Me, too," Demmy said.

"Let's go then," Rufus said, and opened a door off the kitchen Cody hadn't noticed before. "This is the side entrance."

The door opened onto a small wooden deck with a couple of plastic chairs that had been toppled by the storm. Rufus righted the chairs, then led the way down the two steps from the deck to the soggy, muddy ground.

"Ugh, what a mess," Demmy said.

"The island is basically rock and dirt. Storms turn all of it into mud." He raised his eyebrows and looked at Cody. "Still want to come along?"

Cody snorted a laugh. "I don't mind a little dirt."

"It's true," Demmy said from where he leaned on the deck railing. "I think I'll sit this one out."

"All right then," Rufus said. "Let's go, Cody."

Rufus led the way across the open and muddy area to where a narrow path disappeared into a line of small trees. Cody's boots were soon caked with mud as he trekked after Rufus. Bugs buzzed around his head and he was almost immediately soaked from walking through low-hanging branches heavy with wet leaves. By the time they reached the clearing where the utility pole stood, Cody was sweat-drenched, bug-bit, and mud-stained. He wished he'd allowed Rufus to check the condition of the pole on his own.

"Well, shit and shinola," Rufus said. "That's not good."

"What's not good?"

Cody swatted at a large, buzzing fly and moved up next to Rufus. The smoking and sparking remains of what looked to be a small power transformer sat atop a wooden utility pole that had been blackened halfway down its length.

"That doesn't look like a quick fix," Cody said.

"Far from it." Rufus pulled his smart phone from a pocket and took a couple of pictures of the damage, then turned to Cody. "There's a gas generator in the shed. It's not enough to power the whole cabin, but I can attach the refrigerator and well to it so you'll have water and food."

"All the basics of home," Cody muttered.

"I know it's not the way you wanted to start your honeymoon, but it's the best option I have for now."

"Not your fault. And trust me, this is just par for the course for us."

Rufus started back along the trail and Cody followed.

"I'll let the power company know about the damage, but it will probably be a day or two before they can get someone out here."

"Good thing Demmy and I like each other," Cody said.

"This is a true test of the depth of your love." Rufus looked over his shoulder and winked. "Think of how romantic the nights will be by oil lamp and a fire in the fireplace."

"Yeah, I'm sure we'll find something to occupy our time." He already had about a dozen positions and places inside and outside the cabin he wanted to try out. Although from the number of bugs swarming around him, he might rethink the outdoor places.

"I'm sure you will."

Cody slapped a bug on the side of neck and looked at the bloody mark it left on his palm. "Just tell me the water heater is gas."

"Water heater and stove are gas. And there's a gas grill in the yard."

They emerged from the trees and tromped through the mud to a shed a couple of yards from the cabin. Inside was a good-sized generator and a couple of plastic gas containers. Rufus ran an extension cord to the house for the refrigerator, and then hooked up the pump for the well before he started the generator with a single pull. He showed Cody where to fill it and checked that both gas containers were full.

"Think you can handle it?" Rufus asked.

Cody flapped a hand at the generator as if it were no big deal. "I got this."

"All right. You two take care out here. When I come back, I'll blow the horn when I'm about to reach the dock to give you some time to collect yourselves." Rufus grinned and winked.

"You make us sound a lot more proper than we really act."

"I'm giving you the benefit of the doubt."

Rufus clapped a hand on Cody's shoulder and left the shed. Cody looked at the generator working steadily, the rhythmic chugging lulling him into a dreamy state. The blast of the horn from Rufus's boat made him jump, and he grinned as he stepped outside and closed the shed door. He made his way across the muddy yard and sat on the steps to untie his shoes.

"I take it that horn was Rufus saying good-bye?" Demmy asked from behind the screen of the side door.

"You take it correctly." Cody pulled off a boot and looked at the thick mud covering the sole. He turned and held it up for Demmy to see. "Want to go for a hike?"

"Not really. The bugs chased me inside once the two of you went off for your stroll. How's the power situation look?"

Cody explained what they'd discovered and the information Rufus had told him, pausing now and then to wave away a cloud of bugs. He pulled off his other boot, similarly caked with mud, and set both in a corner of the deck before stepping inside the cabin. Demmy stood a couple of feet away, looking him over with a critical eye. Cody did a slow bump and grind, peeling off his sweaty, muddy shirt in the process. He ran his tongue over his teeth and pinched his own left nipple.

"You want to get with this?" he asked in a sultry voice.

Demmy laughed and Cody joined him.

"May I interest you in a shower, sir?" Demmy asked once he'd stifled his laughter.

"Yeah, okay. Let's check out the master bathroom." He leaned in and kissed Demmy softly on the lips. "And once I'm clean, I want to get dirty all over again with you."

"Sweet talker."

"You know me so well."

They made their way up the steps to the open loft master bedroom. A king-sized bed with a tall mattress set and piled with pillows took up most of the room. The white-tiled bathroom was almost as big as the bedroom and had a large claw-foot tub positioned near a floor-to-ceiling window, a walk-in shower area cordoned off behind glass blocks, and a marble-topped double sink vanity. Thick white towels were stacked on a table near the bathtub, and more lined the shelves of a built-in linen closet behind the door.

"I'm afraid to take a shower or bath in here," Cody said. "I don't want to mess it up."

Demmy looked him up and down. "You might as well get over that fear right now, because you're a mess."

"But still sexy, right?" Cody waggled his eyebrows. "Like, dead sexy, am I right?"

Demmy reached out to cup his crotch and ducked his head to lick his nipple. "The deadest."

Cody kissed him, then pulled back and frowned. "Not sure I like that description any longer. Especially out here on an island with no power."

"And don't forget Esther swimming around beneath the surface of the lake."

"I'm not going to spend one minute thinking about that scaly monster."

Cody leaned in for another kiss, but Demmy pulled back.

"How do you know she's got scales?"

"What? I don't know. She's a fish, right?" Cody started to strip. "You in need of a shower after our car and boat rides?"

"I don't think she's a fish."

Cody sighed. "Can we not discuss the local monster while I'm trying to get you in the mood for our honeymoon?"

Demmy watched him slowly unbuckle his belt. He licked his lips and started unbuttoning his shirt as he looked Cody in the eye. "It's going to take a lot of scrubbing on my part to get you clean."

"Oh yeah, there's that nasty guy I married."

Cody stepped out of his shorts and stood in his underwear, his steadily hardening cock tenting the front.

"I will never get tired of looking at you," Demmy said as he dropped his shirt on the floor. His pupils were wide, and Cody could see the long line of his dick trapped beneath his jeans.

"Good thing we got married then," Cody said. "Otherwise our partners might get suspicious."

Demmy stepped up close, put a hand on the back of his neck, and pulled Cody down for a hot, hard kiss as he stuck his free hand inside Cody's underwear and gripped him tight. Cody groaned and was really into the tongue-heavy kiss when Demmy pulled back and gave him a stern look.

"You are mine, is that clear?"

The rough timbre of Demmy's tone made Cody's balls tighten and his cock throb.

"Fuck me, you are so fucking hot when you're possessive."

"You didn't answer my question," Demmy said, and tightened his fingers around Cody's dick. "You are mine, and no one else's. Is that clear?"

Cody nodded as his pulse pounded in his ears. "Crystal clear." He yanked Demmy against him and gave him a long kiss before saying, "And you belong to me. No one else." Another kiss, followed by a gentle bite at the spot where Demmy's shoulder met his neck. "Mine."

"Just the way I like it."

Cody cupped Demmy's face between his palms. "I love you, Demmy. I am head over heels in love with you. There's no going back from this, and no way in hell that I'm ever walking away from us. You've been the most important person in my life for as long as I can remember, and I never want to live without you."

Demmy let out a slow breath. "Now that's a wedding vow."

"Wish I would have thought of it yesterday afternoon."

"It's nice to hear, no matter where we are. And you're never going to be rid of me. We're better together."

"Good." Cody gave him a soft, lingering kiss, then took a step back. "Now get out of those fucking clothes and get in the shower with me."

DEMETRIUS LEFT his clothes piled on the bathroom floor and followed Cody across the bathroom. There was plenty of room for them both in the area behind the glass block, and they used generous amounts of the provided body wash to lather each other up. Demetrius probed Cody's hole and stroked his very hard cock. They exchanged kisses, gentle nips, long licks, and quick sucks as they washed each other and took turns rinsing off. Cody turned his back to the shower and got on his knees to take Demetrius in his mouth and suck him slow and deep.

"Oh, yeah," Demetrius said.

The water beat against Demetrius's back as Cody sucked him. He could feel Cody's fingers gripping his buttocks tight, and thought about the many ways Cody had fucked him the night before. There was probably still cum deep inside him.

"I need to be inside you," Demetrius said. "Right now."

Cody stood up and kissed him. "You're pretty bossy today."

"Less talking." Demetrius kissed him once more, then turned him around and pressed between his shoulder blades until Cody bent at the waist.

The glass block had been built in steps up to the ceiling, and Cody gripped one of the lower levels to support himself. Demetrius saw their reflection In the mirror above the double sinks, and it made his cock jump. Cody's expression was needful and excited, and Demetrius had to remind himself this was all really happening.

He got on his knees and spread Cody's ass cheeks open. The clean, pink ring of his anus clenched and relaxed, clearly an invitation. Demetrius ran his tongue slowly up the length of Cody's crack, then pushed the tip into the dark, musky center.

"Oh, Demmy," Cody said with a sigh. "I love your hot fucking mouth."

Demetrius licked, sucked, and nipped at Cody's hole. He reached around and stroked Cody's long, hard length as he rimmed him, feeling the slick-sticky smear of pre-cum with each pass of his hand.

He delivered a final sloppy kiss to Cody's anus and stood up. The water had gone cold, so he shut it off and reached for the lube he'd placed in the shower once Cody had gone off with Rufus.

He'd just had a feeling they might end up in the shower together.

A drizzle of lube down the crack of Cody's ass sent shivers up Cody's back, and Demetrius soothed them with gentle kisses along his spine.

"Stop teasing and fuck me," Cody said with a snarl Demetrius saw reflected in the mirror.

"So impatient."

"Demmy…"

Demetrius slid his dick in far enough for the head to push past the sphincter. In their reflection, Demetrius saw Cody's mouth drop open and his eyes closed.

"Well, that shut you up."

Demetrius pulled back and pushed in again, deeper this time. He repeated the movement, slowly pushing in deeper each time until he was completely embedded inside Cody. With a soft kiss at the top of Cody's spine, Demetrius gripped him by the shoulders and started to move. Slowly at first, savoring the velvet strength of Cody's body clutching at him, the resistance that yielded to his length. His hips picked up speed without any thought on his part, and the glorious sound of their wet skin slapping together in time with Cody's grunts and his own moans quickly pushed him over the edge.

"I'm close," Demetrius managed to say. "I'm there."

"Open your eyes," Cody said. "Look at me."

Demetrius looked at their reflection in the mirror, locking his gaze with Cody's. He could see Cody jerking himself off while holding tight to the glass block with the other hand. In seconds he was gone, and he drove deep into Cody as he came, keeping his eyes open as his lips parted.

"You're so fucking hot," Cody said, his arm moving fast and eyes on Demetrius. "I'm coming. I'm coming."

Muscles pulsed all along Demetrius's dick as Cody came, squeezing even more cum out of him. When Cody had finished, he rested his forehead against the glass block and worked to catch his breath. Demetrius slowly pulled out and ran a hand up and down Cody's spine until Cody stood up and turned to kiss him.

"Need to clean off," Cody muttered between kisses.

"We drained the water heater," Demetrius said.

"Of course we did."

They shared a quick, cold shower and when he'd finished, Demetrius carefully crossed the tile floor to grab one of the terry cloth robes hanging on the back of the door. He pulled it on and handed the other to Cody.

"Thanks, you filthy beast," Cody said, and kissed him.

"You're welcome, big and girthy."

Cody chuckled as he pulled on his robe. "I've worked up an appetite. Let's check out the food."

Demetrius led the way downstairs and through the living room to the kitchen. The sky was still overcast, and off in the distance he heard a low rumble of thunder. "Sounds like we're going to get another storm."

"I'll check on the generator after we eat," Cody said. "Make sure the tank is full so it can run all night." He caressed Demetrius's ass through the robe. "Like me."

"I'm definitely going to need a big meal and a nap to keep up with your sex drive."

They decided on pancakes, and Cody mixed up the batter as Demetrius lit more oil lamps to push back the gloom. It would be full dark in another hour, and Demetrius figured they'd be able to extinguish most of the lamps and spend the rest of the night in bed.

Cody brought a tall stack of pancakes to the dining table.

"Not sure which mood you were in today," he said as he sat down. "So I brought syrup and powdered sugar."

"I like to have options."

"Oh, I know that."

Demetrius took Cody's hand and ran his thumb along the smooth surface of his wedding ring. "I love you."

Cody grinned, and the sight of it sent a flutter of want through Demetrius. Maybe having no power for a day or two would be a good thing.

"I love you, too."

They talked about the business as they ate, trying to decide on ways to bring in more customers, and whether they could afford to pay Jugs more per job. When they'd finished eating, Demetrius washed the dishes and turned to find Cody sitting on the center cushion of the couch, his robe spread wide open to allow him to slowly stroke his hard-on.

"Watching me wash dishes got you turned on?"

"I love it when you act all domestic."

Demetrius walked up and knelt between Cody's legs. He swallowed the entire length at once and paused with his nose in Cody's pubic hair, tongue pressing against the underside of his dick.

"Jesus, you've got a hot mouth."

He dragged his mouth slowly up Cody's length and sucked hard on the head before taking him deep again. With steadily increasing speed, Demetrius sucked Cody, hand trailing in time along the shaft.

"You've got me right there," Cody said. "Oh yeah. I'm coming."

Thick cum flooded Demetrius's mouth, and he swallowed it all. He sucked Cody a little longer, then placed a soft kiss on the tip and looked up with a smile.

"That was a nice dessert."

Cody grabbed him under the arms and pulled him up onto the couch beside him. He kissed him, tongue pushing into Demetrius's mouth as Cody loosened the belt of his robe and spread it open.

"My turn for dessert," Cody said, and got on his knees between Demetrius's legs.

The hot, wet confines of Cody's mouth closed over Demetrius and he put his head back against the couch and sighed. Cody's strong hand stroked him as he sucked, and it didn't take long until Demetrius came in Cody's mouth with a quiet gasp. Cody kissed and licked him clean, slowly stroking him the entire time, then looked up and smiled.

"Happy honeymoon."

"Yeah, to you too," Demetrius said, then yawned. "You're wearing me out."

"I've got lots of plans," Cody said, then yawned himself. "But not for right now. Right now I could sleep for a couple of days."

Demetrius watched Cody stand and took the hand he offered to pull him up from the couch. They kissed, and then

Demetrius said, "Let's go up to bed. It's going to take us half an hour to remove all the pillows so we can lie down."

Cody laughed. "What is up with all the pillows?"

"I don't know. Guess it's a decorative thing."

"Guess I'm not going to cut it in decorator school," Cody said as he followed him to the stairs.

"Guess not."

It didn't take quite as long as Demetrius had thought to remove the pillows, but they did make quite a pile in the corner where they tossed them. They shed their robes and slid nude under the lightweight sheet. The mattress was perfect, and Demetrius sighed as he lay on his back. Cody blew out the last of the oil lamps before he put a big arm around Demetrius and pulled him in close. They lay in the dark and watched the steadily brightening flashes of lightning until Demetrius fell asleep.

CHAPTER SEVEN

Demetrius awoke slowly. He kept his eyes closed, but through his eyelids he could tell the light was different in their bedroom for some reason. It was brighter. Had he overslept? And when had so many birds moved into their neighborhood? It was like a bird symphony outside.

Cody snored softly, their legs tangled together and his arm across Demetrius's chest. When Demetrius finally opened his eyes, he stared up at the unfamiliar wood ceiling for a confused moment. Then memory returned and he sighed happily.

Honeymoon. He was actually on his honeymoon. And with his best friend, no less.

As comfortable as he was, Demetrius's bladder had other plans. He eased out from under Cody's limbs and slid out of bed. Yawning as he made his way to the bathroom, he left Cody snoring in bed.

After peeing and washing his hands, Demetrius stood to the side of the floor-to-ceiling window behind the bathtub and looked outside. The sun was up over the trees, so it had to be at least nine in the morning. He'd slept later than usual, but that was all right. It was his honeymoon.

He brushed his teeth then returned to the bedroom and dressed in a lightweight long-sleeved pull-over, an old, comfortable pair of cargo shorts, and his work boots. He left Cody sleeping and headed down the stairs and out the front door of the cabin. The air was clean and a bit muggy, and Demetrius paused on the porch to draw in a deep breath. A short hike would help him wake up, and then he'd see what Cody wanted for breakfast.

He followed the walkway made of boards laid over two by fours to the steps and then down to the dock. There he inspected the small motorboat available for their use and figured it wouldn't take long to bail out the rainwater later if they needed it. He stepped off the wooden walkway onto the dirt trail and mud squished beneath his boot. His hike might end up shorter than he'd anticipated.

The island was mainly a rocky shoreline with a small indentation where the dock had been installed and which Rufus had referred to as Hideaway Cove. The island rose to a tall bluff nearly opposite Hideaway Cove, and Demetrius headed in that direction. He followed the narrow, muddy path around the island's perimeter, struggling in places to keep his footing. The climb to the top of the bluff was a challenge, but after slipping several times and falling to his knees twice, he finally stood at the top and paused to catch his breath.

The view was magnificent from that position. Heaversford Lake spread out all around him, calm and sparkling under the bright sun. The buildings of Hempstead were just visible through some morning haze, and Demetrius could see Esther tour boats cruising the lake as well as speed and sail boats. A muscle cramp encouraged him to do some leg stretches, and he was about to set off down the opposite side of the bluff when a rhythmic splashing sound made him pause.

With a hand over his eyes to cut the glare, Demetrius looked around the lake. The surface was smooth and calm, with no sign of disturbance, but he could still hear the splashing. Then he caught movement in his peripheral vision and turned his head.

Dave Lamond, the old hipster from town, peddled his plastic gathering boat a dozen yards or so off the shore of the island. Sunlight gleamed along the shiny red surface of the wide opening at the front, and as the boat came around the side of the island and more fully into view, Demetrius could hear Dave whistling even over the splashing of his plastic trash collection unit. He was able to see the front more clearly from this angle, and it appeared to be a similar design to a snowblower. Blades in the front collection unit rotated as Dave peddled, drawing plastic into the collector. A chute must have run underneath Dave's recumbent seat and came up behind him to spit the trash into a collecting area in the back.

Dave saw him atop the bluff and waved. Demetrius waved back, unable to keep from smiling as he watched Dave peddle his way toward the other side of the island. The example Dave was setting in his efforts to clean the lake boosted Demetrius's spirits even more, and he continued on his hike, determined to make a full circuit of the island.

At the bottom of the bluff, he came to an abrupt halt. An angry buzzing from his right drew him cautiously to the edge of the path. Was it a large bee hive? Movement within the shadows between several trees where the morning sun had yet to reach made him squint. The shape was a dark cloud in constant motion, and he realized it was a swarm of buzzing flies. Curious, and a little nervous about what he might discover, Demetrius stepped into the tall ferns and carefully picked his way closer to the source.

The smell hit him first: fish gone over and rotting vegetation. He covered his mouth and nose before edging closer. Using his free hand, he waved the flies away and parted some fern fronds to discover a large, slime-covered pile of trash. It was roughly oblong in shape, about two feet across and as high as his knees. He turned away to gulp in a breath of somewhat fresher air, then crouched for a closer look. It consisted of grocery bags, water bottles, drinking straws, cellophane, and several plastic toy shovels, the kind used by children on the beach. All of this was covered with a thin layer of slime that seemed to hold it all together. He wondered where the slime might have come from, then decided it must be seaweed that had gotten wrapped up and dissolved amid the floating clot of plastic.

He straightened up, waved away the flies again, and looked out among the trees. Many of the plants and some of the younger trees were bent or completely flattened on the way to a short strip of pebble-covered beach. Gentle, foamy waves stroked the small stones, and a few plastic bags tumbled back and forth in the water.

For all the effort Dave was making, the lake could have used ten or twenty more people just like him.

The flies chased him back to the trail, and he jogged until he'd left them behind. He pondered the slimy ball of trash for a while, but then bird songs and the hammering of a woodpecker pushed it to the back of his mind. Sunlight winked between the leaves, and the distant drone of jet skis started up out on the lake.

In a short while, he 'd made a full circuit of the island and came back to the dock. He was sweaty and mud-splattered, but he didn't care. The hike had been refreshing and given him a nice boost. He braced himself against a tree and scraped as much mud as possible from the bottom of his boots onto a rock. When his boots were as clean as they were going to get, he climbed the wooden steps to the boardwalk leading to the cabin. Now it was time for him to cook up a big breakfast for his husband.

Husband.

The word blazed in Demetrius's brain like neon, and a rush of giddiness went through him.

"Husband," he whispered, and his smile widened. "I have a husband. And I am a husband. As a matter of fact, I'm on my honeymoon. With my husband."

He laughed and continued: "Hiking on my honeymoon while my husband recuperates from hot sex with his husband. Who is me."

Demetrius extended his arms and spun a few times in the middle of the boardwalk, laughing up at the tree branches arching overhead. He stopped spinning and, with one more look back at the lake, completed his walk to the cabin. He took his boots off on the front porch and set them aside then walked in the front door.

The smell of food cooking made his stomach rumble, and he smiled at the familiar sound of Cody whistling. He moved through the living room and stopped as he caught sight of Cody standing at the stove and tending to a skillet of scrambled eggs. He wore only a white apron, and the sun coming in through the kitchen window perfectly illuminated his firm and beautiful ass, making it glow like a work of art.

"Damn," Demetrius said, and gave a low whistle.

Cody smirked. "Good morning. Ready to eat?"

"So fucking ready."

Demetrius came up behind and put a hand on each marvelous ass cheek as he leaned in to place a soft kiss on the back of his neck.

"Your hair is damp. Did you shower?"

"I did. I wanted to be all clean for my husband."

"Your husband appreciates that."

Demetrius kissed his way down Cody's spine until he was on his knees behind him. He gently bit each firm cheek then spread them wide to reveal the tight pink circle glowing in the sunlight. Demetrius slowly ran his tongue up the length of Cody's crack, pausing to flick the tip teasingly over the twitching muscle.

"Okay. Eggs will keep for a bit."

The sound of the pan moving to another burner made Demetrius smile as he licked and sucked at Cody's hole. Cody bent slightly at the waist, pushing his ass more firmly against Demetrius's face. Demetrius kissed and sucked and licked up and down Cody's crack, then ducked his head to suck his balls before returning his attention to Cody's anus.

"You're going to need to slip something more than your tongue up there." Cody's voice was low and deep.

"Yeah?"

Demetrius got to his feet and Cody turned to face him. His erection tented the apron and a wide spot of pre-cum was spreading across the front. Demetrius lifted the apron and stroked the long, hot length of him as he leaned in for a kiss.

"Upstairs?" Demetrius said between kisses.

"That'll take too long." Cody untied the apron and lifted it over his head, then took Demetrius by the hand and led him to the couch. "Right here is just fine."

Cody spread the apron on the cushion and sat on it, then lay back with his legs in the air. "Did you order the freshly cleaned anus?"

Demetrius chuckled as he stripped. "I also ordered a side of sausage."

Kneeling on the couch between Cody's legs, Demetrius swallowed him to the root. Cody gasped and pressed a hand to the back of Demetrius's head.

"Oh, fuck. You must be really hungry."

Demetrius came up for a breath. "Starving."

He moved between rimming Cody and sucking him for several minutes as his own cock throbbed impatiently. When he couldn't wait any longer, Demetrius pushed to his feet and hurried into the kitchen to grab the bottle of olive oil. He drizzled a bit along his dick and stroked himself as he returned to where Cody lay open and waiting on the couch. Demetrius kissed him as he used oil-slicked fingers to prepare Cody's hole.

"Ready?" Demetrius asked.

Cody's pupils were wide as he nodded. "So ready."

Demetrius moved into place and lined himself up. He put one hand on Cody's chest directly over his heart and felt it pounding beneath his palm as he slipped into him. With slow, gentle thrusts, Demetrius pushed deeper into him until he was in to the root.

"God, you feel so good around me," Demetrius said between kisses.

"Less talking," Cody said, kissing him back. "More fucking."

Demetrius complied, building his thrusts up to a fast, hard pounding. Pools of pre-cum surged out of Cody's dick with each push, and Demetrius spread it along Cody's dick with his palm. He stroked Cody in time with his thrusts, watching as Cody's balls pulled up tight to his body. It wouldn't be long now, and he was right on the edge himself.

"Keep going," Cody said through a gasp. "Just like that. Oh yeah."

Just as Demetrius went over the edge and came deep inside him, Cody's dick pulsed in his hand and semen shot up Cody's torso. Demetrius stroked Cody slowly, milking the last drops from him as he reached up with his free hand to rub the cum into his skin.

"You're amazing," Demetrius said, and kissed each calf draped over his shoulders.

With slow movements, Demetrius reluctantly slid out of Cody and pushed himself up. He smiled down at Cody's dazed and slightly sleepy expression.

"There was a mention of scrambled eggs?"

Cody widened his eyes before he attempted to look hurt.

"That's all I'm good for? A hot fuck and a hot meal?"

Demetrius kissed him softly. "No, of course not. You know how to fix things around the house, too."

Cody pulled him down on top of him and kissed him hard, tongue shoving past Demetrius's lips. Demetrius's cock took quick notice, and he could feel Cody's had also started to harden as it pressed against his own. Cody broke the kiss and slid quickly out from under Demetrius.

"Okay, thanks for the fuck."

Demetrius groaned and pressed his face into the throw pillow that had supported Cody's head. It smelled of their shampoo and Cody's unique musk, and he breathed it in before turning his head to glare at Cody's back.

"You're a tease," Demetrius said.

Cody gave him an overly innocent look. "What? Me? I have no idea what you're talking about."

With a chuckle, Demetrius pushed up from the couch and walked into the kitchen. As he passed Cody standing once more at the stove, he swatted him on the ass.

The eggs were good warmed up, and as they sat naked at the table eating, they talked about the island and lack of power.

"If it gets above 80 today, I'm jumping in the lake," Cody said. "No power means no fans, which means crabby Cody."

Demetrius groaned. "I hate when crabby Cody pays a visit."

"Not many people enjoy crabby Cody."

Demetrius sipped his coffee and smiled. "Good job finding a stove top percolator. At least we'll be properly caffeinated."

A yawn snuck up on him, and he leaned back to stretch his arms overhead. "I might be ready to go back to bed for a bit."

"I like the sound of that," Cody said.

They carried their plates to the sink and left them for later. Cody followed Demetrius upstairs where they took turns in the bathroom before getting into bed. Cody pulled him close and Demetrius tipped his head up for a kiss. He snuggled into the familiar space along Cody's side and quickly fell asleep.

The blast of a loud horn startled them awake some time later. Demetrius sat straight up in bed, heart pounding.

"What the hell was that?"

Cody lay sprawled out on his stomach beside him, face puffy with sleep. "I'm guessing it's Rufus coming out to check on us."

"Okay. Yeah. Shit, that scared the hell out of me." He checked the time on his phone: 10:45, and he had twenty percent battery remaining.

They dressed and stepped out on the porch to wait. The day had warmed considerably, but there was a nice breeze making its way through the trees. Rufus came up the dirt-streaked wooden walkway carrying a canvas bag that looked somewhat heavy. Demetrius met him halfway and took the bag from his hands, finding it was, indeed, quite heavy.

"Is this your boat anchor?" Demetrius asked.

"It could very well be. It's some canned goods I figured you might be in need of, as well as a couple of flashlights and battery powered lanterns."

Cody looked in the bag once Demetrius set it on the porch, and then arched an eyebrow. "This bag of gifts has me feeling suspicious about our chances of getting the power back soon."

Rufus nodded and removed his baseball cap to wipe sweat from his brow. "Yeah, you might be right."

"Oh no," Demetrius said. "How long until the power can be restored?"

"Probably another two days." Rufus looked ashamed. "I told them we had guests out here, but the storm knocked out power to a lot of people in the area, so all I can offer is you're on the list."

"And it sounds like a long one," Demetrius said. "Well, thank you for bringing us these items."

"Why don't I give you guys a ride into town? Maybe Darlene has a room left at the hotel you can stay in for a night or two."

"That sounds like an idea," Demetrius said, and looked at Cody. "What do you think?"

Cody sighed and shrugged. "We can at least get something to eat and check out the town. If we decide to come back, will you be able to give us a ride out here?"

"If that's what you decide, absolutely."

"All right. Let us get changed and grab some things."

"I'm going to check the generator while I'm up here, and I'll meet you down at the dock."

Demetrius carried the bag of supplies into the cabin and set it in a corner of the kitchen. He removed one of the flashlights and switched it on, playing the powerful beam around the walls.

"I'll put one of the lanterns on the dock for when we come back," he said. "And I'll take the other one upstairs."

"Hey." Cody took hold of his hand and pulled him close. "I'm sorry about our honeymoon getting all fucked up."

Demetrius frowned. "All fucked up? I don't think it's that bad. I mean, yeah, it's a pain we have extremely limited electricity, but the cabin is nice. And without any distractions, we've been able to enjoy being together even more."

Cody smiled and kissed him. "Thanks for saying all of that."

"It's true. I love the trip you planned for us, both the one in your head, and the one that it turned into. The only thing that would make this trip even better was if we got to see Esther on the boat ride into town so we could brag about it to everyone."

Cody groaned and pushed him away toward the stairs. "You just ruined a perfect moment."

A short time later, they were in the boat and heading toward town. The wind was stronger on the lake, and Demetrius was glad he'd grabbed a hoodie to wear over his T-shirt. They talked with Rufus about the power situation and gave him some background on Critter Catchers and their lives back in Parson's Hollow.

"I've heard of Parson's Hollow," Rufus said.

"Oh?" Cody asked. "Because it's a great place to live?"

"Nah, not that." Rufus looked over his shoulder. "Though I'm sure it is, don't get me wrong. I heard someone say something about an old woman who drives a big old car with a revolving yellow light on top and is the worst driver in the world."

Demetrius and Cody both laughed, then took turns describing the Widow Monroe. By the time they'd finished, Rufus was laughing and shaking his head as he pulled the boat up close to the dock.

"You guys just made my hday," he said. "I appreciate you being patient and understanding with the power situation out on the island."

"It's not your fault," Cody said. "Where's a good place to eat around here?"

"The hotel has a nice restaurant in the back. And if you eat there, I should be able to convince Darlene to comp your meal because of the power. However, if you want to check out the town, the Heaversford Diner is a good spot for casual dining. Ernesto's is a bit higher class, and they don't allow shorts or jeans, so you'd have to come back for that."

"That's pretty much all we packed, so Ernesto's is off the list for the week," Demetrius said. "We're pretty simple in our tastes, and we never turn down a free meal." He looked at Cody. "Want to give the hotel restaurant a shot?"

"Free's my favorite price. Lead the way."

They followed Rufus along the dock, past the line of people waiting to purchase tickets for an Esther tour. Demetrius looked at Cody with his eyebrows raised, and Cody glared back.

There would be no Esther tour for them this week.

At the gate that led to the parking lot, a tall, thin man stood talking to a couple of people. The tall man wore a bright orange life vest over a blue windbreaker and had long gray hair.

"That's Dave," Demetrius said. "The guy with the trash collecting peddle boat. Right?"

"Yep, that's him," Rufus said. "Looks like he's printed up some new pamphlets to pass out."

Dave greeted Rufus as they approached, and the couple he'd been talking with saw their chance and hurried away.

"Dispose of your trash properly!" Dave called to their backs, then turned to smile at them. "Hey Rufus. New deck hands for The Lazy Aye?"

"Nah, these are guests staying out at Hideaway Cove."

Demetrius and Cody introduced themselves and Demetrius accepted a pamphlet.

"Lots of good information in there," Dave said. "Plastic grocery bags can take anywhere from ten to one thousand years to decompose. And plastic water bottles can take up to four hundred and fifty years."

"That long?" Demetrius said. "That's terrible."

"It is!" Dave waved toward the lake. "And there's so much of it in our beautiful lake these days. Not just from people throwing their trash in there, although that's a big part of it, but the wind will blow it in, or it will fall out of a recycle truck. It's having a huge impact on life in the lake. Anything that lives in the water can't tell what a plastic bag is when it's floating around. They think it's seaweed and they eat it, and then it gets tangled inside of them and kills them. It's been hard on the fish and the muskrats and beavers." Dave's voice quieted and he turned his sad gaze toward the lake. "But especially the turtles."

"I saw you going past the island this morning," Demetrius said. "In your trash collecting boat."

Dave's face lit up. "That's Carmen. I named her that after the opera because it looks like she has her mouth opened really wide like she's performing an aria."

"That's a very fitting name," Cody said. "Did you build her yourself?"

"Oh yeah. Designed her and built her. I put the designs out on my website to encourage other people to build their own. So far there's been about twenty downloads."

"You're starting a movement," Demetrius said.

"Everyone has the power to change the world," Dave said.

"Well, I was just taking these guys up to the hotel for lunch," Rufus said. "They've lost power out on the island."

"That storm last night was pretty bad." Dave winked at Demetrius. "I don't have to worry about things like that. I'm one hundred percent solar powered."

"Good for you," Demetrius said. "That's impressive."

"Take care out there on the lake now, David," Rufus said as

he nudged Demetrius in the direction of the hotel across the street. "Lots of boaters around these days."

"And Esther," Cody said in a flat tone of voice. "Can't forget Esther."

Dave laughed. "Oh yeah, gotta watch out for her. Though I think she'd appreciate my efforts to clean up her lake. You guys have a good day now."

They waved to Dave then Rufus led them across the street and up the driveway to the Crescent Hill Hotel. As Rufus talked to Darlene at the registration desk, Demetrius and Cody browsed the pamphlets for local attractions.

"Esther, Esther, Esther," Cody muttered, perfectly mimicking Jan from *The Brady Bunch*. "Do you think all the fish and turtles get jealous that Esther gets all the press?"

"I know you want to catch a glimpse of Esther as much as anyone else," Demetrius said.

"And we'll file that under the You Don't Know Me at All section of our relationship."

Rufus approached and handed them a couple of Crescent Hill Hotel business cards with writing on the back.

"Got you a free appetizer, entree, and dessert. You'll have to pay for your own drinks, but the food is free at least."

"This is really nice, thank you," Demetrius said, then stepped to the side to look back at the desk where Darlene stood. "Thank you, Darlene."

"You're quite welcome," Darlene said. "Sorry about the inconvenience out on the island, but hopefully this will help. Enjoy!"

Rufus showed them to the dining room door and gave them a wave. "Relax and enjoy your meal. If you decide to spend the night here in town, Darlene's got a room available, free of charge."

He headed for the door and the hostess showed them to a booth. Demetrius was happy to have an outlet in the wall above the table so he could plug in his phone. When Cody looked at his own remaining charge, Demetrius assured him they would charge his phone as well.

They ordered a couple of beers with lunch, and as they ate talked about the trip so far and whether or not they wanted to spend the night in town.

"The hotel seems nice," Cody said.

"But?" Demetrius added.

Cody shrugged. "But it's not as private as the island."

At that moment, a couple of families arrived at the door to the restaurant. They were two young couples, each with two small children. They must have spent the previous day sight-seeing or maybe out on the lake looking for Esther because they were a little sunburned and still looked wiped out. The kids were cranky and short-tempered, each dissolving into whines as the parents carried and dragged them to the tables pushed together in the center of the restaurant.

Demetrius looked at Cody. "Let's go back to the island."

"You don't want to see what room they've got? Maybe we could get one sandwiched between the two families."

"Pretty sure I'd rather be out in the middle of the lake with no power."

They finished eating quickly and Cody left money for the drinks and a tip based on the full price of the meals. To escape the suddenly chaotic dining room, they had to maneuver around the table of over-tired children and stressed out parents, and Demetrius squinted an eye as one of the children let out a piercing wail. When they pushed through the doors to the outside, they looked at each other and started to laugh.

"You'd better be using birth control," Cody said.

Demetrius feigned offense. "Oh, it's my responsibility?"

"You're the nurturing one."

"Yeah, okay. Good point."

The sidewalks were packed with tourists, and they waded

into the fray. Up and down the streets of Hempstead they wandered, checking out shops and street side vendors. Cody started collecting carryout menus from different restaurants to get an idea of where they might eat dinner. At an ice cream shop, Demetrius darted inside where he waited in line for two root beer floats, laughing at Cody's bright smile when he saw him returning.

"Marry me," Cody said as he accepted the cup.

"Anytime, baby."

They found an available bench in the shade and savored the floats as they people watched. Demetrius checked the time on his phone and was surprised to discover it was almost five o'clock. Why did time always seem to speed up on vacation days?

Cody nudged him and nodded across the street. "Look who it is."

Demetrius looked over and saw Rufus walking along the sidewalk beside a man in police uniform. This man was a couple of inches taller than Rufus and looked to be in his mid- to late-sixties. He was bald with a band of silver hair running around the back of his head and a neatly trimmed beard to match.

Rufus looked over at them, started to turn away, then looked back and smiled. He lifted his hand in a wave and said something to the man beside him before they both crossed the street.

"Well, look who it is," Rufus said, smiling as he approached. "Just the couple I was talking about. How was lunch?"

"Great until the screaming children arrived," Cody said.

"Isn't tourism wonderful?" Rufus laughed, then gestured to the man beside him. "Gentlemen, this is Hap Blanchard, an officer with the Hempstead police department."

Cody and Demetrius shook hands with Hap and introduced themselves.

"Rufus has told me about your problems out on the island," Hap said. "Have you been enjoying yourselves despite the challenges?"

"We have," Demetrius said, glancing at Cody. They both grinned, and Demetrius saw a light blush in Cody's face as his own cheeks heated. Apparently they were thinking of the same things.

"Well now," Rufus said. "Have you decided whether or not you're going to stay in town tonight?"

"The meal at the hotel was very good, and affordable," Demetrius said. "But we'd like to return to the island if you could manage it."

"Not a problem at all. When did you want to head out there?"

"We don't want to interrupt your dinner plans," Cody said.

"No problem. Did you boys have dinner yet?"

"No," Demetrius and Cody said together.

"All right then." Rufus waved for them to proceed along the sidewalk. "We'll introduce you to the greasiest spoon in Hempstead."

The greasiest spoon turned out to be a diner called Sally's on the Lake. It seemed more popular with the local residents than tourists as nearly everyone greeted Rufus and Hap the moment they entered. A mix of aromas filled the air and made Demetrius's mouth water. There were a lot of options on the menu, but he decided to stick with a burger and fries, which everyone else ordered as well.

"Best burgers for miles," Hap said. "You'll see."

The service was fast, and in minutes they had their burgers and fries. Demetrius wondered if Rufus and Hap were so well-liked their orders were placed ahead of everyone else's, but then he bit into his burger and his eyes closed with pleasure and he decided it didn't matter. It was, indeed, one of the best burgers he'd ever eaten. During the meal, they talked about life in Hempstead and Parson's Hollow, comparing town residents and establishments. Hempstead, it turned out, was a lot like Parson's Hollow. Except for the monster in the lake.

When Rufus finished his burger, he sat back and sighed. "Never get tired of Sally's burgers. So, you boys ready to get back to your little slice of Heaven?"

"Whenever you are," Cody said and counted out cash for their bill, leaving it on the table.

Rufus nodded to the door. "Let's head for the dock."

"Mind if I tag along?" Hap asked as he dropped money on the table as well. "I'm off duty and a boat ride's always a nice way to end the day."

"Not at all," Rufus said. "There's room for all of us."

Once in the boat, Hap sat across from Cody and Demetrius as Rufus eased the boat away from the dock. Hap lifted his chin toward Cody and asked, "You play football in high school?"

"I did," Cody said. "Linebacker."

"I would have taken you for a quarterback," Hap said.

"Funny, I would have, too," Cody replied. "Too bad my coach didn't see it that way. How about you?"

Hap shrugged with a small grin that let Demetrius know he was a man who loved to tease people. "Quarterback. Started on varsity since I joined my sophomore year."

"Well, you must have gotten all the luck that was supposed to have landed on me," Cody said.

"Luck, or skill?" Hap asked, and he and Cody both laughed.

As Cody and Hap started talking about plays and routes

and bad calls from referees, Demetrius joined Rufus in the three-sided wheelhouse.

"They're talking football," Demetrius said.

Rufus smiled and nodded. "That's my Hap."

"How long did you say you two have been together?"

Rufus gave him a side-eye. "I didn't. Let's just say it's longer than you've been alive, how's that?"

Demetrius laughed, then checked to make sure Cody was still fully immersed in his conversation with Hap before leaning in and lowering his voice. "Has anyone ever found any evidence for Esther?"

"Oh, you know, there have been photographs over the years, and one really bad quality home movie, but no physical evidence to speak of. There's a small museum of Esther artifacts in town, and if you two would like a tour I can try to arrange that."

Demetrius glanced back at Cody to make sure he hadn't overheard. "Oh, no, that's okay, thanks."

Rufus glanced back as well, and raised his eyebrows as he looked at Demetrius again. "He scared of lake monsters?"

"No, it's not that. We just…" He tried to think of how to explain everything without going into too much detail. Maybe just a bit of history would help. "We've had some run-ins with what you might call unusual creatures during our years running the animal control business, and Cody hasn't taken a liking to it."

"Unusual creatures, huh?" Rufus pursed his lips, and then looked back to make sure Hap and Cody weren't listening in before he continued. "Hap's always been very tight-lipped about anything to do with Esther. I'm thinking he had an encounter with her when he was really young and it scared him."

"Really?" Demetrius watched as Hap and Cody shared a laugh about another bad play and tried to imagine the outgoing and gregarious officer as a scared young boy. "So you and I are kind of in the same boat."

"Both literally and figuratively," Rufus said with a smile.

Demetrius laughed. "Good point."

"Oh, shoot. I forgot to bring the spare gas cans for the generator with us. When I bring them out tomorrow, I'll bring a couple of books that will give you some of the history of Esther."

"Okay, but don't let Cody see them."

Rufus cocked an eyebrow. "Keeping secrets on your honeymoon?"

"Ugh, nice guilt trip." Demetrius grimaced. "Okay, good point. Maybe the books are a bad idea."

"I'll have them in the boat so you can decide either way." Rufus nodded toward the bow. "Dock's up ahead. You'd better take a seat." He turned to call over his shoulder. "Heading into the dock now."

Cody and Hap continued to talk football as Rufus guided the boat alongside the dock. Demetrius sat beside Cody and tried pushing down a stubborn feeling of guilt around talking about Esther with Rufus. It was their honeymoon, after all. Couldn't he have just avoided the topic of Esther completely? Why was he so obsessed with monsters?

"You guys want me to come up and make sure no hooligans have broken into your cabin while you were gone?" Hap asked.

"I think we'll be okay," Cody said, then reached out to shake his hand. "Great talking with you."

"You too. It's been nice to reminisce about the good ol' days."

"Yes, he never gets a chance to do that with me," Rufus said with an elaborate eye roll that made them all laugh. "Enjoy your evening, and I'll bring out more gas for the generator tomorrow. You should have enough to get you through the night."

Demetrius stood beside Cody on the dock and waved as Rufus slowly reversed the boat away from the dock, then turned it back toward town.

"Think they're going to have sex out on the water?" Cody asked.

"Oh, yeah," Demetrius said.

"Good." Cody picked up the lantern they'd left on the dock and took Demetrius's hand before they walked up the steps and along the boardwalk to the house.

CHAPTER EIGHT

Cody woke early the next morning. He lay on his back with his eyes closed and listened to the quiet sound of Demmy breathing beside him, feeling the warm length of his body stretched out alongside. Birds called and a gentle breeze rustled through the trees and made its way in through the open window. The sun was already up and the breeze would hopefully help keep the bugs away. Power or not, lake monster or not, it was going to be a great day.

He slid out of bed and used the bathroom, pausing at the sink to inspect his reflection. He hadn't shaved since the morning of the wedding three days ago, and he was looking particularly scruffy. Demmy seemed to like him better a little scruffy compared to clean-shaven, so he decided to let the scruff go and see how it looked at the end of the week. Maybe he'd grow a full-fledged beard and become a man of the woods. He brushed his teeth and splashed cold water on his face, enjoying the sting on his skin.

"You're up early," Demmy muttered when Cody returned to the bedroom and started to dress.

"It's a beautiful day. I don't want it to go to waste."

Demmy rolled onto his back and lifted his head to squint at him. "What's wrong with you?"

"I might take offense to that if I wasn't in such a good mood."

"Seriously. What happened? Did you fall and hit your head?"

"You can make fun all you want. I'm going to seize the day." Cody sat on the bed to pull on his socks. "Care to join me?"

"I will join you, but more out of a sense of duty to make sure you're safe once you slip out of this manic state you've entered."

"Ha ha. Come on, time's a wasting!" Cody yanked the sheet off the bed, exposing Demmy's naked body and morning wood. "Oh, my. Looks like little Demmy is way more awake than big Demmy."

Demmy stroked himself. "Too bad you're already dressed."

"You are an evil tempter, but I will not be lured in."

Cody grabbed Demmy by the feet, and then dragged him to the bottom of the bed. Demmy flailed his arms and laugh-shouted in surprise.

"Let me go!"

"First time I've ever heard you say that."

Demmy kicked free of Cody's grasp and popped up out of bed. "Let's hope it's the last time. Wow, you are really wound up this morning."

"And all without coffee." Cody pulled him close for a kiss and squeezed his hard-on. "Let's go seize the day. And later, I'll seize you. I'll meet you out on the porch."

A short time later, Demmy joined Cody on the covered porch. He wore cargo shorts, a long-sleeved T-shirt, his work boots, and a Pittsburgh Pirates ball cap.

"Okay Captain Energy," Demmy said through a yawn.

"What's your plan?"

"What did you do yesterday morning?" Cody asked.

"I walked the perimeter of the island."

"Sounds good. Let's do it."

Cody motioned for Demmy to lead the way.

"Why do I walk in front?"

"I like the view."

"Well, then halfway around I say we switch positions so I can enjoy the view as well."

"I like the way you think."

Demmy led the way to the dock, then set off along a narrow trail that followed the edge of the island. The sun glittered on the small waves and seagulls shrieked as they glided overhead. A number of boats were already out on the water, and Cody could hear the competing hums of a couple of speedboats from somewhere out of sight.

"We're coming up to the bluff," Demmy said over his shoulder. "We can take a break at the top where there's a really nice view of the lake and the town."

"You're the leader."

The bluff was not as tall as Cody had anticipated, and when they reached the summit, they stood side-by-side and looked out over the water.

"I saw Dave, that environmental guy we talked to in town from up here yesterday morning," Demmy said. "He was peddling his red plastic-gathering boat and gave me a big wave."

"He must have legs like a jack-rabbit."

Demmy laughed and nudged him, and Cody thought nothing could ruin the day. But as they turned to descend the other side of the bluff, Demmy noticed something and took a step closer to the edge. Then he took another step and leaned down as he stared along the side of the bluff.

"What is that?" Demmy said.

A nervous feeling crackled through Cody. He sensed the amazing day was in jeopardy, and just as he was about to gently pull Demmy back and tell him to forget what he thought he might have seen as he led him along the trail, Demmy gasped.

"I think that's a piece of Dave's boat down there."

"Oh?" Cody refused to look. "Maybe it fell off while he was making his morning route. Let's hit the trail, we want to keep our heart rates up and the blood pumping."

"But he could be in trouble. We need to check it out."

"Do we?"

Demmy turned and gave him a stern look. "Yes, we do."

Cody gave up with a nod. "You're right, I know. I was just really enjoying the hike."

"We'll finish the hike, but we need to check into this first. Come on."

Demmy led the way down the trail. At the bottom of the bluff, he set off through the undergrowth and around trees toward the water. Cody followed, trying not to worry about ticks and chiggers and lyme disease. Dead leaves rustled and sticks snapped beneath his boots until they left the cover of trees behind and stepped out onto a narrow strip of rocky beach. The beach allowed them to backtrack, and as they neared the larger rocks scattered around the base of the bluff, Cody's nervous feeling deepened into dread. It hadn't been just a piece of the boat that had caught Demmy's eye; it was the whole damn thing. The long, shiny red length of Dave's plastic gathering boat was wedged upside down among the rocks.

"Shit," Demmy said. "What the hell happened?" He started picking his way through the rocks toward the boat.

"Careful, Demmy," Cody called. "You don't know what you're going to find in there."

He hesitated for two seconds before cursing under his

breath and following. About a yard away from the over-turned boat, a horrible smell of rotting fish engulfed them. They stopped and covered their noses and mouths.

"I've smelled this before," Demmy said through his hand. "There's a big ball of slimy plastic I found yesterday just off the trail that smelled like this."

"How about we head back to the cabin and use the short-wave to call Rufus? The police should come out here and look at the boat."

Demmy looked between Cody and the boat a couple times. He took his hand away from his nose and mouth and called, "Dave? Are you in there?"

The only response was the cry of the gulls overhead. Cody tugged on the bottom of Demmy's shirt. "Come on. Let's radio Rufus."

Demmy nodded, and then turned away from the boat. "Yeah, okay. Let's go."

Cody led the way back to the trail and pulled Demmy into a hug. "You okay?"

"Yeah, I'm just worried. Dave really cares for this lake, and I'd hate for something to have happened to him."

"Maybe the boat got loose overnight and drifted out here or something," Cody said.

"Maybe." Demmy stepped back and gestured along the trail. "We're about halfway, so we may as well keep going."

"All right. And if I remember correctly, I'm supposed to take the lead on this half, right?" Cody received a weak smile in response. "Okay, too soon. I know you're worried and distracted. Let's go."

Cody set off at a quick pace. The mood had turned under-standably somber, and Cody struggled between a feeling of disappointment followed quickly by guilt. Their honeymoon had so far been anything but the perfect experience he'd hoped for when he'd booked the cabin. But a man could be gravely injured, or worse, and Cody needed to get his priorities in line.

The same dank smell of rotting fish engulfed him, and he gagged as he covered his mouth and nose. A few steps later on, he stopped and stared at a big ball of slime-covered plastic items sitting part on the trail and part amid the ferns on the beach side. He looked over his shoulder at Demmy and spoke through his hand.

"Is this what you saw yesterday?"

Demmy had also covered his mouth and nose and he shook his head. "The one I saw was farther off the trail. But this one smells a lot worse."

"Of course it does."

They gave the mass of slimy trash a wide berth. Cody thought it resembled a giant hairball made of plastic, similar to the ones occasionally left on a carpet or blanket by the cat his family had owned when he'd been growing up.

"That smell is just awful," Demmy said as they left the trash ball behind.

"I'm glad the cabin is upwind of that thing."

A short time later, the trail they were on intersected with a more narrow path that cut through the woods in the direction of the cabin. Cody stopped to look along it.

"This might be a shortcut."

"Might?"

"Well, I don't have a map of the island handy, but if my estimate is right, this should be the other end of the path that Rufus and I took to get to the power utility pole."

Demmy looked ahead along the trail they had been following. "You think so?"

"One way to find out." Demmy seemed hesitant, so Cody took his hand. "Hey, if Dave was inside that boat, we would have seen him from the top of the bluff or heard him call for help. Right?"

"What if he's… You know."

"If he's "you know," then it's not going to matter how long it takes us to get to the radio, is it?"

Demmy grimaced. "Good point. Okay, let's try this path."

"There's that sense of adventure I know so well. Come on."

The path did lead them to the utility pole — still blackened at the top from the lightning strike — and it came out at the back of the cabin. They took off their muddy boots and left them on the small porch before going in the side door. Cody stood before the kitchen counter where the radio sat and picked up the handheld microphone.

"Now to try and figure out how this thing works," he muttered.

"The dial's glowing. I would guess it's just on and ready to transmit."

"I just hope I don't accidentally get someone in Russia and start some kind of international incident."

"Maybe don't curse out whoever answers or insult their mother," Demmy suggested.

"Always the voice of reason, aren't you?" He cleared his throat and clicked the button on the side of the microphone. "Um, hello. This is Cody Bower out at Broken Jaw Island. Is Rufus around?"

There was no response and he tried again, shrugging at Demmy who paced nearby. Just as he was about to try a third time, a burst of static made them both jump, and then Rufus's voice came out of the speaker.

"Cody, this is Rufus. Everything okay out there? Over."

Cody nodded to himself and looked at Demmy. "I forgot to say 'over'." He pressed the transmit button. "Hi Rufus. We're okay. But we found Dave's plastic gathering boat upside down in the rocks at the bottom of the bluff. Thought Hap or someone from the police might want to come out and take a look." He released the button, then quickly pressed it again and said, "Over."

Silence followed. Cody looked at Demmy who looked right back. Finally, Rufus responded. "I've called Hap. We'll be out to the island soon. Meet us at the dock. Over."

"Got it. We'll see you at the dock. Over."

"We'll be leaving shortly. Over and out."

Cody retuned the microphone to the small plastic hanger on the side of the radio, then gave Demmy a tight smile. "Happy honeymoon, my love."

"Yeah," Demmy said with a tired grin. "Happy honeymoon. Should we go look at the boat wreckage more closely?"

"Nope. Let's leave that for Hap. I say we eat some breakfast because it's going to be a hell of a long day."

"Good idea."

After a quick breakfast of coffee made in the stovetop percolator along with a couple of over-easy eggs for each of them, Cody followed Demmy down to the dock. The eggs hadn't settled well, but he didn't think they had been bad. He just figured he was more than a little tense about the whole situation.

When they stepped onto the dock, Cody could see The Lazy Aye cutting through the small waves, moving fast and leaving behind a large wake. In another few minutes, Rufus had eased the boat up alongside the dock and he and Hap stepped out.

"Morning," Rufus said, and held up two five gallon-sized plastic gasoline jugs. "More fuel for the generator."

"Oh, thanks," Cody said, and took them. "I'll leave them here on the walkway up to the cabin for later."

"How'd you find the boat?" Hap asked, getting right down to business. His serious demeanor reminded Cody of Lucia Durant back in Parson's Hollow, and a quiet sense of homesickness went through him. It was nice to be away with

Demmy and celebrating their wedding, but this trip had quickly turned on them. Like what happened with most of their trips.

"We were hiking around the island," Demmy said. "I caught a glimpse of it from the top of the bluff."

Hap obviously knew the island because he headed off along the trail in the right direction. "Let's check it out."

They fell into a single file, Cody and Demmy following Hap and Rufus bringing up the rear. At the top of the bluff, Hap moved carefully up to the edge and leaned out.

"Easy there, Hap," Rufus said.

"I'm all right, you old worrywart."

Rufus grunted and mumbled so Cody could hear, "He said just before he fell off the side of the bluff."

Cody grinned, but quickly turned serious when Hap stepped back and looked between him and Demmy. "And how did you get close to see the damage?"

Demmy pointed to the other side of the bluff. "We went down that side and approached it a short ways along the rocks."

"Did you touch the boat?" Hap asked and set off down the trail.

"No," Demmy said, and followed.

Cody fell in behind Demmy and Rufus followed again. Hap led them through the undergrowth and around trees to the beach. He stood and looked the boat over, then gestured for them to stay back.

"Wait here."

Hap made his way to the boat, maneuvering around rocks and climbing over some until he reached the wreckage. He stepped around the bow and looked at the passenger area.

"Is he in there?" Rufus called.

"No. And there's no blood that I can see." Hap stepped in and leaned closer, then abruptly pulled back and put a hand over his nose and mouth. "There's some kind of slime on the boat, and it smells disgusting."

Demmy looked at Cody, and then called out, "Like rotting fish?"

"Yeah, like that."

"You smelled it from here?" Rufus asked.

Cody shook his head. "We found it covering a bunch of plastic trash a little farther down the trail."

"And I found another one like it yesterday just off the trail," Demmy added.

Hap returned and stood before them. "You didn't hear anything unusual last night or this morning?"

"Nothing," Cody said. "And I was just telling Rufus we found a couple of large balls of plastic trash covered with that same smelly slime a little farther along the trail."

"Show me."

They led Hap and Rufus to the fly-covered ball of trash that lay partially blocking the trail. The four of them stood around and stared at it, the buzzing of the flies and the quiet shush of the waves on the nearby rocky beach the only sound.

"Forgive my French, but what the ever-loving fuck is that?" Hap said, and Cody felt a sudden surge of affection for the man.

"Oh, come on, Hap," Rufus said, "you know damn well it's a slimy ball of plastic trash that used to be floating around in our lake."

Hap gave him a gentle glare before asking them, "Where's the other one you found?"

Demmy went a little farther along the trail and poked around the ferns until he found it. It was smaller than the one they had left behind, but smelled just as bad.

"All right," Hap said. "Let's go to the cabin. I need to use the radio to get someone out here."

"There's a short cut not too far ahead," Cody said, and took the lead.

When they reached the utility pole, they all stopped and looked up at the damage.

"I'm hopeful the power company will be out tomorrow," Rufus said. "I'll call when I get back to the hotel and make sure it's still on their list."

"We'd appreciate that," Cody said. "Demmy's getting tired of the sound of my voice."

"So tired," Demmy said with a sigh. "So much talking."

Demmy was rewarded with weak and distracted grins from both Hap and Rufus before Rufus led the way to the cabin. He went into the storage shed to check on the generator while Cody and Demmy went inside with Hap. They listened to Hap talk with someone about sending people out to the island, and when he'd finished, he looked them over a moment.

"How long have you two have been together?"

Cody exchanged a look with Demmy, then said, "It's a little complicated. We met when we were both in kindergarten and became friends. We both dated other people all during that time—"

"Cody dated women," Demmy said.

Cody sighed. "Yes, I dated women."

"A lot of women."

"Yes, fine: a lot of women."

"Sooo many women."

"He gets the idea, Demmy."

Hap chuckled. "This story sounds very familiar."

Cody raised his eyebrows. "Oh?"

"Yep. Rufus and I met in high school. He's older than me and wasn't really out, per se, but everybody knew he was gay. I dated all the girls I could. Married one, too, right out of high school."

Demmy linked arms with Cody. "I'm the one Cody asked to marry him." And damn if he didn't look puffed up and proud about it.

"Smarter than I was." Hap shook his head. "My marriage lasted three years before it fell apart. I ran into Rufus at the bar one night and we got to talking and, well, that was a lot of years ago now."

"And the town doesn't know about your relationship?" Cody asked.

Rufus came in the side door and had obviously been listening, because as he stopped at the kitchen sink to wash his hands, he said over his shoulder, "The friendly people in town know about us. The other folks don't acknowledge it at all."

As he dried his hands on a dishtowel, Rufus leaned back against the sink and looked at Hap with a smile. Hap smiled back, and Cody could sense the strong connection between them.

"That's their loss," Hap said, and after looking at Rufus for little longer, turned to Cody and Demmy. "Back to business. So you two didn't hear anything unusual or see anything until you found the boat this morning."

"Not a thing," Demmy said.

"And we've had the windows open at night for the breeze," Cody added.

"All right. I'm going to wait for the boat down at the dock." Hap pushed up from the counter and looked at Rufus. "You need to get back into town for anything?"

"Nothing on my schedule until later this afternoon. I'll wait with you, and we can leave these men to themselves. Don't forget about the gas down by the dock."

"We won't," Cody said. "Thanks again."

He walked with them to the door and watched their backs until the curve in the boardwalk hid them from view behind the trees. When he turned back, Demmy sat on the couch with his head back and his eyes closed.

"Tired?" Cody asked.

"Yeah, but I shouldn't be. It's not even noon yet."

"We could take naps."

"I'm not sure it's that kind of tired."

Cody sat beside him. "Do you want to just say 'fuck it' to this trip and head back home?"

Demmy took his hand and looked at him. "Not a chance."

"Even though it's the worst honeymoon ever?"

Demmy slid close and kissed him. "No way it could be the worst when I'm here with you."

Cody grinned. "Smooth talker."

"Years of study under a great teacher."

Cody raised his eyebrows. "Under a great teacher, huh? I like the sound of that." He leaned in for a longer, deeper kiss.

When they parted, Demmy rested a palm on Cody's swelling crotch. "You may want to hold that thought, big guy. There are going to be people all over this tiny island for a while."

"Dammit."

"But once we're on our own again, it's on."

They weren't alone again until very late in the day. The island proved to be quite conducive to sounds. The endless chug of boat motors and shouts between Hap and the other officers acted as a worrisome backdrop. Demmy found some board games and a deck of cards in a cabinet and they spent the afternoon in friendly competition.

"I wish those guys would leave already so I could beat your ass at strip poker," Cody said.

"I'll let you in on a little secret," Demmy said as he shuffled cards. "I'm kind of a sure thing, in case you hadn't noticed. You don't need a card game to get me out of my clothes."

Cody sat back and massaged his crotch. "You're not helping my condition any."

"Sorry," Demmy said in a tone that let Cody know he really wasn't.

After another hand of poker, Demmy stood up and stretched. He went to the window and looked outside.

"Are you curious to see what they're doing?" he asked.

Cody got up and stood beside him. "You want to go for a walk and check things out?"

"Do you?"

"Yeah. I gotta admit it."

Demmy smiled, and the happiness it conjured within Cody conflicted with his anxiety about the discovery of Dave's overturned and beached boat. Not much he could do about it, however, but he did suggest they take the narrow path out back to the trail and approach the bluff from that direction. Demmy agreed and they set off.

On the trail leading to the bluff, they skirted the slimy and smelly ball of plastic trash, now swarmed with flies, and picked their way through the trees to the stony beach. From that vantage point, they could see two police officers and a man in shorts and a short-sleeved polo shirt trying to get a tow line around Dave's boat. They had turned it right-side up and Cody winced at the crumpled aluminum and shattered windshield.

"I wonder if they found any trace of Dave?" Demmy said.

"We could ask Hap."

"He's busy right now. Maybe when they've managed to get the tow rope secured."

It took the men another hour to get the tow rope secured and the boat off the beach. Hap and the other officer stood with their backs to Cody and Demmy, watching Dave's boat get towed out onto the lake and back toward town. Hap turned and noticed them watching. He said something to the officer who looked their way and nodded. Both men made their way along the rocks and Hap approached them while the other officer turned to head to the trail.

"We'll be gone shortly," Hap said. "Unless you've found something else?"

"No, we were just curious about the boat," Demmy said. "It looked damaged."

Hap nodded. "There was some damage to the passenger area. But there's no sign of blood or Dave. The damage may have been caused when it went up on the rocks, but we're not sure yet. We'll look it over more closely when we get it back to town."

"Any thoughts on the smelly slime that was on it?" Cody asked. "And the big ball of plastic on the path?"

"Could be some kind of algae growing out in the lake. Rufus will probably come out tomorrow to clean it up. He does love this little island."

"Thanks for the information," Demmy said. "We know you've got work to do."

"You guys staying here tonight or do you need a ride into town?" Hap started for the trees and Cody and Demmy followed.

"We hadn't really talked about it," Cody said, and looked back at Demmy.

"I'd rather stay out here tonight," Demmy said. "The stove is gas, and the radio and pump for the well are on the generator. With the battery lanterns and oil lamps we've got enough light."

"Sounds romantic," Hap said.

"Lamp light makes me look younger," Cody said, and they all laughed.

At the trail they parted company with Hap and returned to the cabin via the shortcut by the utility pole. When they got inside the cabin, Cody grabbed Demmy's arm and had him stop.

"What? Do you see something?" Demmy scanned the trees at the edge of the grassy area that surrounded the cabin.

"No. Listen."

Demmy cocked his head and listened. "I don't hear anything."

Cody smiled. "Exactly. We're all alone again."

"Well, what did you have in mind?"

Cody's stomach growled, and they both laughed.

"I guess it's dinner time," Cody said.

"Let's check out our options."

They found pasta and a jar of sauce in the cabinets and were soon eating at the table by the window, each of them enjoying a beer as well. As they ate and the sun started to set, they talked about the island and the pollution in the lake and their hopes that Dave would turn up alive. By the time they'd washed the dishes and put everything away, it was fully dark and Cody had lit several oil lamps.

"Feel like checking out that big bathtub upstairs?" he asked and waggled his brows.

Demmy laughed. "I'm not sure both of us will fit inside it."

They did both fit inside, and after they'd washed each other and rinsed off in the shower, they ended up in bed. Cody took his time as he slid down Demmy's body, the flickering lamplight shining on their skin. The open windows allowed the evening breeze inside to cool things down, and Cody crawled back up Demmy's body and entered him. He started out slowly, with long, drawn out thrusts that pushed quiet gasps out of Demmy as he stared up at him. Building momentum, Cody soon pumped faster into him, then slowed down before speeding up again. He kept Demmy close to the edge until he couldn't take it any longer himself and snapped his hips fast, pushing them both into orgasm.

For a while they lay together and listened to the insects and frogs and nightbirds. Then Demmy got up to pee and clean up and Cody followed suit. Back in bed and under the sheet, Demmy snuggled up to Cody and moments later they both were asleep.

Cody awoke sometime in the night, gooseflesh up and down his body. Was he chilled or spooked? He lay on his back and listened to the quiet outside. The generator was chugging along, but he could no longer hear insects or frogs. He slipped out of bed and left Demmy quietly snoring to go into the bathroom and pee. When he'd finished, he picked up a battery powered lantern and carried it downstairs. The light threw long shadows around him, making everything look alien and threatening.

Halfway across the living room, he heard a sound and stopped in his tracks. A cold needle of fear started in his gut and stitched its way up his spine, pulling his balls up as well. Had he really just heard that? He couldn't seem to move, so he stood very still and cocked his head, closing his eyes as he strained to hear.

The sound came again and made him jump. It was as if something large was gagging and coughing up an object somewhere out on the island. Cody swallowed hard and opened his eyes, forcing his feet to move. He reached the front door and engaged the lock, though whatever was getting sick outside sounded big enough to bust down the door. He crossed the living room and kitchen and had just reached for the lock on the side door when the generator stopped with a quiet sigh.

Dammit, he'd left the gas cans down by the dock.

With no power, the refrigerator clicked off and the glow from the shortwave radio died. Cody stood in the kitchen with the lantern shaking slightly in his grip. The silence was complete now, and it felt oppressive and watchful. Something was outside the cabin, and Cody wasn't about to go out there and fill the generator, even if it meant they didn't have a radio.

The creak of a floorboard from behind startled a shout out of him. He whirled, staggering back and thrusting the lantern out in front of him in an effort to ward off whatever had gotten inside.

Demmy blinked in the light and held up his hands.

"It's me. It's just me."

"Fuck!" Cody's heart banged hard and he feared he might pass out. "Fuck me."

"What's wrong?" Demmy slowly approached and eased the lantern from his hand to set it on the counter. "You're pale as a ghost. What happened?"

"I heard something."

"In the cabin?"

"No. Outside. Something, I don't know, choking and coughing. And then the generator died and you came up behind me and scared forty years off my life."

"I'm sorry, I didn't mean to scare you. I woke up and you weren't in bed so I came down to see what you were doing. I should have said something or called to you."

Cody waved his words away. "I just got really spooked. I'm okay."

"Did you hear anything other than the coughing sound?"

"No. And the insects and frogs had all stopped as well."

"Really?"

They both went quiet, listening to the now comforting buzz of insects and quiet belching songs of the frogs.

"They're back now," Demmy said. "I think we're safe."

"Let's hope so."

Demmy picked up the lantern and took Cody's hand. "Come on back to bed."

"Okay. But I'm not sure I'll be able to sleep."

Demmy grinned. "Even better. Come on."

Afterwards, Cody took a while to fall asleep. When it finally did come, he dreamed about Dave's big boat sucking in plastic trash and coughing it up out the back with loud retching sounds.

CHAPTER NINE

The rumble of an engine woke Demetrius, and he rolled over, blinking in the bright morning light. A steady breeze made the window sheers dance, and the engine sounded like it was coming closer to the cabin. He sat up and looked at Cody's empty side of the bed, then yawned and swung his legs over the edge. Voices slowly being drowned out by the approaching engine came in through the window as he walked to the bathroom to pee. There was no view from the large bathroom window of people or whatever machine was rumbling past, so Demetrius used water and his fingers to smooth down his hair, brushed his teeth, got dressed, and headed downstairs.

Cody walked in the side door as Demetrius was pouring himself a cup of coffee from the percolator.

"Good morning, sleepy head." Cody swatted him lightly on the ass as he walked past.

"Good morning. What's all the ruckus about?"

"The utility guys are here. We'll have electricity again soon."

"No more oil lamp evenings," Demetrius said with an elaborate sigh.

"Well, that doesn't mean we can't light them anyway."

"Such a romantic." Demetrius walked to the table by the window, giving Cody's crotch a gentle grope as he passed.

"Don't wake the beast unless you're prepared for him to attack your town."

Demetrius laughed into his coffee. "Is the town in your analogy supposed to be my ass?"

"Your ass, your mouth, your groin, your armpit." Cody shrugged. "You never know where the monster will strike next."

"Sounds like so many of our Critter Catchers jobs."

Cody snorted. "That's the truth."

"Mr. Bower?" A man's voice called through the screen of the side door.

"Yeah, come on in," Cody called back.

A short, stocky man stomped into the kitchen. He wore a yellow hard hat, and an orange reflective vest over a blue short-sleeved polo shirt. He stopped when he saw Demetrius sitting at the table.

"Oh, sorry. I didn't mean to interrupt," the man said.

"You didn't," Cody said. "What's up, Earl?"

"Um. Oh. I wanted to let you know you're going to lose power for a few minutes because we need to shut down the generator."

Earl shot a quick look toward Demetrius and seemed to have a tough time looking Cody in the eyes. Apparently Earl's world view was reeling because he had just figured out that straight-appearing Cody had reserved the honeymoon island bungalow for himself and his husband. The so-familiar feeling started in the pit of Demetrius's stomach: part queasy guilt and part impotent anger. Demetrius sipped his coffee and kept quiet.

"Oh, sure. No problem." Cody approached the man. "Do you need me to shut it down?"

Earl took a quick step back. "No! I mean, nope. I'm familiar with the generator out here. I'll shut it down in about ten minutes if that's okay with you, um, you two?" Earl cleared his throat and threw a quick glance toward Demetrius. "Both of you?"

Cody looked over and Demetrius shrugged and nodded.

"That's fine," Cody said." Whatever you need to do. It'll be nice just to have lights out here again."

"Okay. Yeah. Just wanted to tell you that."

Earl practically ran from the house. Cody poured himself a cup of coffee and joined Demetrius at the table.

"I think you broke Earl," Demetrius said.

"What do you mean?"

"Did you meet him down at the dock?"

Cody nodded. "Yeah. I'd gone down earlier to get the gas cans, but wanted to just watch the activity on the lake. Earl and two other guys came up in a boat and unloaded a four-wheeler to carry the new transformer to the pole."

"Did you talk to him very much?"

"Where's this going?" Cody leaned in over the table and lowered his voice. "Are you jealous of Earl? Because, Demmy, let me assure you, he is not my type. Like… No."

Demetrius smirked. "I'm relieved to hear that, of course. But what I'm getting at is he got more than a little nervous when he saw me sitting here drinking coffee and looking like I just woke up."

Cody's eyes widened and he sat back. "Oh. And I told him I was here on my honeymoon. And he's probably never met a same-sex married couple before."

"Now he'll have something to tell the grandkids."

"Wow. I didn't even pick up on that. But now that you

mention it, he was acting a lot different in the cabin than he did down by the dock."

"Yep. Welcome to a gay relationship."

Cody took his hand and interlaced their fingers. His brown eyes softened and he smiled as he rubbed his thumb along the side of Demmy's finger. "I wouldn't want to be anywhere else."

The anxious anger in his gut weakened, and Demetrius smiled back. "Me either."

As the men worked outside, they played a few hands of poker and then some backgammon. Finally, Demetrius started to feel restless and suggested they go for a walk. Cody agreed, and as they left the cabin, gave a wave to Earl who stood at the narrow path that led to the utility pole. Earl lifted his hand in acknowledgement and turned quickly away.

"And there it is," Demetrius said, leading the way toward the dock.

"How'd you do it for so much of your life? You were bullied off and on through school. Was any of it easy?"

"Being friends with you helped." Demetrius stepped off the board walk and onto the dirt trail that followed the island's perimeter, and Cody took his hand and tugged him to a stop.

"I wasn't with you all the time," Cody said. "I know some of those assholes from the football team picked on you when I wasn't around."

"They probably picked on you for being friends with me," Demetrius said. "Come on, it's in the past. Let's go for a walk."

As they followed the now familiar trail, both of them were silent. The sound of the men working on the utility pole carried well, and it sounded much too loud after the silence they'd enjoyed the last few days. Demetrius was looking forward to the men finishing up their work and leaving them in peace again. When they came to the path that was a shortcut back to the cabin past the utility pole, they bypassed it without a word. Neither of them, it seemed, wanted to interact with anyone else. When they reached the opposite side of the island from the dock at Hideaway Cove, they found the waves were up and breaking against the rocks.

"Big lake," Cody said as they stopped to catch their breath and look out on the water.

"Deep, too, according to Rufus. Esther must love it."

Cody sighed, and Demetrius grinned.

When they had completed the circuit and reached the dock again, they found Rufus just stepping off his boat. His big smile was a welcome change from Earl's nervousness.

"Look at the two of you, already up and getting in your morning constitutional."

"Not much choice," Cody said. "Lots of activity out here this morning."

"That's why I came out, to make sure Earl and his crew were men of their word."

Cody led the way up the boardwalk to the cabin. Rufus called out to Earl who was just emerging from the path, wiping sweat from his forehead. Earl nodded and approached them, only glancing at Cody now and then as he provided the update, and not once looking at Demetrius.

"Power should be back on in a few hours," Earl said.

"You had to replace the whole transformer?" Rufus asked.

"Yup. Took a direct hit."

"Lucky us," Cody said.

Earl gave him a quick look and a nod before returning his attention to Rufus. "We should be out of here just after twelve."

"Power's going to be up and down during that time?" Rufus asked.

"Right." He gave Cody a bit longer of a look. "I had to go

inside and unplug a few things in the kitchen to keep them from getting blown when the power comes back on. I'll make sure it's all plugged back in and up and running before we go."

"Sounds good," Cody said. "Thank you."

"Yup." And with that, Earl returned to the path.

"You guys want a ride over to town?" Rufus said. "Sounds like it's going to be loud and hectic over here for a while, and it's shaping up to be a nice day. Maybe you could take a drive around the area."

Demetrius exchanged a look and a shrug with Cody, then turned back to Rufus. "That sounds good. Let us get a few things and we'll meet you at the dock."

When they were in the bedroom gathering hoodies, wallets, sunglasses, and phone chargers, Demetrius said, "Did you notice Earl ignored me completely and barely looked at you?"

Cody nodded and shrugged. "His loss. If he can't handle two hot men fucking each other's brains out in seclusion to celebrate their wedding, then he's not worth knowing."

Demetrius chuckled. "I like the way you think."

Cody pulled him into a tight hug and delivered a deep kiss. "You're going to like the way I think even more once we get back here tonight."

"Oh, anticipation. I like it."

After one more kiss, they left the cabin and met up with Rufus. He made sure they both were seated and wearing life vests before he reversed the boat away from the dock and turned toward town. The waves were a bit higher than they'd seen before, and Demetrius held tight to the side of the boat. Rufus talked about the lake and the town's history as he steered, looking over his shoulder on occasion.

When they'd just about reached the halfway point, Cody

leaned forward in his seat and pointed past Demetrius. "Hey, Rufus. What's that over there?"

Demetrius looked to where Cody pointed. Something bright red bobbed in the water and gulls screeched as they circled above it.

"Let's find out."

Rufus steered the boat in that direction. Sunlight glinted off the waves around the object, making it difficult to see. As they approached the shape, however, a nervous feeling started in Demetrius's gut. This trip had started to feel like one of their special cases, and he knew Cody wasn't happy about it. And now he had a very bad feeling about this latest discovery.

Demetrius watched Cody's expression tighten as they neared the object. Cody looked at him, lips pressed tight, and shook his head.

"Should have kept my mouth shut," Cody said.

"Oh, shit," Rufus said. "Aw, man. Dammit all to hell."

"It's him, isn't it?" Demetrius said to Rufus's back. "It's Dave."

"It's a body, I know that much," Rufus said. "But it does look like Dave's jacket."

"Happy fucking honeymoon," Cody muttered.

"Not your fault," Demetrius said.

"Yeah, but still." Cody sighed and dropped his gaze to stare at the deck as Rufus cut the engines and let the boat drift up close to the shape.

Demetrius stood to peer over the side as Rufus came out of the wheelhouse.

"Yeah, that's Dave," Rufus said. "Son of a bitch." He stood with his hands on his hips and stared at the body as it drifted closer to the side of the boat. "Let me call it in and see what Hap wants to do about it."

Demetrius sat beside Cody and took his hand as they listened to Rufus and Hap's conversation.

"You're sure it's Dave?" Hap said, voice sounding small over the radio.

"It's his jacket," Rufus said. "And no one's seen him since his boat was wrecked on the island."

"Shit. Son of a bitch."

"That's what I said."

"He was a good man," Hap said, and sighed. "Fuck. This really sucks. Any sign of trauma from what you can see?"

"Let me check."

Rufus grabbed a long metal pole with a hook on the end and moved to the side of the boat. After a few attempts, he managed to hook the red material and pulled the body up to the side of the boat. Splashing sounds mixed with the lap of the waves and the cry of the birds as Rufus leaned over the side and turned the body over.

"I don't see any trauma," Rufus said. "But he's tangled up in netting and fishing line." He brought a hand up and sneered at it. "And some of the slimy stuff you two keep finding on the island."

"Great," Cody muttered.

Rufus looked over and made a face. "I hate to ask, but could one of you hang onto this pole while I talk with Hap? Or, better yet, get on the radio with him and relay what I say?"

"Yeah, I can do that," Demetrius said and got up to walk to the radio. "Hap, this is Demetrius from out on the island. Rufus is at the side of the boat and asked me to relay information to you."

"Yeah, okay. I'm ready."

Rufus nodded and looked down at the body. "I don't see any marks on Dave's head, and his body is intact. But he's got fishing line and netting wrapped around him."

Demetrius repeated what Rufus had said. Hap grunted and sighed in response. "Well shit. I can't leave him floating out there. And the police boat is out of commission right now. I hate to ask this, but since you two are with Rufus, do you think you can wrangle Dave's body on board and bring it in?"

A chill went through Demetrius and he met Cody's wide-eyed gaze with one of his own. He tried to swallow, but there was a lump in his throat that made it impossible. Rufus looked at them both and must have read their expressions because he leaned farther over the side and tried to haul the body in on his own. A large swell rocked the boat and nearly sent Rufus overboard, and Cody shot to his feet with a shout.

"All right, we can help," Cody said. "Just... Give us a minute to prepare."

Rufus straightened up and nodded. "Much appreciated, guys. I know this is a lot more gruesome of a honeymoon than you had planned."

"You have no idea," Cody said. He took several deep breaths and Demetrius copied him, feeling the cold ball of nerves in his stomach tighten, but the lump in his throat shrink a bit.

"Ready?" Cody asked him.

Demetrius nodded. "Yeah. Okay." He pressed the transmit button on the radio and said to Hap, "We'll help Rufus out. Give us a few minutes."

"I appreciate it," Hap replied.

The water was cold and Dave's body heavy as they struggled to pull it over the gunwale and onto the deck of the boat. What seemed like miles of fishing line had wrapped around Dave's torso and legs. It looked like Dave had been attacked by a group of spiders, or maybe a giant one. Smelly slime covered much of his torso and made it difficult to get a good grip.

"That shit really stinks," Cody said as he turned away to draw in a breath.

"Lift on three," Rufus said. "One, two, three."

They all three groaned as they hauled the body up and over the gunwale. It thumped onto the deck on its back, and Dave's open and cloudy eyes stared up into the sun. Water gurgled out of Dave's open mouth and spread across the deck and Demetrius and Cody moved quickly out of the path.

Slime coated Demetrius's hands and he held them up and away from himself as he tried not to look down at the body. Rufus crouched over the body, forearms resting on his elbows and hands dangling between his knees as he looked Dave over.

"Doesn't appear to be any signs of trauma," Rufus said.

"No, none at all," Cody said over his shoulder as he leaned over the opposite side of the boat, scrubbing his hands in the lake. "Just water pouring out of his mouth and his eyes cloudy and staring. Other than that, he looks great."

Rufus stood with a grunt and looked between them. "This the first body you two have seen?"

Demetrius huffed a laugh before he joined Cody at the side of the boat to wash his hands. "No. We've seen some things."

"It's our honeymoon, okay?" Cody turned and sat on the bench seat, shaking the lake water from his hands as he looked at Rufus. "It's not really what I had in mind for our honeymoon. Dead bodies. Mysterious sounds in the night. A monster legend for Demmy to dig into."

"Mysterious sounds?" Rufus asked.

Cody sighed. He looked so worn down by the day's discovery, Demetrius decided to respond for him.

"Something made some weird noises last night." He faced Rufus and shook the water from his hands as well. "Like a gagging, choking noise."

"You think it's what's coughing up those big balls of slimy trash?" Rufus asked.

Demetrius shrugged. "I guess so."

"He'd like to figure it out," Cody said. "He always wants to figure it out."

Demetrius disliked hearing the defensive tone in his own voice when he replied, but he couldn't help it. "I like a good mystery. There's nothing wrong with that."

"Can't they be more sedate mysteries?" Cody said. "Like who egged Widow Monroe's house? Or who stole the giant fiberglass chicken from in front of Carl's Chicken Coop?"

"Our work doesn't let us get involved in those types of mysteries," Demetrius said, trying to keep his temper in check because he didn't want their honeymoon marred by an ugly argument. At least not in front of Rufus. And especially not with a man's body at their feet. He dropped his chin to his chest and took a breath. In a calm, even tone, he said, "Let's not fight about this, okay? There are more important things going on right now. Dave is dead, for one."

"And staring at me," Cody grumbled.

"I can fix that," Rufus said. He lifted one of the padded benches and pulled a thin blanket from inside the storage compartment. With a flourish, he spread the blanket over the upper half of Dave's body. "Better?"

Cody nodded.

"You two hang on," Rufus said. "I'll get us into town real quick."

The engine was too loud to allow for conversation as Rufus opened the throttle and sped toward town. Demetrius was glad for the chance to just sit and think. He feared either of them might say something he would regret later if they tried to talk things out now.

And, to Cody's credit, he wasn't wrong.

Demetrius did enjoy digging into a mystery, and especially one involving a monster. When he'd been growing up, monster movies scared and delighted him. He'd spent countless weekend afternoons sitting in front of the living room television watching wide-eyed as Godzilla trampled Tokyo. Or the Creature from the Black Lagoon kept pace with Julie Adams as she swam above him. Or Triffids threatened the population. The heroes would always prevail, but sometimes the movie ended with a touch of uncertainty, and a little shiver of excited fear would run through Demetrius. Maybe next time it would be up to him to figure out how to stop Godzilla, or the Gill Man, or the Triffids.

And years later, here he was, solving strange mysteries and chasing down monsters with his best friend turned husband. But they were doing more than just stopping monsters. They were getting to the root of their attacks. The wolf man that had started this whole business had been angry at his fellow senior citizens who had shunned and belittled him. The suspected chupacabra had been Aggie's beloved pet on which her father had performed drug experiments. The swamp monster had been evil brought to life deep in the Everglades and most likely forced from its home due to encroaching human development or pollution. Then there was the Devil of Pinesville, which had begun attacking people as it became addicted to heroin. And the sasquatch they'd encountered out in Colorado had been angry about Cody's father hitting it with his truck.

Monsters weren't really so different from humans. And Demetrius enjoyed figuring out their underlying motivations. And he realized that sometimes he might let it take precedence over his relationship with Cody. Since he knew Cody wasn't keen on monster-hunting, maybe he should take some steps back from anything unusual happening around them on Heaversford Lake.

But Hap and Rufus and the rest of the town weren't

familiar with monster hunting. Oh, sure, they had boat tours and souvenirs related to Esther that had sustained the tourism trade for decades, but they had never really had to work an actual case that involved the monster. Only Demetrius and Cody had that experience. And now someone was dead, most likely because of the monster, and, whether Cody liked it or not, they really should provide assistance.

Now he just needed to convince Cody.

CHAPTER TEN

Hap and a deputy hefted Dave's body onto the dock. It made a solid thumping sound that turned Cody's stomach and made him flinch.

They had talked with Dave just two days ago. Despite the man's overbearing hipster persona, Dave's heart was pure and he had truly loved Heaversford Lake, that much had been obvious. Dave had been outgoing and genuine, and Cody had liked him. And no one deserved to drown all tangled up in fishing line and covered with putrid slime. Especially not in the lake he worked so hard to protect.

Demmy had been quiet after they'd pulled Dave's body onto the boat, and Cody allowed the silence between them to continue even after Rufus had pulled up at the dock. He didn't have the words or temperament to say anything at that moment without risking a full-blown argument, and he didn't want to mar their honeymoon with a stupid fight.

Although it seemed as if Esther had already done that for them. Because Cody was pretty much certain of only two things in this mess of trip: he loved Demmy more than he could ever explain, and he hated monsters with just as much passion.

Monsters had taken the lives of several people back in Parson's Hollow and the surrounding area. They were violent, predatory creatures that lurked in the shadows and stalked innocent people. And no matter how hard Cody tried to keep them clear of monsters, they always seemed to get roped into some kind of creature case.

Correction: *Demmy* always seemed to get them roped into some kind of creature case.

Even though they had some experience digging into these types of unusual cases, Cody didn't want to wind up lying on a dock covered in slime with his lungs full of water and his limbs bound up by fishing line. And he sure as hell didn't want that for Demmy, either.

Hap approached and extended the hand he'd just cleaned with a sanitizing wipe.

"Thank you for helping Rufus out," Hap said. "And Dave. I know things have gone far beyond your idea of a relaxing honeymoon."

Cody shook Hap's hand and gave a single nod. "It was the least we could do. Dave was a good man who really loved this lake. Shame how it had to happen."

"That it is," Hap said, and turned to shake Demmy's hand.

Cody knew he needed to say something to Demmy, to break through the silent tension between them. He didn't want to start a fight, however, and there wasn't much to say other than, "Don't even consider getting involved in all of this."

Which, knowing Demmy, wouldn't go over well at all.

Rufus approached before Cody could figure out what to say.

"Been a busy morning for you boys."

Demmy chuckled and glanced toward Cody but didn't let

his gaze linger. Yep, it was going to take a while for them to work their way through this tension. Welcome to marriage.

"How about I treat you to dinner?" Rufus asked. "I know a great place."

"Would it happen to be the dining room of the hotel?" Cody said.

"Nope. It would be the dining room of my house. What do you say? You really went above and beyond out there today, and I'd like to show my appreciation." He waved toward Hap who stood over Dave's body, talking quietly with his deputy. "I'm sure Hap would like that, too."

Cody made brief eye contact with Demmy who lifted a shoulder in a half-shrug. Turning back to Rufus, Cody said, "Okay, yeah. That would be nice. What can we bring?"

"Just yourselves," Rufus said. "And an appetite. Maybe once you get away from the smell coming off Dave and this dock, you'll discover you're hungry."

"Yeah, maybe."

Cody typed Rufus's home address into his phone and set an alert to remind them about dinner. He then followed Demmy off the dock and into the public parking lot. They stood in awkward silence for a moment, looking everywhere but at each other.

Finally, Cody said, "I don't know about you, but I don't think I could eat just yet."

"I agree. Maybe not even for dinner."

"Let's not get carried away now. Dinner's six hours away."

"Yeah, okay. So what do we do until then? Do you want to drive around the lake and see some sights?"

Cody stared until Demmy finally had to look away with a hint of a smile.

"That goes on the bad teasing topic list."

"There's a bad teasing topic list?"

"There is now. And any teasing about sightseeing along the shores of Heaversford Lake is strictly forbidden."

Demmy chuckled. "Okay. Any other topics I should avoid?"

"I'll let you know. Let's start walking."

Demmy followed him out of the parking lot and onto the sidewalk. "You doing okay?"

"After finding a dead guy floating in the lake and pulling him up into a boat and getting slime on my hands that I think I'll feel until the day I die no matter how many times I wash them?" Cody held up a hand and waggled it back and forth. "Eh. So-so."

"I would guess Dave's boat capsized and he was thrown out of it."

"Seems that way. Though I'm not sure the current would have been strong enough to toss his boat onto the rocks around the island like that. But, who am I to know the ins and outs of this lake?"

"True. Who are we to make assumptions?" Demmy said.

"This also seems like a local situation, so we shouldn't go poking our noses into Hap's official investigation." Cody watched Demmy from the corner of his eye. "Right?"

Demmy didn't look at him, but gave a single nod. "Right. No offering to work with Hap on the investigation."

They browsed some shops for a while, and when they passed a bar, Cody noticed it was open. He checked the time on his phone and was surprised to see it was almost noon.

"How's your appetite?" Cody asked.

"It's recovered a bit. We never did eat breakfast."

"Want to get a bar burger and a beer?"

Demmy's eyebrows went up.

"Hey, we can start drinking before noon if we want to. It's our vacation."

A twist of guilt as he realized he'd said 'vacation' instead of 'honeymoon.' And from the flicker of sadness that flashed across Demmy's face, he'd noticed it, too.

But then he shrugged. "Okay."

Cody held the door for Demmy to enter first. He was glad for Demmy's agreement, but he knew they needed to put this glitch in their honeymoon behind them. Maybe a beer for each of them would grease the wheels of conversation.

Yeah, because nothing helped an argument quite like throwing alcohol into the mix.

And Dave's death was much more than a simple glitch.

The interior of the bar was set up much like The Hollow Leg back home, just a lot smaller. A juke box in the back corner was quiet for now, and three of the five other occupants sat at the long bar. Demmy chose a table in the middle of the place, and the bartender came over. He was a young and handsome guy, and Cody thought the guy smiled at Demmy a little too brightly.

"Welcome to Heaversford House. What can I get you guys?"

They each ordered a draft beer and a burger with fries. When the bartender walked off, Cody drummed his fingers on the table and looked at everything and everyone in the bar other than Demmy. They needed to talk about the monster in the room, he knew that, but he was also reluctant to continue the conversation. He was walking a fine line between strongly requesting Demmy stay out of the investigation into Dave's death and not ruining their honeymoon any further. But if he didn't say something, Demmy would most likely keep working the case over and over in his brain.

The bartender brought their beers, told them the burgers would be up soon, and had just turned away when the door burst open and a woman rushed inside and up to the bar.

"Did you guys hear about Dave?" the woman asked, excitement evident in her voice.

The stools at the bar must have been occupied by locals, because all of them started talking at once.

"Dave?"

"Hippie Dave?"

"What happened?"

"He high again?"

"Did he get arrested for loitering again?"

The woman shook her head as Cody's stomach curled into a tight knot of tension and he met Demmy's gaze across the table.

"No!" she practically shouted. "He's dead!"

Minor chaos erupted, and she waited until the commotion had died down to explain that she had been at the docks seeing to her boat when Rufus had brought in Dave's body. Hap had been there to meet them, and now the county coroner had arrived to take the body away.

Three quarters of the people sitting at the bar got up and rushed out the door. The bartender shouted at their backs, demanding payment, but no one listened. When the door closed behind the last exiting patron, the bartender started writing up tabs as he shook his head.

"Word travels quick in a small town," Demmy said. "Though it got around faster here than it might have back home."

"The public dock seems to be a real focal point of this town."

"Kind of like Margie's?"

At the mention of the town diner, they finally shared a smile.

"Yeah," Cody said. "Kind of like that."

"I don't intend on talking to Hap at all about Dave's death," Demmy said. "Okay? You can relax."

"I'm sorry."

Demmy frowned. "What are you sorry for?"

"I feel like I'm being an asshole."

Demmy sat back and crossed his arms. "This feels like a trap."

"Yeah, yeah. Look, I wanted this week to be special, right? This was the part of our wedding I was responsible for and I got too caught up in my own head worrying about it that I procrastinated, and now we've ended up here and so far it's gone to hell. I'm more than a little guilt-ridden and defensive about it."

"This week has been unpredictable and exciting and full of the hottest sex I've ever had. I don't think it's gone to hell, and I don't blame you for any of it."

Cody nodded, then grinned and leaned forward. "Hottest sex ever?"

Demmy grinned back. "Even hotter than our first time during the drive home from my parents' place in Florida."

The burgers arrived and they were quiet as they ate. Around them, the people left in the bar talked about Dave and wondered how he had managed to drown in the very lake he loved and worked so hard to protect. Cody kept his head down and focused on his food, and across from him he could see Demmy doing the same.

When they'd finished, Demmy paid the tab and they both headed to the restroom. It was empty, and Cody grabbed Demmy by the hand and pulled him close for a quick, gentle kiss.

"I'm sorry," he said.

"You said that already."

"But I didn't get to say it like this." He kissed him again, soft and lingering, his tongue stroking Demmy's bottom lip.

Demmy stepped back, cheeks flushed and erection apparent in his shorts. "Apology accepted. Now I need a minute to be able to pee."

When they'd finished and washed their hands, they

stepped out of the bar and both looked toward the dock. An ambulance waited just behind Hap's police cruiser, lights flashing on both vehicles. They turned away and walked in the opposite direction.

Rufus's house was small but nicely maintained. He greeted them with a bright smile and ushered them into the living room furnished with two recliners facing a large screen television, a love seat, and a low coffee table. A baseball game on the TV was muted, and Hap sat in one of the recliners, feet up, bottle of beer on a table between the chairs. Hap looked around and lifted a hand in greeting.

"I'm not standing up," Hap said. "But I'm welcoming you as a tired and lazy out of shape ex-athlete who's had a long day."

They all laughed, and Cody felt much of his tension drain away.

"I'm working on dinner still," Rufus said. "It's my turn to cook."

"Thank god for that," Hap put in. "Because if it had been my turn, you would be eating carry out from Heaversford House."

"Why don't you guys join Hap," Rufus suggested. "Can I get you a drink?"

"I'll come help out in the kitchen," Demmy said. "If that's okay. Cody's the sports fan."

"Hey, you came to all my games in high school," Cody said.

"Did you see how you looked in those football pants?" Demmy said with a grin, and Cody blushed.

"Even back then?" Cody asked.

Demmy shrugged. "Sorry. I was crushing on you all through high school."

"I knew I should have gone for it back then," Cody said.

"Yeah, yeah. I don't think either of us could have handled it at that age." Demmy's smile was warm and comforting, and Cody was glad they'd accepted Rufus's offer of dinner.

Cody sat in the other recliner and Hap took the game off mute. The volume was low, and they were able to talk about the players and averages and the Pittsburgh Pirates's chances to go to the World Series. Demmy brought them each a cold beer, and they sat in companionable silence for a while.

"Have you and Rufus lived together long?" Cody asked.

"We don't live together," Hap said, quickly glancing away from the game. "I'm here most of the time, but I still have a small apartment closer to the station."

"Oh. Is that so the town doesn't ask questions?"

"No, it's more to give us both space," Hap said. "But like Rufus said before, I don't think we're fooling anyone in town. It's almost like there's an unspoken understanding. No one tries to set either of us up with available women, and we don't show any PDAs."

"PDAs?"

"Public displays of affection."

"Ah. Got it."

On the television, the Pirates hit a home run, and both of them got more involved in the game. When Rufus called them into the kitchen, Hap muted the game again before they got up. A round table was situated in one end of the kitchen, place settings sparkling beneath a dimmed overhead light. The smell of chicken was stronger in the kitchen, and Cody's stomach growled.

Dinner was buffet style, and they filled their plates at the stove and countertops, taking pieces of baked chicken, scoops of mashed potatoes, servings of green beans, and half ears of corn. When they were all seated once again, Rufus tucked his napkin into the collar of his shirt and said, "Dig in!"

The food was delicious, and they were all quiet for the first few bites. Then Rufus set down his fork and asked, "You boys recover from the boat ride in?"

"Yeah," Demmy said with a nod. "We're better now."

"I really appreciate you helping Rufus out," Hap said. "It was good of you to get Dave out of the lake as soon as possible and get him back to shore."

"You're welcome," Cody said. "We were glad to be of help."

Another moment of silence, then Hap said, "Rufus tells me you've heard some strange noises out on the island?"

Cody's stomach tightened around the food, and he knew he wouldn't be able to finish his meal. He sat back and dabbed his lips with the napkin. "Yeah. Not sure what it is."

"Sounded like something big choking or gagging," Demmy said.

"Any more balls of slimy plastic trash?" Hap asked.

"Not that we've found," Cody said.

"Dave was covered in the same slime," Rufus said. "As was his boat. Seems to be a connection."

"Yeah, Doc said he'll have it analyzed and let me know what they find out," Hap said. "You guys are still planning to go back to the island tonight?"

"Yeah," Demmy said. "We don't feel threatened out there."

"I heard from Earl that the power's back on," Rufus said. "So you'll have fans and lights."

"Demmy nodded. "That's good news. And we'll have access to the radio if we get into trouble. We should be fine." He looked at Cody. "Right?"

Cody nodded and wished he felt as sure about his response as Demmy seemed to be when he said, "Right. We'll be fine."

CHAPTER ELEVEN

Demetrius closed the bathroom door behind him and leaned back against it.

This was wrong. He knew this was wrong, but he just couldn't seem to help himself. He had to know.

But first, to make sure he hadn't lied when he'd said he had to use the bathroom, he did just that. He didn't flush, not quite yet, and he quietly washed his hands before pulling the phone from his pocket. There in Rufus's bathroom of white tile and soft, navy blue towels, Demetrius broke his word to Cody.

Not even married a week yet, and he was already going behind his husband's back.

Guilt gnawed at him, but he focused on the wording of his text. He didn't have a lot of time, and wouldn't get this kind of chance for a while once they were back on the island. His thumbs flew over the screen of his phone. In his haste, he misspelled at least fifteen percent of the words and had to go back and fix the errors, but he got it all down.

He took a breath and read it all over again.

Then he looked into the mirror.

"What are you doing?" he asked his reflection. "You're being an idiot, that's what."

He copied the entire text message and pasted it into the Notes app where he saved it. This wasn't the time to set this trouble in motion. They only had two days left out on the island. He needed to relax and focus on spending time with Cody. That was it. Let the people and police of Hempstead do what was needed.

With that all decided, Demetrius flushed the toilet and noisily washed his hands. When he joined Cody on the love seat, no one said a word about how long he'd been in the bathroom. They were all absorbed in the end of the baseball game.

Well, that was a whole lot of pressure he hadn't needed to put on himself.

Half an hour later, the Pirates came out victorious and Rufus lowered the footrest of his recliner so he could stand up. Hap was snoring quietly in his recliner, and Rufus paused to gaze down on him with affection.

"I may be seeing things," Cody said in a quiet voice, "but I think you're sweet on him."

"I just might be at that. Come on, let's get you two back out to your remote love shack."

Rufus gathered his wallet and keys, pulled on his boots, and allowed them to step out the front door ahead of him. He eased the door shut, turned the deadbolt, and they set off down the sidewalk. The sun was hanging just above the water, casting a long orange reflection across the surface of the lake. One of the Esther sighting tour boats cut across the sight, heading in for the night.

"You going to be okay coming back in the dark?" Cody asked.

"I've been out on this lake in the dark about as often as I've been on it during the day." Rufus winked. "I'll be just fine. And my man will be waiting for me when I get back home."

"Good luck waking him up," Demetrius said. "He was sawing some pretty big logs when we left."

"I know how to wake him up, don't you worry."

They all laughed. The good feeling in Demetrius's chest battled with the guilt building lower in his gut. He shouldn't have even written out that text. What kind of relationship could be built on a lie so early on?

Dammit. Why was he always getting involved in things he had no right to?

They reached the dock and all three stopped. A small memorial had begun to take shape in a corner of the chain link fence that separated the parking lot from the dock area. There was no plastic wrap around the cut flowers, but rather fabrics or what looked like recycled paper. Someone had dressed a teddy bear in a rain slicker and boots, similar to that which Dave had worn, and placed it in a red boat.

"Tributes already," Rufus said, emotion evident in his voice. "Dave was a good man. He will be missed."

"He really cared about this lake," Demetrius said.

"Yeah, that he did. Hopefully someone will pick up the mantle and keep up what he started." Rufus looked at the flowers and bear another moment, then turned toward the dock. "Come on. Let's get you boys back."

They were all quiet on the ride across the lake. Demetrius sat close to Cody, enjoy the warmth of his leg. When they reached the dock at Hideaway Cove, they both shook Rufus's hand and thanked him for dinner.

"It was our pleasure," Rufus said with a smile. "We don't get much chance to entertain folks of a similar nature, if you know what I mean."

Cody gave him the perfect puzzled look. "No. What do you mean?"

Rufus chuckled and shook his head as he waved goodbye. "Sleep tight, newlyweds. Or not. It's your honeymoon."

Cody put his arm around Demetrius and pulled him in close to his side. Demetrius slipped his arm around Cody's waist and they stood on the dock watching Rufus's boat head back to town.

"Nice guys," Cody said. "I kind of wish they lived closer to us."

"Yeah, me too."

After another couple of minutes, Demetrius shivered in the light breeze. Cody turned to face him and leaned down for a gentle kiss.

"Thank you," Cody said.

"For what?"

"Being my friend."

"You're welcome. And the same goes for you. We have a lot of history to build our marriage on." Demetrius huffed a quiet laughed and widened his eyes. "Can't believe I just said that about the two of us."

Cody grinned. "It's weird sometimes, huh?"

"Really weird. I mean, I spent so many years telling myself you were straight—"

"Well, not entirely."

"But I didn't know that."

"Granted. But… yeah. Anyway."

"Anyway, I kept telling myself not to even entertain the thought of it because it would never happen. And it would just mess up the way I thought about you."

Cody slid his big hands up and down Demetrius's arms. "Sounds really complicated."

"It was, at times. But we made it work."

"We did. And now we're going to make this next level of our relationship work just as well." Cody kissed him again. "Come on, let's get inside."

They walked up the boardwalk toward the house. Now that power had been restored, the accent lights to either side seemed almost too bright. But Demetrius was glad to see the lamp in the living room glowing through the big window. There was no rush to get inside, so they took their time strolling up the boardwalk.

"I know I should have asked this long before now, but why didn't you tell me you were bi-sexual before all of this?" Demetrius asked.

Cody's arm tightened a little around his shoulders, and he leaned over to kiss the side of Demetrius's head.

"I was scared."

"Of me?"

"Of us."

Demetrius stopped. He took Cody's hand, tugging him to a stop and around to face him. "I don't understand."

Cody pulled him into a hug, and when he stepped back, placed a soft kiss on his mouth.

"You're my best friend. Like, seriously, no lie, my complete and total best friend in the entire world. You, above all others, come to mind first when people ask about my friends. It's always been that way, since forever. And, you trusted me with the biggest, most personal secret of your life."

"I came out to you before I told anyone else."

"I know. And I was honored at that. And so happy for you."

"But you didn't trust me with your secret?"

"I didn't trust myself."

"I'm really not following now."

"You knew who you were and what you wanted. You always have. I haven't always been so sure of that. And, to be completely honest, that part of you scared the shit out of the similar part of me. You were set. You wanted men and you knew it. I had yet to realize where I fell in all of that. I had attractions to both guys and girls and that was confusing enough. I went out with a couple of guys, but it didn't go very far. I dated way more women than men, but I never slept with a guy until..." Cody smiled, and Demetrius saw the glimmer of the path lights reflected in tears in his eyes. "Until you. Until us. I didn't say anything before last year because I was really fucking scared of losing you. None of my ex-girlfriends can stand me, in case you haven't noticed."

Demetrius smiled even though he was on the verge of tears himself. "Oh, I've noticed."

"Yeah. Anyway. You were a part of my life I couldn't risk losing. And I thought if I told you I was dating guys, it would change things between us. I wanted you, for a long time. But even way back in my dimly-lit teenage mind, I knew I wasn't ready for you. I did, however, spend some hot nights jerking myself raw over fantasies of you. But to pursue something real with you? I wasn't ready. Or deserving."

Demetrius squeezed Cody's hands. "I compared every man I dated to you. You've always been the absolute ideal for me. I thought about you so often and in such increasingly dirty situations, it started to freak me out a little. I didn't want to be that gay guy who creepily checked out his straight friend, but I couldn't help it. Besides all that, I never wanted to risk our friendship. That was always the most important thing to me. You'll always be my friend first, I promise."

Guilt surged up within him, and Demetrius dropped his gaze.

"Hey, what happened?" Cody ducked his head. "Your expression completely shut down. Look at me, Demmy. What's wrong?"

Demetrius looked up and gave him a smile that felt shaky. "I'm about to initiate our first fight as a married couple."

Cody put on a stern expression. "Did you make out with

Rufus in the kitchen while I was watching baseball with Hap?"

"Not exactly," Demetrius said with a chuckle. "I started to write a text when I was in the bathroom."

"Who to?"

"Tracey Mumm."

At first, Cody looked confused. "My ex-girlfriend Tracey Mumm? Who works at the library? Why would you...?" Understanding dawned. "Ah. For information. About a lake monster."

The heavy sigh felt like a knife in Demetrius's gut.

"But I didn't send it."

"Okay."

"Really. I promise. I didn't send it."

"I believe you." Cody leaned in for a kiss. "And I understand. Come on, let's go in."

"Wait. You understand?"

"Yeah. I understand."

"What do you understand?"

Cody shrugged. "How much you like digging into these monster situations."

"I know you don't like these things, so I want you to know I didn't send the text."

"You said that already."

"But it's important that you know that."

"Okay. Thanks for telling me that. Come on, let's go in."

Demetrius followed him inside the cabin. "I really didn't send it."

"Demmy, I get it. You're confessing to something you considered but didn't follow through on. It's not a big deal."

"Really?"

"Really." Cody turned away, paused, then turned back. "Let me take a guess, though, okay?"

Demetrius frowned. "What kind of guess?"

"How it all happened. Okay?"

"Yeah. Okay."

"You wrote it out as a text first, feeling guilty the whole time, but needing to get the details down and the questions correct. Then you read it over and started feeling even more guilty, so you didn't send the text. But, it was most likely a long message, and it had some good information. So, did you just leave it unsent?"

"No."

Cody smiled. "Then you copied it and pasted it into another app. The Notes app?"

"How'd you know that?"

Cody gave him a firm kiss. "Demmy, I know you better than anyone else." He moved in close and pulled Demetrius up against him. Leaning down, Cody whispered in his ear, "I know you inside and out. How you feel, how you taste, how you sound. You belong to me."

Demetrius swallowed past a lump in his throat as his cock sprang to life. Cody pressed his thigh against the hard line of his erection.

"Well," Cody said with a smirk, "that got your attention."

"You always get my attention, and you know it."

A hot, deep kiss stopped any further words. When Cody pulled back, he said, "Care to prove it?"

"Think you can handle it?"

Cody arched an eyebrow. "You know better than to challenge me." He took Demetrius by the hand and led him toward the steps to the bedroom. "I hope you're properly hydrated."

Demetrius laughed as he followed Cody up the stairs. Despite the storm, issues with power, and monster legend—or maybe because of all that—this had to be the best honeymoon possible.

CHAPTER TWELVE

S omeone was knocking. It was loud and annoying, pulling Cody up from what had been a very deep sleep.

He groaned and rolled over in bed, bumping up against Demmy.

The knocking persisted, and now someone was calling their names. Someone with a deep voice Cody didn't recognize.

A door opened, and footsteps sounded.

"Cody? It's Hap. You here?"

Cody jerked to a sitting position in bed.

"What the...?" he muttered, and scrubbed his hands over his face. Demmy slept soundly beside him, his breathing slow and even.

Memories came back to Cody, starting with the most recent, and then earlier, and so on, as if his mind was trying to find its place in a movie. Hot sex with Demmy last night before they both collapsed. Demmy confessing to him about the unsent text. Their talk about Cody's history of dating men. The boat ride back from the mainland with Rufus. Dinner at Rufus's house with him and Hap.

Hap.

Sergeant Hap was in the bungalow, calling their names.

They were naked.

"Shit," Cody said, and swung his feet over the side of the mattress. He cleared his throat and called. "We're here. Be right down."

Demmy drew in a deep breath and rolled over, his hand landing on the spot Cody had just vacated. As Cody got to his feet and dug some clothes out of the dresser, Demmy sat up in bed.

"Where you going?" Demmy asked.

"Downstairs. Hap's here."

"Hap? He's here?" Demmy wiped sleep from his eyes and yawned as he looked toward the stairs. "What's he want?"

"Don't know yet."

"What time is it?"

"Good question." Cody grabbed his phone. And groaned. "Ten after six."

"In the morning?" Demmy squinted toward the bright sunlight coming in the window. "What the fuck is he doing out here so early?"

"Don't know that yet, either. Stay in bed. I'll go talk to him."

"You're a very kind man," Demmy said through another yawn, and collapsed back into bed.

Once dressed, Cody stopped in the bathroom for a pee, a quick brush of his teeth, and an attempt to tame the corkscrews in his hair. A little more alert, he descended the steps barefoot and found Hap pacing in the living room.

"Hey, what's up?" Cody said.

Hap approached and stood inches away from him. "Have you seen Rufus?"

"What?"

"Rufus. Have you seen him?"

Cody shook his head, confused. "Since last night?"

"Yes. When did you last see him?"

"Last night. He dropped us off out here after dinner. You haven't seen him?"

Hap's expression changed abruptly. His face went slack and tears filled his eyes as he looked away from Cody and out the window toward the lake.

"No. I haven't seen him. I slept all night in the recliner, and when I woke up at five he wasn't home."

"Hap, I'm sorry. I'm sure he's okay. Maybe he's helping someone out on the lake?"

"He would have left a note. He always leaves a note."

Before Cody could respond, Hap's radio crackled and a woman's voice called his name. Hap tipped his head closer to the mic secured on his shoulder and pressed the transmit button.

"I'm here, Cheryl."

"We've found something you should see."

Hap was moving fast toward the door. "Where are you?"

"The south end of Broken Jaw Island. Opposite Hideaway Cove."

Cody was right behind him and had to stop fast when Hap halted. He turned to stare at him, and Cody watched Hap's Adam's apple bounce as he swallowed hard.

"I'll be there in a minute," Hap said into the mic. He held Cody's gaze a moment longer before turning away and pushing out the screen door.

Cody's stomach was a mess of tight knots. He ran up the stairs and gently shook Demmy's shoulder.

"Demmy, wake up. Come on. Get up."

"What's going on?" Demmy blinked up at him.

"Rufus is missing."

Cody went to the dresser and pulled out a pair of socks

for himself, then grabbed some clothes for Demmy and tossed them on the bed.

"What?" Demmy sat up. "Missing? How long?"

"Since he dropped us off last night."

He sat on the edge of the bed with his back to Demmy and pulled on his socks. The mattress shifted beneath him as Demmy got out of bed.

"Missing? Like he never made it back to the dock?"

"Hap said it looks like Rufus never came home last night. Which I took to mean The Lazy Aye was missing from the dock and his bed hadn't been slept in."

Demmy was half dressed and in the bathroom.

"Have they found anything?" Demmy called over the sound of his peeing.

Cody got up and moved around the bedroom, grabbing hats and sunscreen for them both. "One of the officers radioed Hap that they found something on the west side of the island."

Demmy appeared in the bathroom doorway, lips foamy with toothpaste. "Our island?"

"Our island." He waved the hats and sunscreen. "I've got these things. Meet you downstairs."

In the kitchen, Cody grabbed a few granola bars and a couple of bottles of iced tea. He selected a couple of water bottles as well, and when he turned away from the refrigerator, found Demmy behind him, boots in hand. His blue eyes were wide and lips pressed tight.

"Here." Cody handed over a granola bar, bottle of water, and an iced tea.

"West side of the island?"

"Right."

"If we take the shortcut we could be there in a few minutes."

"I was thinking the same thing."

They carried their boots out the back door and sat on the small wooden deck to lace them up. Cody took the lead and set off along the path, now well-trampled thanks to the utility workers the day before.

As he hiked along the path, Cody started a mental conversation with himself. With each rebuttal, his sense of dread seemed to increase exponentially.

Maybe Rufus had experienced engine trouble and was stuck out on the lake.

Then why hadn't he radioed in for help?

Maybe the radio was out as well. What if it had been an electrical problem?

Someone would have seen him by now. And Hap would have found him by now.

Maybe Rufus had just taken the long way back and run out of gas?

Then why hadn't he radioed in for help?

Around and around his mind went, offering up possible reasons for Rufus to go missing, only to shoot them down again.

"This is bad," Demmy said.

"We don't know that."

"Yeah, we do. It's bad."

"Stop thinking that way."

"I can't help it." Demmy was silent for several steps, then said in a quieter voice, "Such a kind man. A good, kind man."

"He's not gone." Cody pushed a branch out of the way and held it for Demmy before releasing it. He repeated, "He's not gone," and hoped just by saying the words he could make it true.

They came out on the wider trail and followed that toward the far side of the island. As they approached a bend in the trail, Cody heard the thrum of a boat engine and people calling to one another. Maybe it was Rufus?

The thought got him moving faster. After a few steps, he started to jog. He could hear Demmy keeping pace behind him, and not long after reaching the trail, they came to the side of the island opposite the town. Large rocks sat half-buried along the coarse sand. Out on the water, a police boat idled as it rode gentle swells. The waves broke on and around the rocks in the beach, soaking the feet and pant legs of the officers on shore, Hap among them. They stood in a loose circle, looking down at something in the sand.

"What are they looking at?" Demmy asked.

"I can't tell."

"Let's go a little closer." Demmy stepped out onto the sand.

"Wait, Demmy…" Cody sighed as he watched Demmy approach the group. "Dammit." He followed to a point about ten feet from the officers.

"Hap?" Cody called. "Everything okay?"

Hap looked over his shoulder. His eyes were watery and his face drawn. "Don't come any closer, you two. Stay right there."

One of the officers gripped Hap's shoulder and squeezed it. "Get yourself on back to town, Hap. We'll look for him. We'll find him."

Hap shook his head. "I can't just sit and wait. I need to do something." He walked away from the group and strode past Cody and Demmy. His jaw was set and his gaze fixed on the trees beyond the beach.

"Hap, what can we do?" Cody called to his back.

"Nothing you can do, Cody," Hap said without looking back. And then he disappeared into the trees.

"Is that from Rufus's boat?" Demmy asked, voice raised so the officers could hear him over the waves.

Cody turned from where Hap had gone into the trees. With him gone from the group, he could see something lying in the sand that looked like it had come from the side of a boat. A light blue boat with red along the top. He thought that was called the gunwale, but couldn't be sure. Either way, it looked exactly as if it belonged on The Lazy Aye.

"Most likely." The officer stared at them. "Which makes this island a possible crime scene. You two hear anything last night?"

A chill of fear went through Cody. "What? No. Nope, not a thing."

"There's no contact with Rufus at all?" Demmy asked.

"Let's just say it's an active investigation," the officer said.

All three officers gave them hard stares.

Cody tugged on the hem of Demmy's T-shirt. "Let's get back to the cabin."

"Yeah. Okay."

They were quiet on the hike back. Once inside the cabin, Cody went to the radio and slowly made his way through the channels, listening to what back and forth he could find. A lot of boaters were out on the lake now, either fishing, pleasure cruising, or actively searching for any sign of Rufus.

And they weren't finding much.

"I can't believe it." Demmy's voice was low and flat. He sat on the couch, back against the arm and knees pulled up to his chest. "First Dave and now Rufus?"

"We don't know anything for sure," Cody said, but he could hear how desperate he sounded.

"Yeah, I know."

After a time, they cobbled together a meal and ate in silence. The conversations continued on the radio in the background. Muffled sounds from the beach occasionally floated in the open windows with the breeze. Cody opened a beer for each of them and they sat in the shade on the porch, not saying much of anything.

It was mid-afternoon when a boat horn brought them both

to their feet. Cody could see his own hope reflected in Demmy's expression before he headed off along the boardwalk toward the dock at a fast clip. Cody followed, and when they came out of the trees both of them stopped to look at the dock.

Cody's hopes sank, leaving cold empty space behind.

Hap was stepping off a police boat and onto the dock. His face was even more haggard than it had been that morning.

"Anything?" Cody asked.

Hap stomped past them, avoiding eye contact. "Not a fucking thing."

"Hap..." Demmy called to his back, but Hap just kept walking.

"He's blaming us," Cody said. "He's blaming us for Rufus going missing."

Demmy gave a single nod. "We were the last ones to see Rufus alive. We may need a lawyer."

"Fuck. And all we have is each other for alibis."

"I don't know what to do," Demmy said. "I'm at a total loss with this situation."

Things had to be pretty dire for Demmy to say such a thing. He always had some kind of idea in the back of his mind, or had planned out how to handle a situation. Every monster case they'd stumbled into so far, Demmy had always come up with some scheme to get them through. But this situation was different. This monster—and, yes, Cody was admitting, at least to himself, that there was a monster involved—was not something they could just hike around and find. This thing lived underwater, and that made it even more frustrating and frightening.

And now, Cody was ready to admit that he was afraid, for himself and Demmy, naturally, but also for Rufus. The only way to prove their innocence was for them to prove that something else was guilty.

Which meant they needed to go monster hunting.

On their honeymoon.

Fuck.

Cody took a deep breath and let it out. He grabbed Demmy's hand and squeezed, drawing his attention.

"You still have that text you wrote in your Notes app?" Cody asked.

Demmy frowned. "Yeah. Why?"

"Send it."

"What?"

"We need to prove our innocence here. And to do that, we need as much information as we can get about Esther. Send Tracey the text."

"Are you sure?"

"We didn't do anything to Rufus, and we would never hurt anyone," Cody said. "But to this town and to Hap, we're strangers. They don't know us. The only person who knew us even a little bit was Rufus."

"Oh my God," Demmy said, his voice a whisper. He looked out over the lake toward town. "They're going to lock us up."

"Good possibility. Especially if they find Rufus's body or more pieces of his boat washed up on this island."

Demmy looked distraught. "You really think he's dead?"

"Don't you?"

"Yeah. I do. I just didn't want to say it out loud." He gave a sad and quiet laugh as he shook his head. "This is a lot like that first case right after we opened Critter Catchers. The werewolf."

"Wolf man," Cody corrected in a gentle voice, and they shared a quick smile.

"You don't think Hap will stand up for us?" Demmy asked.

Cody shrugged. "If I was in Hap's place, and you

vanished after going out with a couple of strangers, I'd be all over them to get information."

"Dammit." He pulled out his phone and moments later he let out a breath and slid it back into his pocket. "Okay. I've sent it. Let's hope Tracey can find something to help us out."

Cody nodded and looked out over the smooth surface of the lake. Tracey Mumm, yet another of his ex-girlfriends and now a librarian at the Parson's Hollow library, was a bit of stretch for them. But she had come through for them before, on both the wolf man and what they had thought was a chupacabra. With access to a room filled with books that were older and more obscure than those able to be checked out, she was a good source of information on the unexplainable creatures they had come across.

Now Cody hoped she could dig up something about a monster quite similar to the famous Nessie over in Loch Ness. And he hoped they could find a way to prove its existence.

He was quite aware of this shift in attitude about one of their monsters. Not only did he need to prove Esther was real, but he also need to prove she was the cause of Rufus's disappearance. And most likely the reason for the death of aging hipster and lake cleaner Dave.

"I guess we should just go back to the cabin and wait, huh?"

Cody nodded. "Yeah. Let's stay out of Hap's way and hope Tracey gets back to us soon."

They'd gotten halfway up the steps that led to the board-walk when the sound of a boat engine approaching brought them back down to the dock. Cody could see right away it wasn't The Lazy Aye, but it didn't appear to be a police boat either. It was an old metal fishing boat with a loud outboard motor, and it rode low in the water. Once the small boat bumped against the dock, a short, thin woman stepped out. Although there wasn't a cloud in sight, she wore a bright orange rain slicker with a matching hat, denim overalls with the legs cutoff at the knees, a tie-dye T-shirt with the sleeves rolled up, and white athletic socks that gleamed through the holes of neon green Crocs. Large round plastic-framed glasses were connected to a chain that went around the back of her neck.

"Hi," Demmy said. "Can we help you?"

"Don't know," the woman said, her voice rattling in her throat. She turned to haul a large, over-stuffed backpack up from the boat and hefted it onto her back with a grunt. Cody was afraid she might topple off the side of the dock and get pulled under by the weight of it. "You boys know about the recent sightings?"

"Sightings?" Cody exchanged a look with Demmy. "Like, monster sightings?"

"Well I'm not talking about those fucking Kardashians for pity's sake! I'm here about Esther." She tromped up to them and stuck out a hand. "Name's Clarabell Remington. I'm part of the UFO Society, which doesn't stand for Unidentified Flying Objects, but rather for Unusual Fauna Observers Society. Rufus called me earlier this week, said I might be able to help. Is he out here and available?"

CHAPTER THIRTEEN

Demetrius stared at the tiny and oddly dressed woman standing on the dock. Clarabell looked between him and Cody, her chin thrust out.

He was at a loss on what he should do. The correct thing, of course, would be to take her to see Hap. But Hap was busy searching for Rufus, and Demetrius didn't think Hap would want to deal with someone like Clarabell at that point in time. At least not while Rufus was missing.

Cody cleared his throat and approached Clarabell with his hand extended.

"I'm Cody Bower. Can I help you with that back pack? It looks pretty heavy."

Clarabell gave him a long, hard stare. "Believe it or not, stud muffin, I can carry my own bag."

"Ah, okay. Just being polite is all. And it's Cody Bower, though I have heard stud muffin a time or two." He turned his back to her and gave Demetrius a wide-eyed stare as he returned to stand beside him.

"I bet you have." Clarabell lifted her chin toward

Demetrius. "What's his problem? Someone hit his reboot switch?"

Demetrius blinked and stammered through his response. "What? N-no. I just… I'm Demetrius Singleton. And we weren't expecting to see you. I mean, Rufus hadn't told us he'd called you."

"So?" She shrugged and, with quick steps, approached them. She gave no sign of stopping—perhaps it was the weight of the pack driving her forward—and Demetrius and Cody quickly stepped apart to let her pass between them.

"I assume you're going to tell me Rufus is waiting up at the cabin." She paused to look over her shoulder. "And he already told me about Dave Lamond drowning, so if that's what's got you two all jumpy, you can relax." A few shakes of her head and quick purse of her lips. "Shame. Dave really loved this lake."

Demetrius couldn't keep it in any longer. When Clarabell started up the steps to the boardwalk, he called to her back, "Rufus is missing."

"Demmy…" Cody said in a low voice.

"We need to tell her."

Clarabell stopped. She adjusted the straps of the pack and turned slowly to face them. "How long?"

"Since late last night," Cody said. "He dropped us off here on the dock and headed back to town. His boat is missing, and from what anyone can tell, he never made it in."

"She's a night feeder." Clarabell let the pack slide off her shoulders and thump to the boards. Standing there with her arms at her sides and her gaze unfocused, Demetrius wondered if she might have had a stroke or a heart attack. A moment later she continued speaking, and he and Cody moved a few steps closer to hear better.

"We talked about it off and on over the years, Rufus and I. How she had to be most active at night. Late at night, too, not evening or dusk or something like you'd expect. It was like she knew she had to stay hidden as much as possible. Had to be that way, otherwise someone would've seen her more often. As it was there was only the few sightings from the rum runners and mobsters who crossed the lake late at night. You've heard those stories, right?"

She lifted her gaze and latched it on Demetrius. He shook his head, afraid to speak for fear of interrupting the strange mood that had come over the three of them. It was as if they were standing in a tiny bubble of space and time, where she told them tales of long ago.

"Domingo Patrelli ran booze out of Hempstead during Prohibition. It wasn't much, mind you, but it made him a comfortable living. They ran a still in the basement of his bakery and filled barrels with homemade hooch. His bakers loaded the barrels into boats and rowed them out to Broken Jaw Island in the middle of the night. A number of them reported something tracking their boat through the water, and two of the men caught a quick sight of the monster with the lantern they weren't supposed to light.

"Some people think Domingo killed those men for disobeying his orders about the lantern, after which he dumped them in the lake as a warning. But others claimed it was Esther that did it. No one knows for sure."

"Okay, we could go on like this for a while, I'm sure," Cody said. "But we've got limited time. Rufus is missing, and it appears Hap would like to pin it all on us."

Clarabell sniffed and crossed her thin arms. "Hap is not a believer."

"I never thought Rufus was a believer, either," Demetrius said. "Your association with him is kind of a surprise."

"It's not something he liked to spread around. Especially not to strangers."

Demetrius felt a tiny bit hurt by her use of the word

strangers. Rufus had invited them over to his house for dinner. He'd been friendly and outgoing, and Demetrius had talked with him about the unusual cases they'd stumbled across the past two years.

And yet, when he really thought about it, he guessed they really were strangers, no matter how friendly Rufus had acted. Demetrius just wished things could have been different, that they hadn't spent so much time in town last night. Or maybe they could have stayed the night at Rufus's place, or even in a room at the hotel.

Footsteps approached along the boardwalk. A heavy tread moving fast. Demetrius had a feeling he knew who it was, and he was right. Hap came around the bend and stopped dead in his tracks when he saw Clarabell standing on the steps, turned now to face him. His expression shifted to anger in a matter of seconds. He stood where he was, about a dozen feet away, and jabbed a finger at Clarabell.

"You! What are you doing here?"

"Rufus called me."

Hap reeled back as if Clarabell had physically struck him. Even from where he stood, Demetrius could see that Hap had sudden tears in his eyes.

"When?" His voice was thick with emotion, and he angrily swiped away tears.

"Two days ago. After Dave died." Clarabell lifted her chin. "He thought something had changed, and he called to ask me to come out and help."

Hap's laugh surprised Demetrius and, based on the look he got from Cody, he wasn't alone.

"Help? *Help?*" Hap laughed again, a short, bitter sound with absolutely zero humor. "And how in the hell were you going to help? Huh?" He approached and stood a few feet from her. "Fill his head with crazy ideas? Share your *science* —" Hap made air quotes with his fingers. "—with him? Tell him that just because all anyone had was stories and urban legends and no real proof, no hard facts, that it didn't mean some big monster was living in the lake. It never bothered swimmers, never came up to check out or eat any water skiers. Nope. It just hung out some place sonar never spotted it and countless scuba divers never came across it. Yep, that would have been great if you could have gotten him all riled up again and led him to believe that Dave had been killed by something that lived in the deep parts of this lake that he loved more than anything. That would have been just perfect."

Demetrius felt awkward and embarrassed to be standing there listening to Hap chew Clarabell out. But he was afraid to move for fear of pulling Hap's attention off her and onto him. Cowardly as it might be, he wanted to stay as far off Hap's radar as possible. Not only because he didn't want to end up on the receiving end of Hap's tirade, but also because the longer he and Cody could stay free, the closer they might get to figuring out what had happened to Rufus.

"You've lived here long enough to know that something about this lake isn't right," Clarabell said.

Hap nodded. "You're right. It's polluted as hell because of all the damn tourists."

"There's something else going on, and you know it."

"I know nothing of the kind. You stay out of my way as I work on finding Rufus, you lunatic. I don't want any of your bullshit clogging up this investigation, do I make myself clear?"

Clarabell gave a single nod. "Crystal. I will not interfere with your investigation."

"Then we'll get along just fine." Hap stomped past her and up to Demetrius and Cody. Demetrius's stomach was in knots as he watched Hap approach. His phone buzzed in his pocket, but he ignored it.

He exchanged a quick look with Cody and could see by his expression that he was just as nervous about Hap's next move. Were they going to be arrested for suspicion of murder? Taken in for questioning? Had more evidence been discovered on the beach?

Hap stood before them with his hands on his hips. A moment of silence passed during which Hap studied his boots, Clarabell stared at Hap's back, and Demetrius and Cody looked at his bowed head. When he finally looked up, he drew in a deep breath and offered a shaky smile.

"I have trouble seeing the two of you as killers."

A cool sense of relief washed through Demetrius, but Cody still looked nervous.

"I sense a 'but' coming along any minute," Cody said.

Demetrius's relief withered away inside him.

"Yeah, well, you'd be partly right. I have trouble seeing you two as killers, *but*, I need you to come into the station and give a statement."

"Just a statement?" Demetrius said.

"That's all."

"We don't need a lawyer?" Cody said.

"I can't give you that kind of advice." Hap shrugged, but smiled. "I'm going to be the one asking questions and taking your statement. But I have no intention of locking you guys up."

"Is that piece of boat on the beach part of The Lazy Aye?" Cody said.

The question appeared to surprise Hap. He pressed his lips into a tight thin line as he considered how to respond.

"It appears to be."

"I'm very sorry," Cody said, and stepped up to Hap with his hand extended.

Hap shook Cody's hand, but he didn't look happy about it.

"I'm not giving up hope, do you understand me?" His fierce gaze shifted from Cody to Demetrius and back again. "Until we find Rufus, I'm not writing him off. And if you two had nothing to do with it, then you might be able to give me some kind of clue that will point me in the right direction."

"We want to help out any way we can," Demetrius said. "If giving you a statement will help, then that's what we'll do."

Hap nodded before he sighed. "I wish I knew what more to do, but for now I'll have to rely on good old fashioned police work. The dive team will be checking the route between here and the town. But that's going to take a while. I'm not a diver, so I can't be in on that part of it, but I need to do something, you know? I just don't know what happened. It's like he and the boat just vanished."

"Tell us where you want to talk to us," Cody said. "Up at the cabin or back in town?"

Demetrius knew where he'd rather give his statement, but he had a feeling Hap was going to have them cross the lake and do it in the station.

"I'm not the best typist, so I'll probably make a recording of the statement and type it up later. We have digital recorders at the station, so it would be best if you came into town."

Cody nodded. "No problem. Just let us get ready and we'll meet you at the dock."

"Good. Thanks, guys. I really appreciate this. It helps to stay busy."

Hap walked onto the dock without a look back at Clarabell. Demetrius noticed him look into the boat she had brought out and which was now tied to the dock, but that was it for his acknowledgement of her.

"Let's go back to the cabin," Cody said.

Demetrius followed Cody to where Clarabell stood on the steps by her pack. Without pausing or saying a word, Cody snagged the top handle of the pack and lifted it. Clarabell watched him stride away from her along the boardwalk, then looked at Demetrius.

"I take it I'm following?"

"You and me both," Demetrius said.

They walked in silence after Cody. Clarabell's green Crocs scuffed along the boards as birds called in the trees. Off in the distance, Demetrius could hear the faint sound of officers shouting from the police boat to the beach and back again. When they reached the cabin, Cody was already inside, so Demetrius held the door for Clarabell. They found her pack on the floor by the couch, and Demetrius heard Cody rummaging around upstairs in the bedroom.

"There are cold drinks in the refrigerator, go ahead and help yourself. We'll be right down."

"You two a couple like Rufus and Hap?"

"Um, yeah. Yes. We're here on our honeymoon."

Clarabell smiled, and it softened her features. "That's wonderful. Congratulations."

"Thank you. He surprised me with a proposal while we were out in Colorado visiting his family over Christmas. It was a small wedding, but we had the people closest to us there." Demetrius wasn't really sure why he felt the need to explain his and Cody's relationship to Clarabell.

"Sounds nice," she said with a polite smile and a nod.

"Yeah, it was." A long silence dragged out between them until Demetrius finally said, "Well, I should get a few things from the bedroom. Like I said, help yourself to drinks and the bathroom."

"I'll definitely take you up on the offer of the bathroom."

She headed for the bathroom near the kitchen and Demetrius climbed the stairs to the master suite where Cody was pulling on a clean T-shirt.

"Did I hear you telling her about our wedding?"

"Yeah. I have no idea why I did that."

"You and your nervous chatter," Cody said. "Don't get us in trouble with Hap because of it."

"How could I get us in trouble with Hap?" He pulled off the T-shirt he was wearing and searched through a drawer for a clean one.

"Don't say too much. Just tell him what he doesn't know about last night."

"I know."

He found a shirt at the bottom of the drawer and pulled it over his head, then remembered he'd received a text and looked at his phone.

"Tracey responded to my text."

"Oh? What did she say?"

Demetrius shook his head. "She said we're idiots and she's not going to be our paranormal creature bitch any longer."

"She's such a delicate flower," Cody said. "Guess we're on our own with this."

"Guess so. You ready?"

Cody pulled him close for a quick kiss. He kept an arm around Demetrius's waist and pulled back to look at him. "I'm ready. We're going to be okay."

"Yeah. But what about Rufus?"

"I wish I knew. He's a good guy."

"Yeah, he is."

Cody kissed him again. "Let's go."

Cody moved away and Demetrius wished he would have held him a little bit longer. He wasn't sure why, but he really didn't want to cross the lake and go to Hempstead, and he really didn't want to have to talk with Hap. It wasn't like he was hiding anything, but Demetrius got nervous in these kinds of situations. And they'd been in a few of them the last couple of years. If they weren't trying to talk their way out of a mess with Lucia Durant back home, they had been sneaking around the police force in Pinesville, New Jersey as they'd tracked down the Devil.

And they couldn't even stay out of trouble on their honeymoon.

Life with Cody was definitely going to be interesting.

He followed Cody down the stairs. Clarabell was crouched in the living room and digging through her pack.

"We'll see you later," Demetrius said, and gave a quick wave as he followed Cody out the door.

"Good luck!" Clarabell called after them.

He had a feeling they were going to need all the luck they could get.

CHAPTER FOURTEEN

The clock on the wall above Cody's head ticked loudly toward four in the afternoon. He slouched in an uncomfortable chair, waiting for Demmy to finish giving his statement. It had been at least an hour since Hap had finished with Cody and called Demmy into the tiny interview room. Cody was tired and hungry, edging quickly toward hangry, when he'd become so hungry he got angry.

And he hoped to God Demmy wasn't throwing them under the bus in there.

Police officers came and went around him. He recognized a couple of them from having been out on the island that morning. From the looks he was receiving in return, they recognized him, too. It seemed everyone thought they had something to do with Rufus's disappearance. He really couldn't blame them for it. If he'd been in their position, he'd be looking at him with suspicion, too. In the past, he'd been guilty of jumping to conclusions.

Like suspecting Ollie of being a wolf man.

Or distrusting Farmer Reed when they'd been working with Agatha on what they'd thought was a chupacabra case.

Although, come to think of it, with the way things had turned out, he'd been right not to trust Farmer Reed. The guy had tried to kill them, after all.

He shifted position in the chair and stretched out his legs, immediately regretting it when he nearly tripped a female officer walking past.

"Sorry. I'm sorry." He hurriedly pulled his legs back as she delivered a cold glare before continuing her purposeful stride down the hall.

Cody looked after her. A year ago, he might have tried to strike up more of a conversation with her. She was, after all, very attractive. But the man he had been a year ago and the one he was now seemed like two completely different people. And it wasn't just because he was having sex with a man. That was part of it, of course, but the main reason for the change within him came down to one thing.

Demmy.

All their years of friendship had evolved into something so much deeper than Cody had ever thought he would experience. Laughter, conversation, running the business together, and even comfortable silences had completed parts of him he hadn't realized were lacking.

Not to mention how much of a wonderfully dirty and slutty animal Demmy was in bed.

His cock twitched at the thought of it, and he crossed his legs. Time to change the track of his thoughts, or he might be slapped with a public indecency charge. He put a hand on his ankle and tugged his leg a little further along his thigh. Florescent light gleamed off his wedding band, catching his attention. Amazing how quickly things could change. It hadn't even been a year since his and Demmy's friendship had shifted to a physical one. That drive back from Florida had been the longest and most life-changing drive of his life. He'd been terrified to say anything for fear of losing Demmy.

What if Demmy hadn't wanted to pursue a relationship? What if Demmy had only liked him as a friend, and nothing more? What if that fucking swamp monster had killed Cody right away instead of carrying him off?

A wasted life, trying to find something that had been right beside him the whole time.

There was no way Cody could have predicted how things would turn out between him and Demmy. Just like there was no way he could predict how any job would turn out. Even the small animal control jobs went south sometimes. Like his elaborate trap to catch the otter. Or that time he'd crouched in the bed of the truck waving a red towel as Demmy drove slowly down the road, leading the bull back to its pasture.

He chuckled at the memory. Lucia had been so pissed at them. Well, about as pissed as she usually got with them, but still, they'd just been doing their job.

Every day was its own bag of possibilities. And even though this week was their honeymoon, Cody couldn't fight fate. Try as he might to keep their first week of marital bliss monster-free, it was now time to do what had become so familiar to him and Demmy both. It was time to track down Esther and uncover what had happened to Rufus.

The worst part about this job, he supposed, would be learning the truth about what had happened to Rufus. Not knowing any specifics kept open the possibility of him being okay. But they'd worked enough of these cases for Cody to know that was most likely not the case. Which made him feel sad. Rufus had been kind and outgoing, and was apparently well-liked throughout the town.

Not to mention loved by Hap.

Cody hunched forward in the chair and let his hands hang between his knees. It had been a long day, and he had a bad feeling it was going to be an even longer night. As if to prove his point, thunder rumbled in the distance. Of course.

The door opened and Demmy stepped out into the lobby waiting area. He looked better than he had going in, so Cody figured things had gone well.

Hap trailed after him and Cody pushed to his feet as they approached.

"Thanks for coming in," Hap said. "I appreciate the help."

"We were happy to do it," Demmy said. "Whatever we can do to find Rufus. Please let us know."

Hap gave a nod. "I will. Sounds like another storm is rolling in, so be safe. Use the radio if anything shows up out there."

"We will." Cody turned for the door to the street, but Hap's next words stopped him.

"And let me know if that nutcase Clarabell Remington gives you guys a hard time. I'll make sure she leaves town and doesn't bother you again."

"Okay, sure. Yeah," Demmy said.

"Both police boats and half the DNR boats are out on the lake looking for The Lazy Aye. But Darlene has asked Gordon Rawlings to run you out to the island. Just go inside and let her know you're ready to head back. Gordon's boat is in the slip past Rufus's." Hap's eyes shone with sudden tears, and he quickly turned away and disappeared behind the door.

"You do okay in there?" Cody asked.

"It was fine," Demmy said in a low voice. "Let's get back to the island. I have some questions for Clarabell."

"Think she'll still be out there?"

Demmy led the way out of the police station and onto the sidewalk. He turned right and started toward the hotel, walking at a brisk pace. Cody's long legs allowed him to easily keep up.

"What kinds of questions do you have for Clarabell? May I suggest asking if Bozo the Clown is her personal dresser?"

Demmy snorted a laugh. "She is a sight."

"As Amelia would say, 'Oh, pine trees, are you colorblind?'"

That one earned an all-out laugh, and Cody smiled. There was no better feeling than his being able to make Demmy laugh.

They reached the hotel and Cody circled the truck to make sure there were no new dents or scratches while Demmy went inside to ask for a ride back to the island. Cody looked up at the heavy gray clouds that had moved in while they'd been inside the police station. Probably another storm rolling in for the night. He hoped this Rawlings guy had a fast boat, because he really didn't want to get caught out on the lake in a storm.

Especially with a killer monster under the surface.

Demmy pushed out of the door of the hotel with a young and handsome guy right behind him. Cody's jealousy meter ticked up a few notches, and he moved quickly to intercept them.

"Is this our captain?" Cody asked.

"Sure am," the man replied with a dazzling smile. He extended his hand and gave Cody a firm shake. "Gordon Rawlings."

"Cody Bower. Thanks for giving us a lift back to our cabin."

He couldn't help tossing the "us" and "our" into his statement.

"No problem at all. Shame about this mystery with Rufus. I hope they find him soon, and it all turns out to be no big deal."

Gordon looked up at the steel gray clouds. "Looks like we might be in for another blow soon. Let's get you guys back to the cabin right quick."

They let Gordon lead the way along the dock, and Cody

couldn't resist leaning in and whispering to Demmy, "Right quick? I bet that's how he has sex, too."

Demmy stifled a laugh and threw a gentle elbow into Cody's side. Gordon's boat was a smaller speed boat, and it practically flew over the water, delivering them in record time to the dock in Hideaway Cove. Gordon looked over the small fishing boat Clarabell had arrived in as they climbed out of the speedboat.

"This looks like one of Dave's boats," Gordon said. "Did you guys know Dave?"

"Yeah, we knew him by sight," Cody said.

"We were with Rufus when he was found out in the lake," Demmy added. "We helped bring him into the boat."

"Really? Wow. You've had quite a week here in Hempstead." Gordon looked at the smaller boat again, and his expression shifted to something sad and wistful. "I liked Dave. He really cared for this lake, I'll tell you that much. He was a really nice guy, and I think the town will miss him more than they realize."

"I'm sorry about your loss," Cody said, hating how inadequate it sounded.

"Yeah, thanks." Gordon looked up and smiled, though it wasn't quite as bright as before. "Anyway, you guys be careful out here with that storm rolling in. Get on that radio quick if you need help."

"We will," Demmy said. "Thanks again for the lift."

They watched Gordon reverse from the dock, then swing the boat around and aim it toward town. He waved once more and they waved back before he hit the throttle and sped across the water, leaving behind a strong wake.

"Nice guy," Cody said. "Too bad about his impotence."

Demmy gave him a side-eye. "And how would you have any knowledge of his ability to perform?"

Cody shrugged. "I don't know for certain, but look at the

size of his engine, and the way he hot rods that boat all over the lake. It's like he thinks he's drag racing or something. I mean, come on. Talk about overcompensating."

"You're impossible."

"But I can get it up in seconds."

Demmy put a hand over Cody's crotch and pressed gently against him. "Oh, I'm very much aware of that particular skill of yours."

"Yeah? Glad to hear all my efforts haven't gone unnoticed."

"Oh no, not at all." Demmy gave him another squeeze before he dropped his hand. "Let's go find Clarabell."

"You know, I could take that to mean you want to invite Clarabell to join us in bed…"

Demmy's wide eyes were the perfect reaction Cody had been going for.

"But I'm going to assume you just want to find her, let her ramble a bit while we slowly lead her back here to the dock, and then send her on her way so we can get back to being honeymooners."

"You assume correctly. Let's go."

Cody let Demmy lead the way along the boardwalk to the cabin. He kept his gaze on Demmy's butt the whole time, thinking about all the things he wanted to do to and on that fine ass. By the time they reached the cabin, he was half-hard and really hoped they found Clarabell sooner rather than later so he could get to full mast.

After a few steps into the cabin, they both stopped and stared. Cody's cock withered as his brain struggled to understand what he was looking at.

Clarabell had taken over the cabin's living room. Her unzipped pack leaned against the arm of the couch and Cody wondered if it had simply exploded when she'd opened it. Papers, folders stuffed with papers, small boxes that appeared to contain other, smaller boxes, a desk lamp with a flexible neck, and a microscope covered the small dining table. More papers and folders had been scattered across the furniture, leaving no space to sit. Clarabell stood bent over the microscope, tiny hand adjusting the focus as she peered into the eyepiece. Three empty beer bottles stood nearby, and that above the rest of the mess got Cody's brain connected and he found his voice.

"Well, hello. Did you leave any beer for us?"

Clarabell straightened up and looked at them. "There's six left." She crossed her arms tight. "I assume that's enough to get you buzzed."

"Barely," Cody said. He waved at the table. "You've made quite the mess."

"You told me to make myself at home." Clarabell sniffed and returned her attention to the microscope. "Did you know you have an unusual find on this island?"

"Besides her?" Cody muttered, and suffered another gentle elbow from Demmy before he crossed the room to stand near her.

"What is it?" Demmy asked. "What have you found?"

Clarabell set her gaze on him. In the harsh glow of the desk lamp, Cody could see the lines etched around her eyes. "Do you know much about birds?"

"They fly," Cody offered as he approached and sat on the arm of the couch.

"Very good. Many of them also regurgitate what's called a pellet from time to time. This pellet contains the undigestible pieces of their prey, such as bones, feathers, beaks, and so forth."

Cody made a face. "If you try to get us to eat one of these things, I'm going to carry you out of here and down to the dock myself."

"As delightful as that reaction sounds, it's not what I'm

intending. I walked the trail that runs the perimeter of this island. Have you done this as well?"

Demmy nodded. "We have. Several times."

"Did you come across any large, sticky, and somewhat smelly round globs?"

"We have!" Demmy looked to Cody, excitement evident in his eyes before he turned back to Clarabell. "We've seen at least two of them."

Clarabell gave a single nod. "I came across four, and two of them were quite fresh."

"What are they?" Cody asked, interested now despite his irritation with Clarabell.

"I'm calling them pellets, but it's not a very apt description. I'm sure there's a better way to explain it, but I'll tell you my theory."

Cody resisted a snarky comment. Maybe if they allowed Clarabell to spout her theory, she'd pack up her crap and leave them alone. Thunder rumbled in the distance, and Cody could practically hear suspenseful music playing in the background as Clarabell started talking and the storm that might keep her on the island with them approached over the lake.

"I've been coming to Heaversford Lake for many years now. Almost two decades."

Yet another snarky response was held in check.

"During this time, I've come across a number of unexplained items."

"Ever see Esther herself?" Demmy asked.

"Sadly, no. I did, however, discover what I suspect was the imprint of a flipper on the beach of this island one morning. Unfortunately, by the time I had managed to get into town and come back with some molding materials, it had washed away."

"You think Esther can come up on land?" Cody asked.

"If my findings hold true, she most definitely can come onto land for short amounts of time. Tell me, where did you come across the pellets?"

"We found both of them just off the side of the trail," Demmy replied. "On the side of the trail closer to the lake."

"Just a few yards from the shore?" Clarabell asked.

Demmy looked to Cody and he lifted a shoulder in a half-shrug as he nodded. Turning back to Clarabell, Demmy said, "That's right."

"Let me show you something."

Clarabell picked up her smartphone and swiped across the screen a few times before she held it out for them both to see. It was a picture of one of the balls of smelly slime he and Demmy had come across. She swiped the screen for them, going through a progression of images which showed her disentangling the items that had clumped together. Plastic grocery bags, plastic straws, fishing line, and even more plastic bags of various sizes had been peeled away. A few strands of seaweed were mixed in, but what Clarabell had called a pellet mostly consisted of plastic items.

"It's all trash." Demmy's voice was quiet and sad.

"That's right. A few pieces of seaweed in there, but the bulk of it is trash, and the majority of that trash is plastic." She pulled the phone away and tapped the screen as she mumbled to herself. "Where the hell did they go?" She caught herself and glanced up, a light blush coloring her wrinkled cheeks. "I scanned my old photos in with a new-fangled app and it created some kind of folder, but I don't know… Oh, here it is."

She held the phone out once again where they could see it. "These are photos I've taken in the past of the same type of pellet."

Cody made a face. "Are those parts of fish?"

"They are. Fins and bones, to be precise," Clarabell said.

"And notice what else the pellet consists of."

"Seaweed, it looks like," Demmy said.

"Correct. The pellets in years past were mostly made up of organic materials. Very little trash was recovered from these pellets, and more pointedly, no plastic items." She set her phone on the table and sighed. "In the past, it was almost a miracle to come across a pellet. I found maybe three of them in a fifteen year period."

A chill ran up Cody's back. "We found more than that this past week."

Clarabell fixed him with an intense look and gave a single nod. "That's my point."

As if they were in some cheap ass horror movie, lightning flashed, followed seconds later by a sharp crack of thunder that made all of them duck down.

"Looks like I'm stuck out here with you boys for a little longer," Clarabell said.

"Yeah, you can't go out on the lake in a metal boat with this storm," Demmy said, and Cody wished he was in a position to return the elbow he'd received earlier.

"Yeah, you don't do something like that twice in your life and live." Clarabell snorted a laugh as she shook her head. "Okay, so let me show you what else I found."

Cody didn't think he wanted to know, but had to admit—and hate himself for it—that he was interested. Not to mention worried about Rufus. The longer they went without any sign of The Lazy Aye, the worse Cody felt about Rufus's chances. He really liked Rufus, and Hap, too, and he hoped like hell things were going to turn out okay for them.

Unfortunately, his hope was quickly being overshadowed by an even stronger sense of doom.

Clarabell waved toward the microscope. "I've taken samples of the sticky substance each time I've come across a pellet out here. Look for yourself."

Demmy stepped up and leaned in over the microscope. "Not sure what I'm looking at."

"From what I can tell, it's a kind of bile," Clarabell said.

Cody had gotten up from the arm of the couch with the intention of looking in the microscope as well. When he heard the word "bile," however, he lifted a hand and shook his head as he returned to his seat.

"I'll pass, thanks."

"Suit yourself," Clarabell said, and looked to Demmy as he straightened up from the microscope. "What did you see?"

"Some yellow stuff, some clear stuff, and maybe some threads of red stuff running through it."

"Right. I think that red stuff is blood."

"Blood?" Cody and Demmy said at the same time.

"Yep. Won't know for sure until I get it sent out and tested. Never seen blood in the samples before. And the previous samples have all been a lot thicker."

"Girthier?" Cody offered, happy when he received a frown from Clarabell and a half-smile from Demmy.

"Anyway…"

Clarabell was cut off by another bright flash of lightning, which was followed almost immediately by a bang of thunder that shook the cabin and made them all jump. Seconds later, rain started falling in a heavy downpour. It was like someone had opened the spigot on the world's biggest faucet.

Cody got up and headed for the kitchen. "Who needs a beer?" He looked over his shoulder. "Clarabell? Care for a fourth?"

She shrugged. "Why not? I'm not going back tonight from the looks of the weather."

"Perfect," Cody said through a smile that he hoped didn't look too pained.

CHAPTER FIFTEEN

Demetrius could practically feel the frustration coming off Cody.

While Clarabell and Demetrius had examined more of the samples, Cody had boiled water for pasta and opened a jar of sauce.

"Thanks for making dinner," Demetrius said as he carried his and Clarabell's empty beer bottles into the kitchen.

"She's gonna need something to soak up that beer," Cody muttered.

Demetrius leaned in close and whispered, "Happy honeymoon, Mr. Bower-Singleton."

He received a quirk of a smile in response and decided that was about the best he could hope for, considering the situation. With fresh beers in hand, he returned to where Clarabell was making notes.

"How did you and Rufus meet?"

Clarabell stopped writing and lifted her head. She smiled as she looked out the window at the heavy rain. "We met at a conference. This was many years ago, before all these online groups and chat rooms and bots and whatever they have now."

"Fire, running water, indoor plumbing," Demetrius heard Cody mumble from where he stood in the kitchen. It appeared Clarabell hadn't heard him, or had chosen to ignore his remarks as she continued to speak.

"We belonged to a group interested in the investigation and gathering of evidence for creatures of a more, shall we say, unusual lineage."

"Monsters?" Demetrius suggested.

Clarabell shrugged. "Some might call them that. We thought they were just solitary beasts that were most likely lonely and afraid of the changes going on around them. Rufus had lived in Hempstead all of his life, so he had grown up hearing the stories about Esther. He loved having an urban legend living in the lake. He wanted nothing more than to see her for himself, just once. I had recently returned from a hike through mountain trails in Colorado looking for a sasquatch, with no luck, I might add, and we met at this conference in the Adirondacks and hit it off."

Demetrius decided not to bring up their encounter with a sasquatch over Christmas, and instead said, "Sounds like you and Rufus have known each other a long time."

"Seventeen years," she said, and her expression turned sad. "I hope he's okay, I really do. But I fear something terrible has happened to him."

"Things are looking grim," Demetrius said. "He was a very nice man. He invited Cody and I to dinner at his house with him and Hap."

Clarabell's expression brightened. "He finally got Hap to move in with him?"

"Not officially, no. But it seemed pretty obvious that Hap spends most of his nights there."

She gave a satisfied nod. "Good. They both deserve the

chance to be happy." She turned in her chair to look at Cody, then returned her gaze to Demetrius as she lowered her voice. "What's the story with the two of you? How long have you been together?"

A blush warmed Demetrius's cheeks though he wasn't sure why, and he cast his gaze into the kitchen. Cody stood at the stove—tall and masculine and more fucking handsome than anyone had a right to be—and as Demetrius watched, Cody tasted the sauce then pulled back with a hiss as he burned his tongue.

"As friends, since we met in kindergarten. We've been best friends since then and opened a business together a couple of years ago. A year after that, things shifted in our relationship, and now we're here on our honeymoon."

"That's wonderful. I love hearing stories like that. The friendship is the most important part of any relationship." She gave Cody an assessing look that made Demetrius feel a little uncomfortable. "Though he does look like all his parts are in fine working order. And in all the right places." She smiled at Demetrius and winked. "You both do."

"Ah. Yes. Well. Thanks, for that. We're happy. What about you? Anyone special in your life?"

Clarabell made a quiet sound of dismissal, "Pfffft," and waved a hand. "Comes and goes, you know? Like the stock market, or fashion."

Demetrius couldn't help glancing at her bright green Crocs. Fashion?

She had continued to talk, either not catching his glance or choosing to ignore it.

"There've been a few lovers over the years. A couple of them have lingered longer than others, including a sassy and sexy Filipina who tolerated me for almost ten years."

"Oh, really?"

Clarabell squinted at him. "Don't get your spice rack in

disarray, Demetrius. Us older folks have been bisexual for longer than you've been alive." ·

"I didn't mean to suggest—"

"Yeah, yeah. No harm no foul. But let me say this: I may be small and wrinkled, but I've been a swimmer all my life and I can hold my breath a long time."

Cody brought a big bowl of pasta and sauce mixed together to the table. "Just in time to overhear something I can only assume was a sexual reference. Perfect time to eat."

Clarabell let out a high-pitched cackle and headed into the bathroom.

"Holy hell, she's a character," Demetrius said in a low voice.

"Get used to her, because it looks like she's going to be spending the night with us," Cody muttered, then picked up Clarabell's newly emptied beer bottle. "And she's drunk half of our beer."

"She's tiny, but she can really put away the beer."

Clarabell stepped out of the bathroom and patted her stomach. "Let's eat, boys!"

Dinner was lively. Clarabell told stories about the many countries she had visited, and Demetrius talked about some of their more unusual animal control jobs. Cody even opened up about the chupacabra and Devil of Pinesville. Despite the number of beers she'd had, or maybe because of them, Clarabell's eyes were wide and her attention fixed on them as they talked.

"I'm assuming you don't have evidence for any of this stuff," she said. "Otherwise my chat groups would have been blowing up with it, I'm sure."

"It all kind of happens really fast," Cody said. "Some of the wolf man stuff is on security footage from the senior home, but I don't even know if that survived all of it."

"Video? Of a wolf man?" Clarabell's voice went up on the

last word. "You've gotta check on that and get it released. People need to know!"

"We took care of it," Demetrius said.

"How?" She waved her hands excitedly. "Don't tell me!" She leaned in over the table and dropped her voice. "Silver bullets?"

"That did the trick," Cody said. "Cost us a pretty penny, and my great-grandmother's silverware, but we got him."

"Did you know him?"

Demetrius nodded. "In a manner of speaking. He was a resident of the senior living facility."

"Really grumpy fucker, too," Cody said. He caught Demetrius's look and said, "What? He was, you have to admit that."

"Yeah, you're right. He was a grumpy fucker."

They all laughed, but then Demetrius turned serious. "He killed quite a few people when he turned. Made me wish we'd figured it out more quickly."

"You can't blame yourselves for that," Clarabell said. "You stopped him from killing even more people."

"We got turned around in the investigation," Cody added. "There was more than one suspect, and..." He glanced at Demetrius. "It got complicated."

"No. Complicated? When dealing with a wolf man?" Clarabell chuckled.

"I think that's why I feel drawn to these kinds of cases," Demetrius said, feeling as if a low wattage light had suddenly been flipped on in the back of his mind. "I think it comes from that first case we got mixed up in. So many people died, and if we'd been more open to what was happening, we could have prevented some of those deaths."

He felt a sudden strengthening to the bond between them when he saw the love and understanding in Cody's gaze. Why hadn't he been able to explain all of this to Cody over the last year? Maybe it had taken this case and talking about their history with Clarabell for him to really understand the driving force behind his interest in their unusual cases.

"But you did what you could," Clarabell said, pulling Demetrius's attention from Cody.

From his husband.

A flush of heat went through him as all of it seemed to hit him at once.

The wolf man case sparking his drive to dig into these kinds of cases.

The fact that he was married, and not just to a man he loved, but to his best friend.

What a time for a revelation.

But he was glad that with Clarabell's help, they were on the path to understanding more about Esther than anyone before. He just hoped it wasn't too late to help Rufus.

After dinner, they piled the dishes in the sink and Demetrius and Cody sat on the couch with a couple feet of space between them, both nursing their third beer. Clarabell lay sprawled across the love seat across from them, her feet hanging over one arm, head propped up with a pillow against the other. Her bright green Crocs had slipped off an hour ago, and now she clutched her bottle of beer in one hand and waved it around as she talked.

"I'm telling you, this is all leading up to something big. I can feel it."

"Sure it's not just the beer?" Cody asked, and grinned at Demetrius.

Clarabell extended the index finger of her hand holding the beer and pointed at him. "You're a real sassy cat, aren't you?"

"Oh, he's sassy all right," Demetrius said.

"That's right. I don't just wear sassy pants, I've got a whole fucking sassy wardrobe!"

They busted out laughing, and Demetrius reached across the couch cushion to grab Cody's hand.

A garbled rumble floated in on the rain-drenched breeze through the partially open window.

"That was some weird thunder," Demetrius said.

Clarabell pushed up to a sitting position, head turned to look out the picture window that overlooked the covered porch. It had gotten dark an hour ago, and all they could see was the light streaming out from inside reflected by the steady rain.

"That wasn't thunder."

Fear wriggled into Demetrius's gut, and he couldn't help lowering his voice when he asked, "What was it?"

Clarabell's eyes were so wide when she turned back, he could see the whites all the way around her irises.

"I think it was her."

"Esther?" Demetrius said, barely able to breathe.

"Abso-fucking-lutely." Clarabell stood and stuffed her sock-covered feet into her Crocs. She strode across the room and was out the front door before Demetrius could get off the couch.

"Where the fuck is she going?" Cody stomped to the door and pushed outside.

Demetrius stood rooted in place for a moment. His breath came in shallow pants, and a tingling sensation spread from the top of his head, down the back of his neck, and along his arms to pool in his fingertips. They'd dealt with creatures that defined explanation before, many times, but Esther was something entirely different. She was ancient and even more mysterious because she lived underwater.

And if the legends had any truth to them at all, she was massive.

Clarabell yanked open the door and rushed inside. Her sudden appearance startled Demetrius out of his immobility, and he stepped around the arm of the couch to stand in her way. Rain had flattened her hair and spattered her glasses. Her plastic shoes squeaked and squelched with every movement. A feverish blush tinted her cheeks, bringing out the sharp angles of her face.

"What are you doing?" Demetrius asked.

Cody stepped in the door and shook the rain from his hair, making Demetrius think of a dog he had had growing up. After Cody wiped rain from his eyes, he looked over Clarabell's head at Demetrius and asked, "What's she doing?"

"I'm getting a flashlight," Clarabell snapped.

She moved around Demetrius, squeaking and squelching with every step. When she bent over to rummage around in her pack, Demetrius crossed the room to talk with Cody in low tones.

"Did you hear anything out there?" Demetrius asked.

"Maybe." Cody lifted his chin in Clarabell's direction. "She thought she heard that weird choking sound. But it's tough to hear things clearly over the rain."

"Think she's just drunk?"

"Well, she is drunk. But we all heard the first sound, and it wasn't any kind of thunder I've ever heard before."

"Fuck."

"I really wish we could." Cody sighed. "I'd much rather be fucking than—"

Clarabell walked between them, shoes noisy as before, only this time she wore a lamp fastened to a plastic band that sat around her forehead. The top of her head came up to the middle of Demetrius's chest and Cody's belly, and they both looked down to watch her walk past.

"Where the devil are you going?" Cody asked.

She stopped and turned with her hand on the door. "Hunting."

Clarabell switched on the headlamp and a bright beam of

light made Demetrius and Cody both squint and hold up their hands to block the glare. The door opened and shut and she was gone.

"Fuck me running," Demetrius said.

"Uphill," Cody added, then said, "I'll get the lanterns."

He moved to the kitchen, leaving wet tracks behind him. Demetrius looked out through the screen in the door and watched Clarabell's headlamp bob along the boardwalk until it vanished from sight around the bend. He cursed, then jumped when Cody came up behind him.

"I could only find one of the lanterns. But I did find this light with a loop for your wrist. Must have rolled out of her pack when she was digging out her miner hat."

Demetrius took the plastic, palm-sized flashlight and switched it on. The beam was bright and he figured she had replaced the batteries for her trip. He slipped the loop over his hand and onto his wrist, then turned for the door. Cody put a hand on his shoulder and turned him back.

"We're not doing anything foolish."

"Yeah, I know," Demetrius said, and turned for the door again, only to have Cody turn him back around.

"I mean it, Demmy. We keep our wits and live to see tomorrow morning."

"I get it, okay? Come on, Clarabell's already down at the dock by now."

"Better her than us," Cody said, but followed Demetrius out the door.

Just as they reached the steps leading from the porch down to the boardwalk, they heard the strange sound again, like a combination choking and gargling. Demetrius reached back to grab Cody's hand as his heart pounded and a chill went up his spine.

"Where did that come from?" Demetrius asked.

"Fuck if I know," Cody whispered. "Sounded like the depths of Hell."

"We found those other pellets by the bluff. Clarabell's taking the path to the dock, so if we take the short cut past the utility pole we should get there about the same time."

Cody groaned, then nodded. "Fine. Let's go."

Demetrius was drenched in less than a minute. The rain chilled him and his shoes grew heavy with mud, but he focused on following in Cody's wake along the narrow footpath. They passed the utility pole where the transformer hummed high overhead, and not long after that they had reached the wider trail. It was just as muddy as the footpath, but wider, so the going was a bit easier.

"There she is," Cody said, and pointed to the bobbing light of Clarabell's headlamp coming toward them.

"Okay, good. That's good."

Something moved in the trees to their left.

Something big.

It snapped smaller trees and shook the larger ones. Demetrius and Cody both were drenched by the water coming off the shaking leaves. Clarabell shouted something but it was drowned out by the sound of Demetrius's blood rushing in his ears.

He directed his flashlight into the woods and it revealed what looked like a wall of scales. When the wall shifted, it startled a gasp out of him, and he took several steps back. His foot landed in something thick and sticky, and he cried out as he instantly became stuck.

"Jesus Christ, it's her. It's really her." Cody's voice was low and trembled a bit as he backed up to stand next to Demetrius.

"Don't move," Demetrius said.

"What?" Cody swung the lantern around and held it up, throwing out a wide apron of light. "Are you hurt?"

"No. But my foot's caught in what I think is one of her pellets." He made a face and tried to pull his foot free, but it was stuck good.

Cody crouched and set the lantern on the trail near the pellet. "Holy shit, that's some gross stuff. And your foot's buried deep inside it." He looked up, suddenly concerned. "Does it burn? Is it acid?"

"No, it doesn't burn." Demetrius tried to pull his foot free again, but it was no use. And now it did feel like it was burning, at least a little. Damn Cody's imagination.

"Holy fucking shit, but she's beautiful!"

Clarabell stood beside Demetrius, hands moving all around as she stepped up and down in place. "Did you get a good look? Did you? I only saw part of her as she turned back toward the lake. Do you think she's gone back in the water?"

"God that stuff stinks." Cody was bent over, hands tight around Demetrius's calf as he tried to pull his foot free.

"You're stuck?" Clarabell bent over, hands on her knees, headlamp illuminating the thick gelatinous mass of plastic trash and seaweed. "Look at the size of this one." She looked up at Demetrius, the lamp blinding him. "How's it feel?"

"Like my foot's caught in a disgusting sponge." Demetrius held up a hand to block the glare of her light. "Can you aim that somewhere else?"

A crackling-crashing sound from very close by in the woods between the path and the beach shut them all up. Demetrius gasped and Cody straightened up, standing in front of him protectively with his arms to the sides. Demetrius held onto Cody's arm for balance, as well as wanting to remain grounded to someone strong and tangible. Someone solidly in this world. Clarabell ducked under Cody's arm and moved closer to the trees.

"Clarabell, come back," Demetrius hissed.

"I just want to get a look… Oh." Clarabell took a couple of steps back.

The light from Clarabell's headlamp illuminated a large eye, golden-green in color and surrounded by dark green scales. It blinked and then faded back into the darkness. Demetrius got the sense of a large body moving through the trees, just out of the reach of Clarabell's lamp. A heavy choking cough trailed after the monster, and right after they heard a loud splash.

"She's in the water! I can't lose sight of her!" Clarabell ran off down the trail, heading toward the dock.

"No!" Demetrius shouted. "Goddammit! Clarabell, wait!"

A surge of adrenaline flooded his system, and he hauled his foot out of the gummy ball holding him in place. His foot felt three sizes larger and like it had been replaced by a bowling ball. He tried to wipe it off on wet leaves and ferns as Cody held onto him.

"Okay, that's good enough," Demetrius said when he'd managed to clear off some of the gunk. "Let's go."

"What? Where?"

"The dock! We can't let her go out in her boat. She'll drown."

"Better her than us."

"Cody!"

"Demmy!"

Demetrius waved a hand in the direction of the docks. "We need to help her."

"We need to get someone out here to help us."

"She's going to try to get that rusted old boat out into the lake."

"She's lived this long making all her own decisions," Cody said. "We should radio Hap and get him and everyone in that police station out here. With guns."

"That won't help Clarabell."

Cody crossed his arms. "Refer to my previous statement about her living this long making her own decisions."

Demetrius glared, then turned to stomp away. Bits of the slimy gunk fell off his foot with each step, and soon he was able to jog without much trouble. The path was completely muddy and the rain seemed to be falling even harder now. Maybe he'd luck out and the rain will have filled Clarabell's boat and prevented her from going out.

He reached the boardwalk and glanced over his shoulder, disappointed to find Cody not behind him. Well, he'd made his point very clear. Deep down, Demetrius knew Cody was right about them needing to get Hap and other officers out on the island, but he also felt personally responsible for Clarabell's safety. They had allowed her to drink a lot of beer, after all. And fed her dinner. And, when he was really honest with himself, he had taken a liking to the odd little woman.

Demetrius came out of the trees and saw Clarabell's headlamp wobbling back and forth beside the dock. Dammit, she was in her boat already. He broke into a run, blinded by rain as the damp air pushed into his lungs. Could he drown from breathing too heavily in the humidity?

"Clarabell!" he shouted. "Wait!"

The lamp aimed steadily at him, and he felt a surge of hope that he wasn't too late.

He reached the dock and slowed his pace, treading carefully on the slick boards. When he reached the spot Clarabell had tied up her boat, he saw it had taken on a lot of rain and rode low in the water.

"You can't go out in that boat," Demetrius said, raising his voice to be head over the falling rain. "You'll sink!"

"I'll be fine! Go back to the cabin."

She sat down and picked up the oars. Apparently she hadn't been able to get the engine started and intended to row. Demetrius cursed and dropped to his hands and knees on the dock.

"Clarabell, it's not worth it!"

"It's the only chance I've got to see her! I need to try!"

Demetrius cursed and rose up so he was on his knees and looked toward shore. There was no sign of Cody, and when he looked back down, Clarabell had already moved a short distance from the dock. He knew he was going to hate himself for it, but he jumped from the dock and landed in the boat. It shuddered beneath him and tipped from side to side. He managed to keep his balance and plopped down onto the seat facing Clarabell.

She grinned at him as she pulled on the oars. "Welcome aboard, sailor!"

"This is crazy. You know that, right?"

"Life is crazy, Demetrius. It's full of danger and risks and trouble and impossibilities. You need to seize it while you can."

"This is not seizing life. This is trying to put an end to your life."

"Shut up and row for me."

She thrust the oars at him and then moved up a seat. Demetrius clambered up to the bench where she had been sitting and started to row. He was amazed at how far she had gotten them already. Damn, for a short thing, she was strong!

He faced the dock now, and as he rowed, he saw Cody step into view. He held up the lantern, looking like a character from a spooky comic book investigating an old graveyard.

"What the fuck are you doing?" Cody shouted.

"Chasing the white whale!" Clarabell shouted back.

"Demmy, come back! I've called Hap and he's on his way!"

"We should go back, Clarabell," Demetrius said over his shoulder.

"Soon. Just keep rowing."

Demetrius looked over his shoulder to where she leaned over the side of the boat. "What are you doing?"

"Just trying to get her attention, that's all."

He stopped rowing and leaned over the side. "Tell me you're not chumming the water."

"What? No! I'm not adding fish heads and guts to the water. She's more sophisticated than that. I've created a device to transmit sound to draw her in."

"Sound? What kind of sounds?"

"A combination of whale and dolphin calls. Kind of my own little recipe of underwater communication."

Something bumped against the bottom of the boat. It was a soft thump, but was quickly followed by a harder jolt.

"I think you got her attention," Demetrius said as he held onto the sides of the boat. He looked at Cody standing on the dock fifty or so yards away and suddenly wished he'd listened to him and not come down to the dock with Clarabell.

"I see her," Clarabell said, followed quickly by, "Oh no."

Demetrius felt the boat flip as something came up beneath them. He tried to hang on, but the metal was too slippery and he lost his grip. The water that covered the bottom of the boat washed over him as it overturned, and he managed to draw in a deep breath before he plunged into the cold, dark lake.

He struggled out from beneath the overturned boat and kicked for the surface. When he came up, he took a deep gulp of air, then looked around. His flashlight still dangled from his wrist, the beam barely piercing the gloomy lake water. He located Clarabell by the lamp still sitting on her head. She swam toward the overturned boat, and he started for it as well.

"Are you okay?" Demetrius asked once they'd both reached the boat.

"Yeah, I'm good. I'm good." She clung to the side of the boat and looked at him as the headlamp sputtered and died. Apparently, it hadn't been built to be submerged. She'd lost her glasses when they'd flipped and now wiped rain and lake water from her eyes. "I did not expect that reaction."

"This is why you should never tease animals," Demetrius said.

"What makes you think I was teasing her?"

"Do you know what you were saying to her?"

Clarabell spit out a mouthful of water. "No."

"Then it's safe to assume you pissed her off."

"Demmy!"

Demetrius looked toward the dock. Cody stood at the very end, lantern held high to shine the light as far out onto the water as possible.

"Here!" Demetrius called back and stretched his arm high overhead to wave. "We're here!"

Cody moved the lantern and leaned out over the water. "You okay?"

"I'm wet, but okay."

"Can you make it back in?"

Demetrius looked over his shoulder to where Clarabell hung onto the side of the overturned boat. She looked worn out. There was no way she was going to be able to swim in with him. It had been years since he'd taken that water life-saving class at the YMCA, but it was raining too hard and the waves were coming in too fast for him to attempt it.

"I don't think we can," he called back. "The boat's upside down and we're holding onto it."

"Hang on, Hap's on his way."

Demetrius looked at Clarabell. Her lower lip was quivering as she tried to keep her teeth from chattering. She held onto the edge of the boat with her fingertips and lifted her chin up with each swell of the lake to avoid dunking her head under.

"Cody called Hap on the radio and he's heading out," Demetrius said. "We just need to hang on a little longer."

She nodded then gasped as a larger wave washed over them both. Lightning sketched an arc across the sky, and in the stutter of illumination, Demetrius saw a large head rise out of the water several yards behind Clarabell. It was supported by a strong, slender neck that lifted high into the air. Icy fear squeezed Demetrius's throat tight so that he couldn't speak.

Esther was beautiful and terrifying.

"What is it?" Clarabell asked. "What's wrong?"

She looked over her shoulder, but without the lightning, wasn't able to see any sign of Esther. Looking back at Demetrius, she inched closer along the boat. "Did you see her?"

Demetrius had time to nod before Esther came up beneath them. He felt the strong push of her approach first, like a swell of water coming up from below. It spun the boat around and out of his grasp, separating him from Clarabell. The push from beneath him intensified and lifted him up and out of the water. He tried to swim to the side and escape, the flashlight still on his wrist throwing the beam around in crazy circles.

"Demmy?" Cody shouted. "What's wrong?"

High into the air he went. He was able to look down and see in another staccato lightning flash the boat and Clarabell holding onto it. Her head was tipped back as she looked up at him, her mouth a big round "O" of surprise. Demetrius felt a shiver of fear at the height, then a cold, tight feeling closed on him as Esther's jaw closed around him.

Claustrophobia pushed a terrified scream from his lips as he felt the weight of Esther's tongue press him up against her rough palate. His arms were pinned at his sides and his head canted at an awkward angle that made him fear his neck would snap. He could barely breathe in such a compressed position, and he couldn't draw enough breath to scream again.

The flashlight on his wrist was pointed down into Esther's gullet. Demetrius saw plastic bags clotted around small pieces of wood and something larger that had wedged down deep in her throat. As he jostled about inside her mouth from her movements, the bags beneath him floated side to side in still and stagnant water, and he realized that what he'd at first thought were pieces of wood were in actuality fingers.

In the few quick seconds he had, Demetrius saw the hand stretching up toward him, fingers spread out and stiff. Another hard shift as Esther hit the surface of the water, or maybe the boat, he couldn't be sure, and the beam of his light picked out a gray-skinned face submerged in the water beneath the outstretched hand. The eyes were wide and right as water rushed in around him and Demetrius opened his mouth for a final breath, he realized that Rufus's body was wedged inside Esther's throat beneath him and he screamed.

CHAPTER SIXTEEN

"DEMMY!"

Cody's heart slammed as a flash of lightning revealed the monster coming up beneath Demmy and lifting him high into the air. Demmy seemed to hover there, like one of those weird old movies with the actress poised on a tall platform over a pool. Cody was able to see the mouth start to close around Demmy before the lightning faded and left him dazed and seeing spots. All he heard was the hard splash of it hitting the water and a ragged screaming that he realized moments later was coming from him.

"No! Demmy! No, God no!"

Cody dropped the lantern on the dock and dove into the lake. The cold shock of the water hit him like a slap and he gasped when he came up for air. But then his muscles took over and he swam toward the spot he'd last seen the overturned boat.

"Help!"

The voice was weak and choked, and he swam toward it, hoping for a miracle. His hand struck something and he stopped, finding the rusty hull of Clarabell's overturned boat.

Wet, heavy coughing from his right got him moving again, and he sent up prayers to whatever entity might be listening.

Not Demmy.

Not now, just when they'd gotten a chance together.

Never Demmy. Please, never Demmy.

A figure struggled in the water, and when he arrived, was disappointed to realize it was Clarabell.

She cried out at the sight of him. "Oh, thank God!"

Clarabell grabbed onto him, sending them both underwater. Cody managed to break her grip and pushed her away before he broke the surface again.

"Don't grab me, you'll drown us both," he said.

"I can't stay up much longer," she said. "Tired."

"Where's Demmy?"

"Help. Can't keep. Up."

Clarabell went under and popped back up again, coughing out water. Cody cursed and swam around behind her. He put an arm around her shoulders and pulled her along as he swam toward the boat. He dragged her through the water until they both got a hold of the side of hull. Cody looked out over the dark water, desperate to see or hear something.

He cupped a hand to the side of his mouth and shouted, "Demmy!"

"She took him down," Clarabell said. "I saw it. She came up beneath him and took him. He's gone."

"No! Shut up!"

Cody pushed off from the boat and dove beneath the waves. He couldn't see a thing in the murky water, but he swam down as far as his lungs allowed before kicking back to the surface. A plastic bag snarled around his fingers and he shook it off before diving again. And again. And yet again. He knew he was desperate and panicking, but he had no idea what to do. Demmy couldn't be gone, he just couldn't. He couldn't imagine his life without Demmy right there.

A sound from farther out in the lake stopped him from diving again.

"Demmy!"

A light swept past, blindingly bright, then snapped back to focus on him.

"Stay there. We'll pick you up."

The voice was amplified by a bullhorn, and now Cody could hear the heavy thrum of a powerful boat engine. The Hempstead police had arrived.

"Get her first!" Cody pushed himself as far up from the water as he could manage and pointed toward Clarabell. "Get her!"

The light swung away from him and onto Clarabell where she lay pressed against the hull of the boat. Cody watched the police boat swing in that direction then resumed diving, searching for Demmy, blindly reaching out ahead of him in the dark water for the possibility of a touch.

Nothing.

When he was worn out and barely able to keep his head above the swells, Hap and another officer hauled him out of the water and onto the deck of the boat.

"Where's Demetrius?" Hap asked.

"Gone," Clarabell said where she sat in a corner of the stern with blankets wrapped around her.

"What?" Hap looked between them as Cody lay on his side coughing up water.

"No," Cody managed between heaves. "He can't be."

"Something in the water starboard," an officer called.

"Get the light over there," Hap shouted, and moved out of sight.

Cody pushed to a sitting position and let his head hang with his chin to his chest as he tried to get his breath. His lungs ached and his arms and legs shook with exhaustion. He didn't think he could stand.

"What the fuck is that?" a female officer said.

The tone of her voice got Cody to his hands and knees, and he crawled to the side of the boat where he hauled himself upright to peer over the gunwale. The long, slick hump of Esther's back rose and fell through the waves, heading toward the western side of the island.

"She's got him," Cody said. "Demmy. She's got Demmy."

"Follow her," Hap commanded.

The boat swung around and everyone moved to the bow. Cody had some of his breath back and pushed to his feet to follow, Clarabell right behind him. With the searchlight trained on Esther's back, the officer piloting the boat stayed a short distance behind.

"I don't believe it," Hap said, and looked at Cody. "Can you?"

"You'd be surprised what I believe these days," Cody said. "I don't care about her. I want Demmy back."

"She's up out of the water!"

Cody pushed through the few officers crowding the bow until he got to the front. He leaned on the gunwale and watched as the monster lifted her head. Water drained from her mouth as she coughed and choked. A quick flash of light from the back of Esther's throat sent a surge of hope through Cody, and he pointed.

"There! I see Demmy's flashlight."

"What? Where?" Hap pushed aside officers and stood beside Cody. "Where?"

"At the—"

A heavy gasping wheeze cut Cody off. Esther slowly turned over in the water, and the muscles in her neck appeared to give out as it bowed beneath the weight of her large head. She collapsed in the rocky shallows of the island, one large front flipper sticking up from the surface of the water. It waved slowly a few times, then folded down over her side and she lay still.

"Is she dead?" someone asked in a low voice.

"Looks that way," Hap said. "Approach slowly."

"No, we gotta get in there," Cody said. "We gotta get Demmy out of her mouth. He's still in there, I saw it, I know I did."

"I'm not going up to that thing and stick my hands in its mouth until I know for sure it's dead," Hap said.

"I could fire a shot into her backside," the female officer said. "See if she reacts."

Hap gave a single nod, and she pulled out her gun and took aim. Cody jumped at the sound of the shot, and saw the bright red splash of blood high up on Esther's side. There was no sign of reaction.

Hap glanced at Cody before he said, "All right, let's put the raft in the water."

"I'm going, too," Cody said.

"This is police work," Hap said. "We're trained for these situations. You both—" He pointed between Cody and Clarabell. "—Will remain onboard. No argument."

"You're trained to pull people out of the mouths of lake monsters?" Cody said.

"You'd be surprised," the female officer said as she brushed past him.

Cody paced the deck as two officers plus Hap launched a rubber raft. They fired up a small motor and maneuvered around rocks until they eased up close alongside Esther. Hap reached out to skim his hand along her scale-covered body as they went. Cody estimated that Esther was about fifty feet long, maybe ten of which was her neck. He clenched and released his hands as he waited for them to reach her mouth, which was partially submerged in the shallow water.

"Come on," he whispered. "Come on."

He nearly screamed in frustration as the group worked to pry open Esther's mouth. It was taking too long! Demmy needed to be pulled out right that damn minute. What were they screwing around for?

Between the three of them, the group in the raft finally managed to push down her lower jaw and prop her mouth open with a nightstick. Hap shone a flashlight into the dark mouth, then slowly slid inside, appearing to be careful around the teeth. The female officer joined him, and moments later they pulled a body out and into the raft. The body was limp, unmoving.

A flashlight dangled from the left wrist, beam still shining.

Cody's heart seemed to jump into his throat.

"No." He moved to the point of the bow and clutched the metal edge. "No!"

The raft headed back toward the police boat at top speed. Hap was bent over the body, and Cody ran to the stern to await them.

"Demmy," he said as the raft pulled up alongside the boat. "No, Demmy. Don't do this. Demmy!"

"He's not breathing," Hap said to the officers on the boat. "I need someone to continue CPR."

Hap and the two officers in the raft helped lift Demmy's limp body up onto the boat. The officers taking him up carefully stretched him out on the deck and one of them knelt to resume CPR.

"Get him back to town," Hap said. "We're staying with this thing."

He said something else, but Cody wasn't listening. He knelt opposite the officer giving CPR and held Demmy's hand. It was so cold, and he rubbed it between his palms.

Clarabell gripped his shoulder as she moved past him, blankets still draped around her. He was barely aware of her talking with Hap and then climbing down into the raft before the police boat turned toward town.

The boat plowed through heavy swells, but that didn't bother him.

The steady rain washed away his tears, but he didn't care.

What he cared most about lay very still and pale on the deck of the boat before him.

Rubbing Demmy's hand, Cody muttered over and over, "Stay with me. Don't go."

CHAPTER SEVENTEEN

Halfway across the lake, Demmy finally took a breath.

He pushed the officer aside and turned his head away from Cody to cough up water. Cody and the officer rolled him onto his side to help him clear his lungs, and Cody placed his palm flat against the middle of Demmy's back just to feel him shake as he coughed.

When they rolled him onto his back again, Demmy squinted up at Cody through the rain. His mouth quirked up into a smile, and then his head rolled to the side and he was out again.

"Demmy!" Cody shook his shoulders, but there was no response. He looked up at the officer. "Is he breathing?"

The officer picked up Demmy's wrist to check his pulse, then pressed his ear against his chest. He lifted his head and nodded. "He's breathing on his own. Pulse is weak, but steady. We'll get him to the hospital once we get to shore."

Lightning forked across the sky and spray from another big wave drenched them all. Cody sat on the deck with his back against the gunwale and pulled Demmy up between his legs and onto him. He kept one arm tight around him, hand pressed against his chest over his heart so he could feel the beat of it. With the other hand, he held onto a rope to keep them both in place.

He wasn't going to lose sight of Demmy again.

THE SOFT PING of the hospital intercom plucked at Cody's nerves. Doctor names were called and medical staff walked past where he sat, their shoes squeaking on the clean tile floor. The sound brought up a memory of Demmy complaining that professional basketball games sounded like furious mice at war with each other because of the shoes squeaking on the courts, and Cody smiled, then choked back a sob.

He couldn't lose Demmy. He just couldn't.

He pushed to his feet and paced. From the nurse's desk in the middle of the floor to the window at the end of the hallway he stomped back and forth. The storm had finally calmed but the night was overcast, clouds blocking any sign of the moon and stars.

Once they'd arrived at the hospital and Demmy had been taken off on a stretcher, Cody had given his statement to the officer who had ridden with them in the ambulance. Cody didn't have his cell phone or wallet with him, so there was no way to call anyone back home.

Demmy's was the only number he still had committed to memory.

The officer had shaken Cody's hand and wished the best for him and Demmy, then left Cody there on his own and returned to Broken Jaw Island.

Cody had known their insurance carrier, and was glad Demmy was the one to keep track of paying their premium so they'd be covered. Now he just needed to do what the doctor and nurses told him to do, and wait.

But he wasn't any good at waiting.

He got the stink eye from a few patients and visitors as he passed their rooms for the umpteenth time, so he forced himself to sit back down. Why was it taking so long to get Demmy stabilized? He'd started breathing on his own out on the boat. What weren't they telling him?

"Long night?"

Cody looked up from his study of the floor. A young and pretty nurse smiled down at him.

"Yeah." His voice sounded as used up as he felt, and he dropped his gaze again.

"Time is weird in hospitals," she said. "For some people, it speeds past before they can grasp what's happening. For others, it slows to a crawl."

"Good description. You know anything about Demetrius Singleton?"

"Not much. Are you his friend?"

Cody took a mental breath, then looked her in the eye. "I'm his husband."

She didn't even blink, just smiled and nodded. "Let me see what I can find out for you."

"Thank you."

She walked off—more squeaking that brought to mind Demmy's statement about basketball which left him aching—and Cody watched her go. There would be good news, and she would take him to see Demmy who would be awake and sitting up in bed eating hospital pudding and smiling at the sight of Cody in the door to his room.

But when she returned, her face looked pinched. Cody stood up, and she seemed to falter a bit when she saw him at his full height.

"The doctors are still working with him," she said.

"Why? What's wrong?"

"They're not sure. Once they understand what's going on, the doctor will come out and speak with you."

"But, he came to on the boat," Cody said. "He was breathing on his own."

"I'm sorry, but I don't have any more news to share with you. It might be a good idea for you to get something to eat. I'll let the doctors know to look for you down in the cafeteria."

In other words, she wanted him to stop prowling the hallway.

"I don't have my wallet," Cody said.

"Oh. Here." She pulled some cash from the pocket of her scrubs.

"I can't take that from you."

"Call it a loan. Go on, you need to get away and get some coffee and food." She held out the money and Cody took it with a sigh.

"My name's Cody Bower. I'll be waiting down in the cafeteria."

"I'll make sure the doctor comes to see you right away."

He turned for the elevator and pressed the call button. It was going to be a very long night.

CODY SAT in a corner booth of the sparsely populated cafeteria, already regretting the microwavable burrito and flavored iced tea he'd purchased with the nurse's money. He put his head back and crossed his arms, intending to rest his eyes for just a moment.

The next thing he knew, someone was gently shaking the toe of his shoe.

He snorted awake and sat bolt upright. Confusion swamped his brain as he looked bleary-eyed at the man in front of him. He knew this man, but couldn't find a name for him yet. And where the hell was he anyway?

"Doctor Colebrook, report to five west. Doctor Colebrook, five west."

The call over the PA system brought it all back.

The hospital.

Demmy.

He looked at the man who had shaken his foot. It was Hap, and he looked as wrung out as Cody felt.

"Hey there, looks like you're back on Earth now." Hap slid into the booth across from him.

Cody had to clear his throat before his voice would work. "Hap. Hi. Sorry. I must have nodded off."

"No problem. Hated to wake you, but you were really gassing up this corner of the cafeteria. Did you have the burrito?"

A laugh bubbled up from somewhere deep inside him and he nodded. "Regretfully so."

"Had a few of them myself in my day. Never a good way to end a shitty day. So to speak." He twirled the plastic salt shaker on the table. "Any word on Demetrius?"

"Nothing yet. What have you guys found out there?" Cody looked around. "What time is it anyway?"

"Five in the morning."

"Jesus. You've been out there all night?"

"Yep. More to do." Hap looked up at him with tears in his eyes. "We found Rufus. He was lodged in that thing's throat along with about a hundred pounds of plastic bags and other trash."

Cody's heart dropped and he reached across the table to grab his hand. "Hap. I'm so, so sorry."

The tears spilled over and ran down Hap's cheeks as he nodded. "I know. Me too. He was the best man I ever knew."

"Jesus that's so awful. I… I don't know what to say."

"Nothing you can say. I just wanted to come by and see what you knew about Demetrius and give you that update." He wiped the tears from his cheeks, but even more fell right after. "And to apologize for even entertaining the idea you two might have had something to do with it."

"No need to apologize. I would have been the same way if our roles had been reversed."

Hap took a deep breath. "Who would have guessed it? Esther, down there for all these years, finally done in by our own foolish disregard. And taking the man I loved with her."

A woman wearing a doctor's coat stepped into the cafeteria and looked around. She caught sight of Cody and headed for their booth.

"Oh shit." Cody got to his feet and stood at the side of the table. He was vaguely aware of Hap standing up beside him, both of them looking at the doctor as she approached. She reminded him of Amelia with her silver hair cut into a bob and her reading glasses on a chain around her neck, and he wished now that he'd figured out a way to get in touch with her. Wished she were there with him right now.

"Mr. Bower?" Her voice was soft and smooth.

"Yes. I'm him. I am he. This…" Cody stopped himself, took a breath, and nodded. "That's me."

"I'm Doctor Henrietta Barrington." She nodded to Hap. "Hello, sergeant. I've heard about Rufus. I'm so terribly sorry for your loss."

"Thank you, Henrietta." Hap stepped aside and waved to the seat he'd vacated. "Would you like to sit?"

"Thank you, yes." She slid into the booth and Cody sat across from her.

Hap leaned over to clap a hand on Cody's shoulder. "I'll leave you alone for now. Come see me before you leave town, okay?"

"Yeah. Okay. Hap, I'm sorry again."

Hap gave him a quick, sad smile, then walked off and Cody looked back at the doctor.

"How's Demmy?"

"He's resting well now."

"Now?"

"He went through a very traumatic and unique event, Mr. Bower. He took in a lot water in that cramped space inside the creature's mouth. It stopped his heart for several minutes."

Cody's hands went cold and his brain sputtered as he tried to take in what Doctor Barrington was saying.

"In the simplest of terms, Demetrius drowned. It was only the efforts of the Hempstead police department that saved his life. We cleared the water from his lungs and have him on oxygen right now. There are some cuts and contusions, as well as a severely pulled muscle in his neck and shoulder. He's been given a tetanus shot and a strong round of antibiotics via IV to stave off any infections from the stagnant water and open wounds in such an unclean area."

Open wounds. The words clattered around inside Cody's brain as he tried to take it all in. Demmy was hurt. Hell, Demmy had died and been brought back. He'd almost lost him.

His frantic brain managed to latch onto the last words he'd heard. "Unclean area. So, Esther's mouth."

"Yes, strange as that may be to say aloud." She patted Cody's hand. "He went through quite an ordeal. Most extraordinary and terrifying. I wasn't sure he'd make it for a time there, but Demetrius is a fighter."

Cody snorted a laugh as tears blurred his vision. "You have no idea."

"Oh, I think I do. I want to keep him for a day or two. He's been through a lot, and I want to keep an eye on him to ensure there's no underlying infection. He will need time to process what he went through, but for now he's resting comfortably. He's asked for you. Repeatedly."

"He's awake?"

"In and out of consciousness. He's asked for you each time he comes around. And once he asked about a woman named… Clarice? Clara?"

Cody rolled his eyes. "Clarabell. She's a pain in the ass."

Dr. Barrington smirked. "Be that as it may, he's been concerned about her. Shall we go see if he's awake?"

"Really? Yes."

Cody felt as if he moved through a dream as he followed Doctor Barrington out of the cafeteria and down the hall to the elevators. Lack of sleep was to blame, surely, but also the complete absurdity of what had happened out on Broken Jaw Island.

A lake monster had tried to swallow Demmy.

Demmy had drowned and been revived.

Rufus was dead, drowned inside the same lake monster.

There was actually a lake monster. Or used to be.

Hallways blurred together, as did hospital rooms occupied by faceless voices as Cody followed the doctor. At the end of what had to be the longest hospital hallway in existence, the doctor turned into a room and Cody's heart rate doubled. It was a semi-private room, but only the bed near the window was occupied. Demmy lay with his torso slightly elevated, skin almost as pale as the white sheet covering him. His eyes were closed with dark circles underneath. He wore a neck brace, and an IV needle had been inserted in the back of his left hand while an oxygen tube was secured beneath his nose. An EKG monitor stood by the head of the bed, tracking his heart rate. Demmy looked small and vulnerable lying there alone in the big, empty room, and tears filled Cody's eyes at the sight of him.

Doctor Barrington gave him a gentle smile, touched his shoulder, and said, "I'll give you some time alone."

Cody hovered in the doorway, uncertain about stepping further into the room. Maybe if he didn't go in none of this would be true. Demmy looked peaceful but frail, and the sight of him in that condition was unnerving. He was used to seeing Demmy vibrant, sarcastic, and refusing to take any shit from him. This version of Demmy looked broken and so very wrong. Cody didn't know how to put this Demmy into perspective with the one he'd always known.

He took a couple of steps into the room then stopped. And stared some more.

Demmy was breathing, Cody could see the rise and fall of his chest. And the monitor looming on the other side of the bed showed a steady heart rate. But Demmy had been through so much. Almost more than he'd been able to come back from.

His legs went weak, and Cody moved to the space between the beds. He sat on the edge of the empty bed, wincing at the loud crinkling sound of the plastic liner beneath the sheet. After a few minutes of just watching Demmy, Cody said very quietly, "Demmy?"

There was no response. Cody pushed to his feet—more crinkling—and stood over him.

"Demmy? You awake?"

Demmy's eyes fluttered open and darted back and forth, his expression frightened and slightly wild. He tried to turn his head, but stopped with a wince and a gasp.

"Hey, you're okay." Cody leaned over him and put his hand on Demmy's shoulder. "I'm here. It's me. You're safe."

Demmy's gaze latched onto Cody's face and his expression softened. "Cody."

Fresh tears though Cody tried to hold them back. He

managed a smile as the tears ran down his face. "Yeah. It's me. I'm here."

"I never thought I'd see you again." Now Demmy was crying, but he was also smiling, and it was more than Cody could have hoped for.

"Oh, baby, you can't get rid of me that easy. You think some stupid lake monster is enough to keep us apart? You're going to have to do a hell of a lot better than that if you want to get rid of me."

They both laughed quietly at that, then Demmy flinched and put a hand on his stomach.

Cody instantly turned serious. "What is it? What's wrong? Do you need a doctor?"

He turned for the door, intending to shout for someone, but Demmy called his name, encouraging him to look back.

"It's okay," Demmy said. "Just a scrape on my stomach and sore from all the stuff they did. And this neck brace is a pain in the ass." He smiled again, and it looked stronger so Cody relaxed a bit.

"Okay. Let me get a chair."

He rounded the foot of the bed and pulled an armchair around to the other side near the window, positioning it so Demmy could see him without turning his head. Sitting down, he leaned forward and took Demmy's hand between both of his own.

"Guess we put that whole Esther debate to rest, huh?" Demmy said, then yawned.

"Yeah, you made sure of that."

"Clarabell okay?"

"Oh, she's fine. She's worried about you, but she wanted to stay back on the island and oversee everything."

"So what happened?" Demmy asked. "I remember the boat flipped, and Clarabell and I were holding onto the side of the boat. Then I was going up in the air and everything went… Dark?"

He blinked back tears and his gaze darted away from Cody and across the room. His brows knit together, and those little lines so familiar to Cody appeared. Demmy's deep-in-thought lines, and the sight of them sent a flash fire of love and want and need through him that was so strong and bright he nearly started crying again.

Jesus, he was a mess.

"I saw something when I was in there. Inside her… Throat, I guess? My head was bent at a really bad angle, and it hurt so bad. I was afraid my neck was going to break." He lifted a hand to touch the brace as a tear rolled down his cheek. "The flashlight was still on and it shone down her throat, and I saw a lot of plastic trash and…" He looked back at Cody, eyes wide and shining with tears.

He cleared his throat and said in a quiet, shaky voice, "Rufus? Did they find him inside… In her?"

"We can talk about all of that later," Cody said. "You need to rest."

"Cody…"

He sighed and hung his head a moment. Demmy would never get back to sleep if he had such an important question unanswered. Cody lifted his head and nodded once.

"Hap came by and told me they'd found Rufus. He was… Jammed, I guess? Wedged? Anyway, he'd gotten stuck in with the plastic and prevented you from going any further."

"Oh, no." Demmy blew out a long, slow breath. "Oh, Rufus. He was such a kind man."

"I know."

"Hap must be really torn up."

"He is," Cody said with a nod. "But he's holding together well. For now."

"Do you think he'll come by the hospital?"

"If not, we'll see him before we leave town."

"Yeah. Okay. I'd like that." He yawned and his eyes closed for a moment, then he looked over at Cody again. "You going back to the island?"

"You kidding me?"

"I was just wondering where you're going to spend the night."

"Not much night left," Cody said. "And I'm going to spend it right here with you."

Demmy frowned. "I'll sleep most of the time. You should see if they have a room at the hotel."

"Let me be the judge of that."

Another yawn. "Okay. I like that you're here, don't get me wrong. I just want you to get your rest, too. You had to be worried."

"Me? Worried? Come on."

That got a small grin. "Smart ass."

"Just the way you like me."

"That's the truth." Demmy closed his eyes, then popped them open again. "Oh my God. Amelia. And my parents."

"Our phones are on the island. We'll call them later."

"I don't remember anybody's number any more. Damn mobile phones."

"I know, right? But you stop worrying and get some sleep. I'm not going anywhere anytime soon."

"Okay." His eyes closed again. "I love you," he whispered, and then was out once again.

"I love you, too." Cody kissed the back of Demmy's hand, skin cool to the touch.

He tucked Demmy's hand under the sheet and slouched in the armchair. In that position he watched Demmy's profile as he slept until, with a few yawns of his own, he drifted off himself.

Someone gently shook Cody awake and he groaned as he

felt the kink in his neck. The room was flooded with bright sunlight and he blinked and raised a hand to cut the glare as he looked over at the bed. Demmy was sound asleep, lips slightly parted.

Satisfied Demmy was doing well, Cody looked up and discovered Hap standing beside him.

"Hey there," Cody said, his voice a low growl.

"Hey back. You were really sawing some logs when I came in."

Hap smiled, but Cody could see the grief beneath the surface. It could very well have been Demmy wedged deep in Esther's throat instead of Rufus. And if it hadn't been for Rufus being there, Demmy probably would not have made it.

It was terrible and fortunate all at once.

Cody pushed to his feet and grabbed Hap in a tight hug. "I'm so sorry. I'm so very, very sorry."

Hap held onto him for a long time, shoulders shaking as he cried. After a time, Hap delivered a final squeeze and stepped back. He shyly dropped his gaze to the floor and cleared his throat.

"Thanks for that."

"Absolutely."

Hap met his gaze a moment, then looked down at Demmy. "He doing okay?"

Cody looked at Demmy as well. "Better than he was. How are things out on the island?"

Hap huffed a quiet breath. "Crazy. News helicopters have been flying overhead all morning. Boats are coming by and people are stomping all over the place. Clarabell's been running them off as she works on the thing, but there's a lot of 'em now that word's got out. Most of my force has been out there all night and we were all just relieved by the State Police, so I sent 'em all home to get a shower and some sleep."

"On the news now, huh?" Cody lifted his chin toward the dark television on the wall. "Haven't had the thing on once."

"Don't bother. Nothing to see you don't know. I was worried all those trespassers might get into your stuff, so I took the liberty of packing up your things."

"Oh yeah?" Cody felt a rush of relief that he wouldn't have to return to Broken Jaw Island or Hideaway Cove.

"Don't expect things to be folded all nice and neat, but I checked all the drawers and packed up everything out of the bathroom and kitchen. Looked like I got it all. Bags are in the trunk of my patrol car."

"Thanks, Hap. That was really nice of you."

Hap pulled a phone from his pocket and handed it over. "Found this plugged in on a counter in the kitchen. I'm assuming it's yours."

It was Cody's phone, and he smiled at the picture that came up when he touched the button. It was of Demmy, and Cody had caught him in the middle of a laugh while they'd been eating at Margie's Diner one evening not too long ago.

"Yeah, this is mine. I guess it's time to make some calls."

"How about I drive you to the hotel and we'll get you a room? You can shower and get some sleep in a real bed and then drive your truck back here later."

Cody looked over at Demmy, uncertainty weighing on him.

"He'll probably sleep another four or five hours," Hap said. "Leave him a note. You won't do him any good if you run yourself down."

"Yeah, okay. Good point."

Hap left to get some paper and a pen from the nurse's station, and Cody leaned over to gently kiss Demmy's forehead. When Hap returned with the paper, Cody wrote a quick note, folded it in half, and slid it under Demmy's hand. He paused at the door to take one more look back.

Demmy's chest rose and fell evenly, and he lay very still. Cody mentally wished him only good dreams, then turned away. He hated like hell to leave Demmy alone, even for just a few hours, but he knew Hap was right. The drive home was going to be long, and he wanted nothing more than to be back home and sleeping in their bed with Demmy beside him.

Cody told the nurses at the station about his plans, gave them all a wave, then turned away to follow Hap to the elevator.

CHAPTER EIGHTEEN

Demetrius pushed up from the wheelchair and turned, awkwardly because of the neck brace, to smile gratefully at the nurse. "Thanks, Suzanne."

"You take care of yourself, Demetrius," Suzanne said, then looked around him to Cody. "Listen to Cody and follow his orders."

Cody stopped and smiled as he looked between them. "Hear that? You have to follow my orders. That came from a nurse, so that means it matters."

Demetrius shot Suzanne a narrow-eyed look. "Thanks for that, Suzanne."

She laughed as she spun the wheelchair around and disappeared back inside the hospital.

Cody helped Demetrius up into the passenger seat of the truck and closed the door. As he waited for Cody to round the truck to the driver's side, Demetrius noticed a couple of helicopters hovering in the distance, then a news truck drove past the end of the driveway several yards away. It was headed, no doubt, for the main hospital entrance to join the rest of the reporters waiting to get some footage and hope-fully a comment from Demetrius as he was released.

Suzanne had thwarted all of that by wheeling Demetrius to the mechanical room access door at the end of a long, narrow driveway.

Demetrius was definitely going to send Suzanne and the rest of the nurses a nice gift once they got home.

Cody climbed in behind the steering wheel and looked over at him. Demetrius saw Cody's gaze drop to where his seat belt was buckled, and he tugged on it to show it was secure.

"I'm all buckled in. You can start driving."

"Just checking."

"I know."

"Gotta keep an eye on you."

"I know."

"Last time I took my eye off you, you nearly got eaten by a lake monster."

"I know."

"Just saying."

Demetrius snorted a quiet laugh. "You're just saying quite a lot of things the last couple of days."

"And those were just the things I said out loud." Cody patted Demetrius's thigh. "Ready to head out?"

"Well… I was thinking."

Cody's expression tightened. "I don't like the sound of this."

"Yeah, I don't think you'll like it. But I think it will be good for me, in the long run."

<hr>

"I HATE THIS."

Cody's voice was low and filled with tension.

"I know," Demetrius said. "But I really need to do this."

Helicopters swayed above Broken Jaw Island, each trying to line up a better shot than the other. Hap stood at the wheel of the police boat, his expression tight as he maneuvered through the many pleasure boats cruising around the island. There were so many it took all of Hap's focus to find a path through them to the island's dock.

Hap hadn't been too keen on the idea of taking them back to the island. After several minutes of back and forth, however, Demetrius had finally worn him down, just like he'd worn down Cody in the truck as they sat outside the hospital.

He needed to see Esther. Needed to stand next to her, touch her, know that she was real. Pictures and video from the countless news outlets weren't going to cut it. Demetrius needed to be there.

Netting had been strung through the water, effectively blocking access to Hideaway Cove. A police boat idled in almost the same spot Demetrius and Clarabell had overturned, and the officer waved to Hap before lifting the netting out of the way for him to pass. Minutes later, Demetrius was standing on the familiar dock once again and following Hap as he led them to the right toward the bluff and the rock-strewn beach beyond.

"We found The Lazy Aye," Hap said over his shoulder. It was the first words he'd spoken since leading them out of the station and down to the boat. "It sunk about halfway between town and the island."

"I'm sorry," Demetrius said. "Rufus was an awesome guy."

"That he was."

Hap was quiet after that.

They climbed the bluff, and at the top Demetrius had to pause to catch his breath and adjust the brace around his neck. His skin felt hot and itchy beneath it, and he was going to be so glad to be rid of it. Two more days, the doctor had said, at most three. She had also warned him he might experience trouble breathing and general fatigue, and she'd been right. He looked up at the helicopters—one of which seemed to be getting video of them, great—and then at the water where the sun sparkled on the few open patches between boats.

Demetrius was about to suggest they continue on when something down below caught his eye. He moved a few feet back and stepped closer to the edge of the bluff, leaning a bit to see around a clump of trees.

"Demmy…" Cody's tone and the fact he moved closer suggested Demetrius was getting a little too near to the edge for his liking.

"Look." Demetrius pointed. "You can see her pretty well from up here."

Sunlight shimmered along Esther's scales as she lay stretched out in the shallow and rock-strewn water. Seabirds circled overhead, lower than the helicopters that were trying to line up the perfect and unbelievable shot. Esther's head lay on the beach, mouth agape, and people moved around her like busy ants. One figure was shorter than the others and wore denim overalls and green shoes.

"Clarabell's still down there," Demetrius said.

"She's been there the last two days," Hap said. "I don't think she's stopped to sleep or eat."

"Bet she smells as rank as Esther," Cody said.

"Whole beach stinks of dead fish and rotting meat." Hap shook his head, then gestured toward the bluff. "Come on. Let's go."

At the bottom of the bluff, Hap led them along a freshly made path trampled down by the dozens of people going to and fro. They picked their way around the rocks on the beach until they came to a clear spot about ten yards away from Esther's head.

Demetrius stopped and stared.

His heart pounded and his breath caught in his throat.

Esther's head was large and rounded, angled down just enough for them to be able to see her cloudy bright green eye. The teeth Demetrius could see in her open mouth weren't sharp or pointed, but small, rounded nubs.

"Her teeth." Demetrius moved closer.

At that moment, Clarabell came around from the other side of Esther's head. She held a measuring tape and muttered to herself as she walked toward them. When she was a few feet away from Demetrius, she looked up and came to a stop as she blinked in surprise. Then a big smile blossomed and she stretched out her arms as she hurried forward.

"Demetrius!"

She threw her arms around him and hugged him tight. Demetrius laughed as he hugged her back, careful how he moved his neck and trying not to breathe through his nose because she did smell as bad as Cody had suggested.

"Good to see you," Demetrius said when she finally released him and stepped back.

"Not as good as it is for me to see you. You saved my life out on that lake. I owe you everything."

"You would have done the same, I'm sure," Demetrius said.

"I would have tried, but you really did it. Until Esther came up under you and..." She must have seen the change Demetrius felt in his own expression, because she waved a hand dismissively and turned away. "Anyway. It's good to see you again."

"What have you learned about her?" Demetrius asked.

Clarabell looked at him again, but now with a bit of

sadness in her eyes. "She was a magnificent creature. And we killed her."

Demetrius gasped. "We did? How?"

"Well, not we as in you and me," Clarabell explained. "But we as in people in general. Sorry, I haven't really slept since that night, and I may be getting my wires crossed."

"Yeah, that's the reason," Cody muttered, and Demetrius turned to find him standing close behind.

Clarabell continued on as if he hadn't said anything.

"She's got what I estimate to be about a hundred pounds of plastic trash in her stomach. It's packed in so tight it had started to come up her throat. From what I can tell, she ate lake weed and fish, but with all that garbage in her stomach, she wasn't able to keep it down. She was basically starving to death. I think that's what drove her to attack Dave in his boat, and Rufus, and us. She was desperate and starving and alone and had no idea what was happening to her."

A tear ran down Clarabell's cheek and she wiped it away. Demetrius was surprised to find himself close to tears as well.

"Sounds like an awful way to live out the last of her days," Demetrius said.

"It had to be. She didn't intend to be a killer. It was people who turned her into a killer."

She looked past them, and Demetrius turned to see Hap glaring at her.

"She's dead now, and that's the best place for her," Hap said. He shifted his hard look to Demetrius. "You about ready?"

"Just another couple of minutes, if that's okay," Demetrius said.

Hap gave a single nod. "I'll be down at the dock. Don't be too long."

Demetrius and Cody watched him go.

"Can't say that I blame him for that attitude," Cody said,

and turned back to Demetrius. "I'd feel the same way if you weren't standing here with me."

"Yeah, me too," Demetrius said, and gave his hand a quick squeeze before turning back to Clarabell. "You going to get some sleep soon?"

She gave an indignant sniff and waved her hand. "Who needs sleep when you've got the find of the century laid out right here in front of you?"

"Do you have a way to get in touch with us?" Demetrius asked.

Clarabell nodded. "Oh yeah. Stretch here gave me both of your phone numbers. You've not heard the last of Clarabell Remington, I can assure you of that."

"Music to my ears," Cody muttered, then placed a gentle hand on Demetrius's shoulder. "We should get on the road."

"Yeah, okay."

Demetrius pulled Clarabell into a tight hug. "Be careful, okay?"

"Don't worry about me. I'm a tough old broad." Clarabell smiled up at him, then reached over to hug Cody as he bent nearly in half to reach her. "You boys have a safe trip home. I'm trying to keep your names out of all of this, but the reporters are sure to get it from the hotel."

"Yeah, well maybe we'll get some business out of it." Cody gave her another squeeze before releasing her. "Get some sleep. And for God's sake take a shower. You smell worse than the dead lake monster that's been cooking in the sun."

"Smooth talker," Clarabell said, then laughed her high-pitched cackle as she turned back to her work.

Cody led the way back to the dock. They were both silent as they walked. There wasn't really anything to say, Demetrius figured. Just another monster case they had stumbled into. Only this one had come at a terrible cost. And

Demetrius wondered if he'd ever really get over his experience.

Hap was talking with another officer at the end of the dock, and he looked relieved to see them come out of the woods. They were all silent on the ride across the lake back into town, even as one of the news helicopters followed them halfway there before turning back. Cody looked at him and shook his head before turning his face into the wind and closing his eyes.

When they reached the dock, Hap shook their hands and wished them well, his eyes clouded with grief that Demetrius wished he could do something to take away. He shuddered at the memory of seeing Rufus beneath him, mouth open wide and hand stretched out toward him, plastic bags snarled around his fingers. That was going to stay with him for the rest of his life.

He adjusted the brace around his neck as he made his way through the crowd of people on the dock, all of them trying to find a boat to take them out to the island.

"You come in on a boat?" a woman practically shouted in Demetrius's face. "Is it for hire?"

"No," Cody said, stepping between the woman and Demetrius. "It's not for hire."

She glared at him. "You don't have to be a dick about it."

"Can't you see my friend is injured?" Cody looked at Demetrius, then back at the woman. "Correction. My husband is injured. Give us some space."

The woman sneered. "Faggots. I wouldn't ride in any boat you've been in anyway."

"Too bad we've planted our gay asses on every boat in town." Cody smiled and winked. "Enjoy your ride."

"Fags!" the woman shouted after them as they threaded a path through the crowd and into the packed public parking lot.

"Monsters bring out the nicest people," Demetrius said. "She's a classy broad."

They managed to cross the road without getting hit by any of the cars lined up and looking for parking. As they reached the truck waiting in the shade of a tall oak tree in a corner of the Crescent Hill Hotel parking lot, an SUV pulled up behind them and the turn signal popped on as the driver waited for them to leave.

"Hap's going to have his hands full," Cody said as he climbed behind the wheel.

"Maybe it'll help him get through the loss," Demetrius said, then winced as he heard how it sounded. "That sounded wrong. It's not going to help him at all."

"I know what you meant," Cody said. "Buckle up, baby. It's going to take us a while to get out of town."

Demetrius put his head back and closed his eyes. He smiled at the familiar sound of Cody's muttered curses as he worked his way through the congested roads toward the highway. Once they reached the highway, traffic thinned out and the hum of the wheels on the pavement lulled Demetrius to sleep.

The dream came on fast. He was back floating in the lake and looking at Clarabell right across from him. The rain beat steadily against the top of his skull as a flash of lightning buzzed across the dark sky. A figure rose up out of the water between him and Clarabell, and he gave a shout of surprise and backed away, kicking his feet as he feared the monster had come to swallow him up once again.

But it wasn't Esther. This was Rufus, and he turned his head to look at him with his dead and cloudy eyes, and he stretched out a stiff-fingered hand with plastic bags wrapped all around it.

"You did this," Rufus said, his voice a watery ruin as green water dribbled down his chin.

Demetrius turned away to begin swimming toward the dock, only to find Dave, the town's plastic gathering hippie, right behind him. He glimpsed Dave's cloudy blue eyes and rictus smile just before Dave lunged for him.

He awoke with a jerk, immediately wincing at the pain it produced in his neck.

"Whoa, easy Demmy," Cody said, and reached over to massage his shoulder. "You're okay. You're safe."

"Yeah. Good. Whew." Demetrius rubbed his hands up and down his face. "Bad dream."

"Rufus?"

"Yeah. And Dave, too."

Cody made a face. "Double the fun."

"Yeah. Right."

Demetrius's phone buzzed in the cupholder, and he picked it up, then smiled.

"It's Amelia."

"Oh boy." Cody glanced over at him. "I haven't called anyone. You going to tell her?"

"How long until we get home?"

"Few hours."

Demetrius smiled. "Why not." He accepted the call and put it on speaker. "Hi Aunt Amelia."

"Demetrius! How's my married nephew?" Amelia giggled. "Oh, am I on speaker? Is your handsome husband there, too?"

Cody grinned. "Hey you sexy lady."

"Now Cody, don't you go changing teams again!"

They all laughed.

"I saw something crazy on the news just now," Amelia said. "And I wondered if you'd heard about it."

Demetrius exchanged a look with Cody. "Oh? And what did you see?"

"Some kind of Loch Ness monster washed up in a northern Pennsylvania lake. Can you imagine? I mean, I know you boys have seen some strange things. Well, we've all seen some strange things. But this kind of thing is a lot bigger than what you've dealt with. Have you seen these reports?"

"Aunt Amelia, how much time have you got?" Demetrius said, and exchanged a grin with Cody as he guided the truck toward home.

CHAPTER NINETEEN

Cody followed Amelia to the front door of the house she'd pretty much given him and Demmy. She stopped fast and he nearly ran into her, then he took a step back as she whirled on him, finger up and pointing into his face.

"You should have called me." Her expression was stony and serious, and Cody could see tears threatening. If Amelia started to cry, he'd really feel guilty about everything.

"I know," Cody said in a low voice. "I'm sorry."

"He died, Cody. That boy who has been more a son to me than a nephew his whole life drowned in that lake. Inside that monster. He was in the hospital for two days and you didn't call me or his parents." She shook her head and crossed her arms. "I'm very disappointed."

The words cut deep into Cody's heart. Amelia was family to him, and he felt closer to her than many members of his own family. He hated that he'd disappointed her, but he had done what he'd thought was for the best under the circumstances.

"I know you're hurt by my decisions, but I hope you can understand why I handled things that way," Cody said.

"I don't," she said. "Not really."

"It was crazy up there. Police were everywhere, reporters were everywhere. And there was nothing you could have done."

"When you married Demetrius, I expected you to do what's best for him. In that situation, having family with him would have been what was best for him."

A simmer of anger started low in Cody's belly. He tempered it, for the most part, but he did allow a touch to color his tone.

"I will always do what's best for Demmy. And now that he and I are married, I am his family, too. You've got about five and a half years on me for how long you've known him, but I'm right up there with you. I was focused on getting him well enough to get out of that place and bring him home to you and everyone here in town."

Amelia stared. She blinked a couple of times, then took a deep breath and slowly let it out.

"Oh, Juniper Trees. Cody, I'm sorry. I'm so sorry."

She pulled him into a strong hug that he gratefully returned. When she finally stepped back, she had tears in her eyes and she pushed her fingers up under her glasses to wipe them away.

"I'm a bit on the cranky side, and hearing about this pushed me over the edge. I should not have taken it out on you. I absolutely know you have Demetrius's best interests at heart." She adjusted her glasses and looked up at him. "Can you forgive me?"

Cody smiled and hugged her again. "Nothing to forgive. You're as protective of him as I am. Just so long as we trust each other when it comes to Demmy, we'll be all set."

"I agree." She turned for the door, and Cody noticed she was favoring her right leg.

"Are you limping?"

"Oh, just a bit." She leaned over to see around Cody, apparently checking to make sure Demmy was out of earshot, because she lowered her voice and moved a step closer. "I was walking along one of the trails around Parson's Pond a couple of evenings ago and got bit."

"Bit? By what?"

"It was a dog. Stupid thing came out of nowhere and clamped right onto my calf. I screamed like the dickens and gave it a swift kick to the head and it ran off yelping. Joshua tree, but it gave me a scare."

"Did you have it looked at?"

"Oh yeah. Went to the nurse in the senior center and they cleaned it up."

"What about rabies? Are they concerned about that?"

"She didn't mention rabies. Think I should ask her about that?"

"Um, yes please. A strange dog runs up and bites you while you're in the woods? You would definitely want to ask about rabies."

Amelia nodded thoughtfully. "All right. I'll stop by the office on my way home."

"Tell Otis we said hello. And tell him he owes me a beer. The Pirates beat the Devil Rays this week."

"Oh you two and your baseball. I'll tell him." She turned for the door, then back again. "I'm sorry again for the things I said, Cody."

"It's already forgotten. Go on home and get to that nurses's office."

He followed her out onto the porch and helped her down the steps, then watched her cross the yard to her car. After she drove off, Cody went back into the house and down the hall toward the bedrooms. Demmy opened the bathroom door and stepped out into the hall. He'd removed the neck brace and was slowly turning his head left and right.

"Did she yell at you?" Demmy asked.

"Of course."

"Sorry."

Cody shrugged. "I expected it. I pushed back a bit and she apologized and ended up hugging me. We're good." He considered telling Demmy she had been bitten, then decided to keep that to himself. Maybe in a couple of days, once Demmy was a little stronger. "Where's the neck brace?"

"In the bedroom. I can start removing it for a few hours a day now."

"All right, but I'm timing you."

"Yes, sir." Demmy yawned and leaned in the bathroom doorway. "So what do you want to do tonight?"

"You are going back to bed."

"It's five in the evening."

"Exactly. It's your nap time, grandpa."

Demmy scowled. "Watch it, husband."

"Husband? Now you're talking. And, you know, we never did this marriage thing right."

"We didn't? What was all that sex we had during our honeymoon?"

"Oh, that part we got right. May I?" Cody bent and picked Demmy up in his arms. "But I never carried you over the threshold."

Demmy laughed and put his arms around Cody's neck. "Oh, you're assuming you're the one who carries me over the threshold?"

"Do you want to carry me?"

Demmy huffed. "No."

"There you go. And since I don't want to carry you outside and back in again, how about we settle for the threshold of our bedroom for now?"

"That works."

Cody carefully angled him through the bedroom door and

set him gently on the bed. Demmy wore a pair of basketball shorts and a long-sleeved T-shirt, and from the line of his steadily lengthening cock, it appeared he was free-balling.

"Were you not wearing underwear while visiting with your aunt?"

Demmy gave him a wide-eyed and overly innocent look. "Would I do that?"

"Hmm." Cody got on his knees beside the bed and placed his mouth over the bulge in Demmy's shorts. He blew warm air over it and Demmy groaned. When he lifted his head, Cody said, "It doesn't feel like you're wearing underwear."

"You know, we were in the woods a lot during the trip," Demmy said. "We should check each other for ticks."

"Think you're up for that kind of scrutiny?" Cody got to his feet and pulled off his T-shirt then pushed down his shorts.

Demmy laughed. "I do. And thank goodness, because you're ready to go."

"How's your neck feel?"

"It's okay, but a bit stiff." He made a face. "Sorry."

"Don't you worry about a thing. I'll do a thorough tick inspection on you. When you're up to it, you can inspect me." Cody stepped up and dropped his cock into Demmy's palm. "Until that time, you can employ the tug and stroke method."

"I'm not sure I'm familiar with that method." Demmy slowly stroked Cody's dick, using just enough of a grip to create the perfect amount of friction. "Is this right?"

Cody closed his eyes and moaned. "Yep. That's it." He took hold of Demmy's cock and stroked it in time, surprised to discover he was already close.

"You might want to ease up a bit," Cody said. "Or this is going to be over real quick."

Demmy's eyebrows went up. "I must be really good at this tug and stroke method."

Cody's knees went a little weak and he put a fist on the mattress to support himself. "Pretty much an expert."

"Professional grade, huh?"

Faster stroking, which Cody copied on Demmy.

Cody closed his eyes and groaned low in his chest.

"I'm really close," Cody said.

"Me, too."

"Yeah?"

"Oh, yeah. Right there. Oh, right there."

Demmy's cock pulsed in Cody's grip and he came onto his belly. Moments later, Cody came, shooting across Demmy's already splattered belly. He let out a long, slow breath and leaned down to kiss Demmy's lips.

"I love you," Cody said.

"I love you, too."

Cody eased himself out of Demmy's hand and headed to the bathroom. He ran a washcloth under warm water, wrung it out, and returned to find Demmy with his eyes already closed and lips parted, breathing deep. When Cody gently wiped him clean, Demmy stirred and smiled up at him.

"Thanks," he muttered.

"You sleep."

"Okay. What about you?"

"There's a baseball game on. Thought I'd get the laundry started and watch it."

Demmy rolled onto his side, being careful with his neck and turning his back on Cody. "Sounds nice."

And he was asleep again.

Cody pulled on his shorts and T-shirt and eased the bedroom door closed behind him. He checked the status of the refrigerator—empty—and decided pizza or a trip into Margie's Diner was on order once Demmy woke up. After he unpacked their bags and sorted the laundry, Cody started the washer and headed upstairs where he grabbed a beer, sat on the couch, and turned on the game.

It was still the first inning and he was able to follow the first few batters, but then his mind wandered. He thought back to those moments when he'd stood on the dock in Hideaway Cove and watched the monster come up from beneath Demmy. That horrified and helpless feeling washed through him again at the thought of losing Demmy just when they'd started their life together. There was no one else who could ever step in and fill Demmy's place. If Cody would have lost him, he would have been devastated.

He did, however, understand a bit better why Demmy was so drawn to these unusual cases. Demmy liked the mystery of them, being the one to dig into the lore or the legend and figure out the truth.

And he had also brought a greater understanding to the creatures they'd encountered. Demmy had great compassion for all living things, and tried to find the good in them.

Too bad they hadn't been able to find anything good about cranky old Mr. Kelmer, the wolf man that had been their first outside the norm animal control case.

But, Mr. Kelmer aside, Cody wasn't as against the monster cases as he had been. If they could figure things out and reveal the truth around the rumors and stories and, maybe, prevent anyone else from suffering a loss because of these creatures, then he was all in. As long as they were careful. And as long as he and Demmy worked out a plan ahead of time.

It would also be nice if they got paid for these cases.

The hard crack of a bat meeting the ball brought his attention back to the game, and he smiled as one of the Pirates ran the bases for a home run. If they kept playing this well, Otis might owe him another beer.

Cody settled back into the couch and decided he'd been

thinking way too much lately. He needed to relax and just enjoy the moment.

As Demmy slept in their bed down the hall, Cody sipped his beer and watched the game, feeling grateful for what he had and looking forward to what was yet to come.

THE END

DREAD OF NIGHT

CRITTER CATCHERS BOOK SEVEN

Demetrius and Cody return for an all new adventure in DREAD OF NIGHT: Critter Catchers Book Seven, available now!

DREAD OF NIGHT

A vengeful monster. An unsuspecting small town. Two men willing to sacrifice everything to save those they love.

Cody and Demetrius's quiet days of marital bliss are disrupted by the surprise arrival of Cody's teenage niece, Summer, and the continually strange behavior of Demetrius's Aunt Amelia. As the two juggle family drama and critter catching, they learn a number of people around Parson's Hollow have either been bitten by a mysterious large dog or gone missing, while others have been brutally attacked, including one of their clients.

Sheriff's Deputy Lucia Durant, refusing to entertain any notion of paranormal involvement, questions them mercilessly before calling in a State Police sergeant for assistance. As the evidence the Critter Catchers uncover points to a werewolf hiding in plain sight somewhere in town, Cody and Demetrius must try to convince Lucia and the mayor the truth about what is happening, and what it could mean if those bitten were to leave town.

When Cody's obnoxious brother Roman shows up unannounced to take Summer back home, the attacks take an even more personal twist, and Cody and Demetrius race against the clock, narrowing down their suspect list and counting down the days until the next, possibly fatal, full moon.

Dread of Night is available in digital, print, and audio from these retailers: https://books2read.com/crittercatchers7

ABOUT THE AUTHOR

Hank Edwards (he/him) has been writing gay fiction for more than twenty years. He has published over forty novels and novellas and dozens of short stories. His writing crosses many sub-genres, including contemporary romance, rom-com, paranormal, suspense, mystery, wacky comedy, and erotica. He has written a number of series such as the funny and spooky Critter Catchers, Old West historical horror of Venom Valley, suspenseful FBI and civilian Up to Trouble, and the erotic and funny Fluffers, Inc. Under the pen name R. G. Thomas, he has written a young adult urban fantasy gay romance series called The Town of Superstition. He was born and still lives in a northwest suburb of the Motor City, Detroit, Michigan.

For more information:
www.hankedwardsbooks.com
hankedwardsbooks@gmail.com
www.facebook.com/groups/hankshangout

ALSO BY HANK EDWARDS

<u>Critter Catchers Series</u>

Terror by Moonlight

Chasing the Chupacabra

Swamped by Fear

The Devil of Pinesville

Screams of the Season

Horror at Hideaway Cove

Dread of Night

Critter Catchers Box Set 1

Critter Catchers Box Set 2

<u>Critter Catchers Universe Stories</u>

The Mystery of the Morelock Motel

<u>Critter Catchers: Level Up Series</u>

Grave Danger

Wet Screams

<u>Williamsville Inn Gay Romance:</u>

Snowflakes and Song Lyrics

The Cupid Crawl

Fake Date Flip-Flop

Star-Spangled Showdown

<u>Lacetown Murder Mysteries</u>

(co-written with Deanna Wadsworth)

Murder Most Lovely

Murder Most Deserving

Venom Valley Series

Cowboys & Vampires

Stakes & Spurs

Blood & Stone

Up to Trouble Series

Holed Up

Shacked Up

Roughed Up

Choked Up

Fluffers, Inc. Series

Fluffers, Inc.

A Carnal Cruise

Vancouver Nights

Standalone Gay Romance

Buried Secrets

Destiny's Bastard

Hired Muscle

Plus Ones

Repossession is 9/10ths of the Law

Wicked Reflection

Holiday Gay Romance:

A Gift for Greg (A Story Orgy Single)

Mistletoe at Midnight (A Story Orgy Single)

The Christmas Accomplice

<u>Story Orgy Singles Gay Romance</u>:

A Gift for Greg

By the Book

Cross Country Foreplay

Mistletoe at Midnight

The Cheapskate: Bad Boyfriends

With This Ring

The Story Orgy Singles Boxed Set

<u>The Town of Superstition (YA urban fantasy series)</u>

<u>Published under pen name R. G. Thomas</u>

The Midnight Gardener

The Well of Tears

The Battle of Iron Gulch

A Tangle of Secrets

<u>Gay Erotic Short Story Collections</u>:

A Very Dirty Dozen

Another Very Dirty Dozen

A Third Very Dirty Dozen

A Fourth Very Dirty Dozen

<u>Salacious Singles Gay Erotic Short Stories</u>:

Bear Market

Convoy

Double Down

Exchange Rate

Finding North

Hotel Dick

Kindred Spirits

Sacked

Stroking Midnight

Vanity Loves Company

Wet Lands